Also by Brenda Adcock:

One Step At A Time

Brenda Adcock

Yellow Rose Books
by Regal Crest

ISBN 978-1-61929-408-0

First Printing 2019

9 8 7 6 5 4 3 2 1

Original cover design by AcornGraphics

Published by:

Regal Crest Enterprises

Find us on the World Wide Web at
http://www.regalcrest.biz

Published in the United States of America

Acknowledgments

For the most part, this story is loosely based on an event that happened to a young man, someone I knew quite well. Other than that unfortunate event, everything else is something I invented in my own mind. Unlike the other stories I have written recently, I truly enjoyed writing this one because it allowed me to return to the darker side of characters that I love and the entire story came together without feeling like I was struggling. Perhaps we all have a light side and a darker side. I know I do, but have always found the darker side fascinating. Some of you might identify with that side and that's okay because sometimes bad things happen to otherwise good people. It's how we handle those things that make us who we are.

The biggest problem I had writing this story was wondering whether it would be accepted by my readers because my main character isn't the most likable woman, but I hope I was able to keep her true to herself throughout the story.

Because my wife doesn't read anything I write and isn't terribly interested in lesbian literature, I have always wanted to have someone I could talk to about a story I was working on. To that end I contacted my friend and editor to ask her to read my first draft. As a result, we have had several phone discussions about various parts of this story. Having someone to toss ideas around with is an enormous help to any writer. Therefore, I am eternally grateful to Patty Schramm for her invaluable input on this story.

I would be an ingrate or a moron if I didn't thank my publisher, Cathy Bryerose, for her unwavering support, even when I occasionally stumbled. I hope my readers will enjoy this story and will always be grateful for your support.

Dedication

To Cheryl, for giving me the gift of her unwavering love and making it so easy for me to love.

Chapter One

MADDIE JAMES LAY on her bunk, arms folded beneath her head, and stared at the grey cinderblock walls surrounding her. The monochromatic cubical where she would spend her last night caged like an animal was depressing, but not as depressing as the last ten years at Sand Ridge Women's Correctional Facility. She hated being caged and she hated the thought of having to report to some underpaid bureaucrat once a week. So, she sucked it up and did her whole dime. It could have been worse, she thought. The judge had slapped her with the bargain basement price for a man's life. She'd paid her debt in full. Tomorrow she would walk into the sunshine of freedom, look up, and never see another bar or wall of chain link topped with razor wire.

"Hey, Madwoman," a voice rasped. "Got a smoke?"

Maddie reached into a pocket of her overalls and took out a battered pack. She rolled over and slid it across the cell block floor.

"I'm as nervous as a damn cat," the inmate in the cage across from her chuckled as she shook out a generic cigarette.

"Keep it," Maddie said. "How long since you breathed free air, old woman?"

"Thanks. Longer'n you been alive, kid," the older woman said as she stuck a cigarette between her lips and rolled it around with her tongue, unlit. "Probation?"

"Nope."

"I never listened because I was a smart-ass punk, but don't you never come back here."

"I won't," Maddie said as she rolled onto her back and took a deep breath. Tomorrow. Tomorrow her life would start over. The truth was she didn't remember much about her life before she arrived at Sand Ridge. Too much money too fast. Too much booze. Too many drugs available for the asking. Too many young girls eager to get in her pants looking for the thrill of screwing a celebrity. Too fucking many excuses. Everyone promised to come visit, but no one had. When her money was gone, so was anyone who pretended to give a shit. They moved on to the next big thrill. She would just be moving on.

Ten Years Earlier

"LET'S GO, JAMES!" a loud voice ordered. "Beauty nap is over!"

Maddie squinted as she sat up in her cell in solitary confinement and rubbed her face. She turned her head toward the female guards in their gray and blue uniforms and grunted out a laugh. The bandage covering a row of stitches on the guard's forehead was evidence of their last encounter when Maddie arrived the week before for intake, and her reaction to an unnecessary cavity search. What did they think she'd secretly crammed up her ass or pussy during the bus ride from whatever town she'd been in to her new home in the middle of fuckin' nowhere? Within an hour of her arrival at Sand Ridge, she had smarted off and refused to obey virtually any order she'd been given, as her body rebelled against its loss of the drugs it was accustomed to and made her irritable. She found the idea of being told when to bathe, eat her meals, go to sleep or get up, all according to someone else's schedule, repugnant. She hated being told what to do. Always had. Always would. Her failure to comply when ordered to strip and grab her ankles for a cavity search was almost the last straw. The last straw fell when a strutting, butchie guard slapped her baton in the palm of her hand and shoved her face into Maddie's and hissed, "Would you like a little assistance, inmate?" Before Maddie could start to form another smart-ass retort, the guard poked her in the abdomen with her baton hard enough to double her over. "Now strip!" the guard ordered loudly. Maddie stood up slowly and began unbuttoning her shirt, watching as the guard grinned at her.

Maddie glanced quickly at the guard's nameplate. "Turn you on, Lassiter?" she grinned and slowly ran her tongue over her lips. She whipped her shirt off and dropped it to the floor. Then she reached out and grabbed Lassiter's shirt, jerked her closer, and planted a sloppy kiss on the startled punk ass guard.

When Lassiter pulled away, Maddie grabbed her again, ignoring the other guards behind her attempting to force Maddie to release her grip, and head-butted Lassiter, causing blood to stream down the woman's face. "Fuckin' pussy!" Maddie crowed triumphantly. "I didn't hit you that damn hard." A blow across her back and a second glancing blow to her head ended the altercation and Maddie was dragged off.

That little outburst landed her a week in solitary for "an attitude adjustment" and the prison administration considered adding time to her sentence for assaulting Lassiter. Her learning curve on the correct way to respond when ordered to do something would be steep. Hell, she would never learn, but could fake it, rebelling in subtle ways whenever possible.

A WEEK LATER, two guards appeared outside her cell to escort her to the shower room.

"What? No coffee, Lassiter?" Maddie asked the injured guard with a grin.

"Shut up and get your shit, James. Last private shower for a long time."

After being shoved into the changing area, Maddie stripped and stepped out, twisting the knobs on the white wall to adjust the water temperature. The guards waited in the hallway and she could hear them talking. She felt sweaty and gritty. She shampooed her blonde hair. It was short and had always been cut into a spiky, cocky style that fit her public image. She leaned her head back to rinse away the soapy water and a hand covered her mouth while a second arm wrapped around her upper body, trapping her arms tightly against her sides.

"Welcome to Sand Ridge Women's Correctional Facility," a low, hard voice growled in her ear. The arm tightened and something hard and metallic encircled her right wrist, biting painfully into her skin. Her left wrist was wrestled behind her back and the metal snapped closed. The person behind her held her head in a vise-like grip against their body. Maddie struggled, but the hand only tightened.

"Keep fightin' and I'll snap your skinny fuckin' white neck like a chicken, bitch," the voice growled in her ear.

The soapy, wet floor made standing tricky and Maddie couldn't get away without falling. The woman behind her grabbed the handcuffs holding Maddie's hands together and jerked them up, hooking them over the shower control. Pain shot through her shoulders. She breathed hard through her partially obstructed nose as her head was pulled forward under the water pouring from the showerhead.

"We hear you don't like cavity searches," another voice rasped. "Then you'll love this one, bitch, so get used to bendin' over."

Suddenly, the hot water disappeared and freezing cold water pelted full force against her back like a million tiny knives and poured over her head. Her legs were kicked apart and the pain in her shoulders brought tears to Maddie's eyes. She wasn't prepared and grunted, squeezing her eyes tightly shut when she felt her body being penetrated hard and fast. Whatever it was plunged deeper with each thrust before being pulled out slowly.

"She's bleedin', man," someone said.

"Figures. Sharpened my nails this mornin' just for her," a voice laughed.

She struggled to scream, but a hand was clamped tightly over her mouth while a second hand squeezed her throat. Fingers pinched her nostrils closed and held on. "Hand me that clip," a voice ordered. Maddie twisted her head back and forth until a blow to her abdomen stopped her. Something metallic was clipped over her nose and was followed by a strike to her abdomen that forced the air from her lungs. She began to panic without a way to suck in a breath and flailed around for a few seconds until her legs felt like spaghetti and she slumped, held up by her aching arms.

"Next," the now familiar voice said. Instantly, fingers roughly parted her ass cheeks and a thick finger worked its way into her ass while another object slid into her sex painfully, alternating their thrusts in and out of her body. Seconds before she passed out from pain and the lack of air, the clip slid off her nose and the hand over her mouth disappeared, leaving her gasping and shaking from the cold water.

"Hurry up in there, James! We ain't got all damn day," a guard called from outside the shower room.

She groaned when rough hands grabbed the hair on either side of her head and pulled it up. She blinked hard to clear her eyes, but the water blurred her vision. "You're my bitch now," a voice breathed. "Remember that, James." Maddie jerked as a tongue outlined her ear.

Her arms were pulled up, her shoulders throbbing as the handcuffs were released and she fell to the floor onto her knees, her sex and asshole throbbing. A hand grabbed a fistful of her hair and lifted her head, laughing, then let her head fall to the tile floor. Before she could move again she was alone, cold water beating down on her naked body like needles.

Maddie pushed her body up. She washed quickly and dried. She made her way slowly to the changing area and pulled her issued clothing on. Her eyes were glazed over when she rejoined the guards in the hall.

"Next time, make it faster, James," one of the guards said gruffly. "You only get ten minutes to shower."

The guards accompanied Maddie to the cafeteria and showed her the procedure for meals. Maddie picked up a tray of disgusting looking food and carried it to an empty table. She sat carefully, biting her lower lip, and pushed her food around. She kept her eyes down and stared at her tray. Occasionally, she glanced up and saw guards and inmates looking at her and snickering or talking behind their hands while watching her. She was humiliated and filled with rage. She wouldn't be anyone's fuckin' bitch.

The table moved slightly as another inmate sat down. Maddie glanced up and saw a large, ebony-skinned woman smile at her. There was something in the smile that reminded Maddie of a shark. The woman's eyes were cold and hollow. Maddie ignored her.

"We have rec time after this. Stay close to me," the woman said in a low voice.

"Who the fuck are you?" Maddie sneered.

"Your new best friend." Her eyes scanned the top half of Maddie's body. "Unless ya'd rather be Bree's new bitch. She claimed ya, right?"

"Nobody's claimed me," Maddie answered, her tone defensive.

"Ya got two choices, girl. Ya can let me he'p ya or ya can get fucked every night by women ya won't like. Your choice." She casually nodded toward another table. "See that chunky bitch over there. That's Bree. She owns ya."

"Nobody owns me!" Maddie snapped between clinched teeth.

"She does unless ya stop it now."

"How?" Maddie shivered when she looked at the woman. She was almost Maddie's size, but obviously had bigger friends. At least two.

"How many took ya?"

Maddie swallowed hard and felt tears forming in her eyes. She fought them off. "Three," she admitted with a soft voice. "I think."

"Sit up straight and don't be afraid to look at your attackers," the woman ordered.

"Who are you?"

The woman flashed a broad smile and shoved a plastic spoonful of food into her mouth. She looked much older than Maddie, but this place could make anyone look old. "Aggie. Which guards set ya up?"

"The two that brought me in here."

"They protect Bree and her group. Ya any good at fightin'?"

"When the odds are even," Maddie muttered. "I can hold my own."

"In a street fight?"

"Yeah."

"My girls'll keep the guards away and give ya a shot at Bree."

Maddie shook her head. "I...I hurt too much to..."

"Ignore it. If not, you'll have a visitor. Soon. Bree's prob'ly already sold your services for tonight."

Maddie glanced toward where Bree sat, laughing as she slowly licked her food from her fingers. The same fingers that had violated Maddie less than an hour before. A calloused hand grabbed her wrist, drawing her attention back to Aggie.

"Don't go at her mad. Just let the others know she don't own ya. Even if ya lose...and ya prob'ly will...they will know they're in for a fight if they wanna rent ya." Aggie shrugged her shoulders. "Everthin' in here's 'bout respect. They'll either respect ya because ya won't take no shit or use ya."

"I don't like to be touched," Maddie said.

"That's up to ya, baby girl." Aggie stood and picked up her tray. She carried it to a conveyor belt and set it down before sauntering slowly to the rec yard.

Maddie finished what she could of her unappetizing lunch

and wiped her hands down the sides of her loose uniform pantlegs. She could feel the other inmates staring at her as she wandered out the side door of the cafeteria and blinked at the sudden intrusion of bright sunlight. She didn't want to do what Aggie had suggested. She hurt. Her ass and sex throbbed with each beat of her heart and there had been nothing sexually enjoyable about the invasion of her body. It inflicted pain without pleasure.

Her crotch flexed involuntarily, reacting to the memory of the many times she had endured pain when expecting pleasure. Inflicting that pain seemed to bring her bedmates some kind of perverse pleasure and she allowed it to continue rather than be alone.

She closed her eyes and tilted her head back, remembering that her search to achieve some kind of pleasure was what landed her in prison.

She'd been out of control after tweaking all day. The flicker of strobe lighting caused her eyes to alternately constrict and dilate. The music from her electric guitar was so loud that when people spoke to her afterward, she couldn't really hear them. She'd pushed her way through the surprisingly large number of fans in the backwater burg and into her dressing room. She'd barely locked the door when Courtney jumped into her arms and nearly smothered her with an all-consuming kiss.

Maddie pulled away when her body became starved for air. Courtney's pupils were dilated as she wrapped her body around Maddie's until Maddie succumbed to the arousal that began to flow through her body. She carried Courtney to a chaise lounge and dropped her as she jerked at the skintight pants that seemed molded to the laughing woman's body. Maddie fell to her knees between Courtney's legs and began feasting on what she wanted at that moment.

Everything was in the moment. There was never any thinking, just seeking. She was definitely out of control, but didn't care. This was what she wanted, what she needed at that particular moment. Maddie pulled Courtney's legs over her shoulders and held her in that perfect spot as Courtney's body began to writhe and grind against Maddie's mouth, begging to be taken harder and faster. No matter what, tonight Maddie would take it all. She would keep Courtney trapped in her arms until there was nothing left, no matter how much Courtney begged her to stop. Maddie felt over the top, ready to claim anything she wanted, and would take Courtney with her.

"That's it, baby!" Courtney called out as she began to lose control. "Take me now!"

Maddie looked down at Courtney, the sides of her mouth curving into a smile. She sucked in Courtney's clit and whipped it with her tongue until she knew pain and pleasure had become one. Moments before Courtney's orgasm took control, Maddie released her and plunged two fingers inside her, eliciting a deep moan as Courtney reached out and grabbed Maddie's hand, shoving it faster and deeper.

When Maddie felt Courtney's muscle walls tighten around her fingers and the flow of hot liquid, she withdrew her fingers and lapped the heat up, sucking it from Courtney's body. Somehow Courtney managed to roll over and get Maddie beneath her, still draining the sweet, hot nectar from her body. Courtney moved her hips to give Maddie access to every inch of her sex. By the time they were both too exhausted to continue, Maddie's face was coated with the sticky proof of Courtney's pleasure.

Courtney leaned down and consumed Maddie's mouth with long, devouring kisses, before biting painfully along her neck. "Let's get out of here, baby," Courtney said. "I need more of that."

"I'm tired, Court," Maddie said drowsily.

"But I still need you," Courtney whined.

Maddie smiled and rubbed her face against Courtney's expensive blouse. "You always need me." She laughed. "You're a very needy girl." She sat up and nuzzled against Courtney's breasts. They were young and firm, and incredibly sensitive. Maddie knew Courtney wasn't wearing any undergarments and the thought of that soft, pulsing skin against her mouth aroused her again.

"Let's go home," Courtney whispered as she tongued Maddie's ear and sucked it into her mouth. "I want you to take me in the shower and then in bed until I won't be able to move."

"I can barely move now," Maddie grinned crookedly.

Maddie rested her forehead against Courtney's chest. Courtney reached to the table next to the chaise and picked up a glass tile. She cut a line of cocaine and lay a tightly rolled twenty next to it. "Take this, baby. It'll make you feel better."

Maddie shook her head. She was just coming down from her last hit. "No more, Court. I need to rest first."

Courtney picked up the rolled twenty. "Just a short one, baby."

Maddie took the bill and snorted the line of coke. It hit her system hard and her eyes rolled back in her head. She leaned her head back and closed her eyes. A few minutes later, she whispered, "Take me home, baby, so I can fuck you like you ain't never been fucked before."

Courtney pushed her body up and straightened her clothing as Maddie watched her. "I want you all the fuckin' time," Maddie muttered. "I wanna fuck you all the fuckin' time. Does that make me weird?"

"Not to me, stud, because I want it all the fuckin' time." Courtney took Maddie's hand and pulled her up. Maddie washed her face and straightened her clothing.

There were still a couple dozen fans, mostly teenage girls, waiting outside the theater door that opened into an alley behind the auditorium when Maddie and Courtney left the building. Maddie had her arm draped over Courtney's shoulder. Her signature sunglasses covered her eyes. She grinned when she saw the young girls as they surged toward them. Courtney pulled Maddie closer. "Don't get any ideas," she whispered as her lips covered Maddie's.

"This is where I found you," Maddie said with a wink. "Afraid I'll find someone to replace you?"

Courtney poked her hard in the ribs. "You'll never find anyone as hot as me and you know it."

"Ow!"

"Remember that, bitch."

Maddie leaned back and stared incredulously at her companion. "Bitch?" she asked the young woman she fucked just minutes earlier.

Courtney drew Maddie into a sweltering kiss for their audience. She grinned when the kiss ended as she clamped Maddie's bottom lip between her teeth. "You're my bitch, Maddie James, and no one else's."

Maddie released her and pulled her car keys from her pocket.

"I'm nobody's bitch," she seethed. She stalked away, stopping halfway to her car, to stare at a girl. "How old are you, honey?" she asked as her lips curled into a killer grin.

Maddie could see the excitement run down the girl's body as she stammered, "Eight...eighteen."

Maddie placed her finger in the girl's belt loop and jerked her closer. "Got a name, sweetheart?"

"Danielle," the girl answered, her body trembling.

"Cool," Maddie breathed as she glanced at Courtney before she delivered a deep, probing kiss. Afterward she took the girl's hand and led her toward her deep purple and silver Dodge Challenger, revving the powerful engine while the girl got hesitantly into the passenger seat. Maddie flipped a switch and motioned the girl closer.

Danielle waved at someone who had apparently accompanied her to the concert and sank into the seat next to Maddie. Maddie slung an arm around her and drew her into another demanding kiss before peeling out of the parking area.

"What about your friend?" Danielle asked, her eyes widening as they drove away, tires squealing as they accelerated.

"You're my *new* friend, baby," Maddie said with a grin.

"Where are we going?"

"My place," Maddie smiled as she slid her hand up Danielle's leg and squeezed it. "We can get much better acquainted there, without any distractions."

Danielle acted nervous as she readjusted her clothes. Maddie quickly pulled to the shoulder of the road and turned to look at her passenger. "You ever drive a car like this?" she asked, her fingers playing with Danielle's hair. She could see the nervousness in the girl's eyes.

"No, but it's awesome."

"Trade seats with me for a while." Maddie unbuckled her seat belt and raised the steering wheel. "Crawl over me," she whispered and then laughed. "I want you to crawl all over me, baby."

Danielle raised her butt and tried not to let it touch Maddie. Maddie grabbed her around the waist and pulled her down, growling in her ear, "You afraid of me, baby?"

"A little," Danielle admitted. "I've never met anyone like you before."

"Just relax, baby. I can take you back if you want. I promise I don't bite...much," Maddie laughed as she pulled the girl against her and kissed along the back of her neck while her hands moved up to cover and knead her young breasts. Maddie could feel the first twitches of her body's arousal thrumming through her pelvis.

Maddie released Danielle and let her get behind the wheel. She sat next to the girl and stroked her long brown hair. It was soft and fell between her fingers like water. "Take the next ramp onto the highway and open her up." She leaned over and nibbled along the side of Danielle's neck. "She's built for speed, just like you."

Danielle gained confidence the longer she drove and she accelerated onto the ramp. It was nearly two in the morning and traffic wasn't heavy as she wove in and out of the lanes. She yelped when Maddie's hand slid under her skirt and along the inside of her thigh.

"Your skin is so smooth. Like a baby's butt," Maddie muttered softly. The taste of the girl's skin was intoxicating and Maddie pressed herself closer, her hand creeping closer toward its goal. When her fingers reached Danielle's panties, they were damp. She smiled as she carefully pulled them to the side and stroked her clitoris.

"Stop it," Danielle said, trying to push the probing fingers away.

"You feel so fuckin' good. God! You're so wet." With each statement Maddie increased the pressure of her fingers against Danielle's sex. The vehicle continued to accelerate as Danielle tried to fight off Maddie's advances. She shoved Maddie away and the car swerved. Maddie glanced up and her eyes widened.

"Brakes!" she yelled.

Danielle looked up and slammed on the brakes, but it was too late. She turned the steering wheel. The left front of the Challenger struck the right rear quarter panel of a much smaller Toyota and it spun out of control. Maddie saw a blur fly out of the car and land in front of the Challenger. Before either of them could do anything, the thump-thump under the wheels made it obvious they'd run over something. Maddie stretched her long leg out and pressed the brake pedal until the muscle car slid to a stop.

"Let me under the wheel," Maddie snapped. "When the cops arrive tell them you were asleep. It'll be fine. Just stay calm."

Danielle crawled over Maddie and Maddie waited a minute before she opened the driver's door and stepped out. Traffic was streaming around the site, some barely seeing it in time to avoid it. She pulled Danielle out.

"Go stand on the shoulder so you don't get hit," she ordered before she turned to approach the second car. She checked the front of the Challenger and only saw minor damage. She trotted toward the second car, but didn't see anyone in the driver's seat. Other cars were slowing and stopping to render assistance. Maddie looked toward the shoulder of the highway, but only saw Danielle with her arms wrapped around her middle, crying. She reached the Toyota and looked inside. She saw no one. She heard sirens rapidly approaching the scene and walked back to join Danielle.

As soon as she was standing next to the trembling girl, she said, "Just stay calm. Don't offer any information unless asked," she continued. "We didn't do anything wrong." She looked around and chuckled. "Probably a stolen car anyway. The driver's nowhere around. If anyone asks, I was driving. Got it?"

When Danielle didn't say anything, Maddie nudged her shoulder. "Got it!" she hissed.

Danielle nodded. "My...my mother is going to kill me."

"Shit happens," Maddie shrugged and stuck her hands in the pockets of her tight leather pants. "It's your fault anyway for being so fuckin' hot." She leaned down closer and ran the tip of her tongue over Danielle's ear.

Danielle pushed her away and glared at her. She lowered her voice and said, "I'm sixteen."

"What?" Maddie asked, as if she hadn't heard the girl.

"I said I'm sixteen."

"I asked you how old you were before we left."

"I lied so I would have a chance to get closer to you." Her eyes drifted up and down Maddie's thin body. "I thought you'd be so cool. Instead all you wanted was to...to grope me." Danielle looked back at the wreck. "If this hadn't happened you'd probably have raped me, you sick fuck." Danielle's voice grew louder with each sentence.

Maddie grabbed Danielle by the arm and pulled her closer.

"Calm the fuck down," she cautioned in a low voice. "I'll take care of it."

Danielle jerked her arm away. "I bet you will. I could have you arrested for statutory rape."

"Shut up!" Maddie ordered. "Twenty people heard me ask your age and heard your lyin' answer. Don't worry, kid, I'll make sure you get a few bucks for keepin' your yap shut." Maddie smiled. "Besides, you're kinda cute and almost worth the money."

A motorcycle officer approached the two women. He glanced at Danielle before asking Maddie, "Were you the driver of the Challenger?"

"That's right, officer." Maddie pulled her California driver's license from her wallet and handed it to him. "My insurance and registration are in the car."

"Can you tell me your version of what happened?"

"I finished a concert and was on my way to my hotel. I was givin' Danielle here a lift after her friends left without her. Guess I was a little more tired than I thought. I don't remember what my speed was. After I entered the highway everything seemed to be fine until that car was suddenly in front of me. The taillights were really weak. I tried to swerve out of the way to avoid an accident, but clipped the rear panel." Maddie looked around. "I went to check on the other driver, but couldn't find him. Guess he ran away or somethin'." She smiled. "Probably didn't have any insurance anyway."

"Well, you'd be wrong about that, Miss James. He's still on the scene."

Maddie looked at him. "Apparently he's under your vehicle," the officer continued with a frown. "We're waiting for someone to remove the body now."

"What?" Danielle exclaimed. "We ran over him!" she accused.

"No, I didn't! I never even saw him!" Maddie said firmly.

"And who are you, ma'am?" the officer asked Danielle.

"Danielle Hunter. I was in the car with Maddie. I felt us bump over something, but didn't know what it was."

Maddie secretly breathed a sigh of relief. If Danielle hadn't known, how could she have? She watched as the officer wrote down information from Danielle's driver's license and asked her more questions. Then he turned to Maddie.

"You admit you were the driver?"

"Yeah," Maddie answered. She looked around and saw other officers questioning witnesses. A couple pointed in her direction and said something. She frowned. She rubbed her hand over her short, spiky blonde hair and took a deep breath. She was coming down from her last hit and was exhausted.

"Have you had anything to drink or used any drugs, prescription or street, tonight?"

"Nope," she answered.

He flashed a penlight across her eyes and the light felt like a knife stabbing into her eyeballs.

"I'll need to take you in for a blood sample," he said.

"For what?"

"To prove you weren't under the influence when the accident occurred."

But she had been. She couldn't remember how many lines Courtney had given her before the concert, during breaks, and after she left the stage. She remembered a couple of short pick-me-up lines after she'd fucked Courtney. How long ago had that been?

"I'm afraid I'll have to turn that kind offer down, officer," she said.

"Then I'll have to place you under arrest and take you to a local hospital for a blood test after I secure a warrant."

"You can't do that without my permission and I'm not givin' it, so knock yourself out, bubba."

The officer pulled his handcuffs from his belt. "Turn around," he said.

He grabbed her wrist and pulled it behind her as he recited her Miranda rights. She acknowledged she understood them and asked that her attorney be contacted. He motioned for another officer to handcuff Danielle.

"You don't need to arrest her," Maddie said. "She's just a kid. I was the one drivin'."

"Call her parents to meet you at the station," the officer said. "We can get her if we need her later."

He held Maddie's arm as he led her to a cruiser. He pushed her against the side of the vehicle a little rougher than he needed to and the front door handle mashed into her lower back.

"Cool it, Dudley," she said.

"What did you say?" he asked, placing his hand in the middle of her chest.

"Nothin'," she answered, refusing to look at him.

"I asked you a question."

"I answered it, so back off, man," she snapped defiantly.

He opened the back door and guided her inside. Maddie watched as a wrecker backed up to her Challenger and slowly lifted it off the ground. She closed her eyes when she saw the bloody, broken body of a man beneath. She turned away because he seemed to be staring at her. Then something clicked in her fuzzy mind and she forced herself to look as forensic technicians turned the body onto its side, shaking their heads. The man was wearing what appeared to be a uniform, but she couldn't identify it.

Despite the best efforts of her attorneys at trial, Maddie knew she would be found guilty of the charges against her. Vehicular manslaughter while under the influence of cocaine. The forensic experts had found drug paraphernalia in the Challenger and witnesses, especially Courtney, that bitch, testified she had inhaled a number of lines in the hours leading up to the death of the victim, who turned out to be a deputy with the local sheriff's department.

He was a pillar of the community, leaving behind a wife and two young children. She listened to what the prosecutor said about her emotionlessly for three long days. She was a popular music figure who was out of control the night Deputy Bryan Melendez was killed. She had endangered the life of a young, under-age girl by speeding until she struck the back of the deputy's car. His seat belt malfunctioned and he was ejected from his vehicle. Because of Maddie's impaired judgment, she was unable to stop and drove over the deputy, dragging his helpless body beneath her car for several feet.

Periodically, during the closing argument, Maddie rubbed her forehead between her thumb and forefinger to shut out what was being said about her. No one felt sorry for her. She was just another instant celebrity who'd acquired too much money too fast and threw it away. She had a way out, but refused to take it. Danielle was driving when the accident occurred and she was a minor. Maddie would rather be known as a murderer than a child molester.

She had already decided what she would do when she was found guilty. She needed to cleanse herself of what had quickly become an addiction to drugs, alcohol, and a desire for the fast life. And she would. Her lawyers were certain she would receive a probated sentence. The day she stood to hear the sentence imposed by the judge she hadn't been as ready as she thought. But a man lost his life because of the decisions she'd made.

Ten years in the Sand Ridge Women's Correctional Facility was the price.

She placidly stood and waited to be handcuffed and taken away while her lawyer pledged to appeal her conviction and demand a new trial. A sheriff's deputy began to lead her out of the courtroom. Even that cunt, Courtney, tearfully promised to visit her often. As she stepped from behind the table to be led away, the victim's widow moved in front of her and, with tears in her eyes, slapped Maddie with every ounce of strength she possessed. Only the sheriff's hand on her arm prevented her from falling.

Eighteen months later a civil court gave the widow virtually every cent Maddie had ever earned as compensation for her loss and pain and suffering. Now when Maddie saw herself in a mirror, she was once again a struggling performer, desperate to escape the life she'd been forced to endure after her parents were killed, ironically by a drunk driver.

Chapter Two

MADDIE LOOKED ACROSS the walkway of the cell block and watched Aggie chew on the unlit cigarette. Aggie taught Maddie how to survive, how not to become anyone's bitch, and Maddie had the scars to prove it. She smiled. It had been hard to take a beating over and over, but they had to know she *would* fight back. She wasn't the pampered punk they thought she was. She was stronger than she thought and stayed mostly to herself, killing time by working out in the rec yard and learning the intricacies of automobile engines.

Killing ten long years.

Now she was a day away from freedom. She'd served every minute of her sentence and lost touch with everyone who had once seemed important to her. She read and learned. She entered Sand Ridge as a twenty-one-year-old punk rocker and would leave as a thirty-one-year-old adult who'd paid the price for youthful, self-absorbed recklessness.

From time-to-time she met another inmate who appealed to her and fucked her. But after that day in the shower, no one ever fucked Maddie James. She wouldn't allow anyone to touch her again. She hadn't known being touched could be anything other than painful since she was a teenager. She was strong and buffed from hours spent in the rec yard lifting weights. She walked with a confident new swagger that dared anyone to mess with her.

"Hey, Aggie," she whispered.

"Yeah," Aggie breathed.

"Do you remember what it felt like to have someone touch you? Someone you wanted to touch you?"

"Dream about it ever fuckin' night," Aggie chuckled.

"Is that what it is, a dream?"

"After all these years, that's all it can be for me. But you're young, Madwoman. Ya got plenty of time to get your engine goin' again."

"What if I don't want to?"

"Then ya don't have to! Become a fuckin' nun or somethin'."

"You goin' home?"

"Ain't got no home. Gonna live with my daughter in St. Louie. Says she's got a room I can rent. Pretty close to a park, lots of little kids and animals. Not far from the Mississip. Reckon it'll do me just fine. No more fuckin' bars."

"Was it worth it? What you did?"

For a few moments there was no response and Maddie wondered if Aggie had heard her. Finally, she responded. "It was to me, I guess. My man was hurtin' my baby and woulda killed her if I didn't do somethin' first." Maddie heard Aggie take a deep breath before continuing. "I coulda done a bunch of legal shit, but no piece of paper woulda kep' him from breakin' down my door. She's still alive because he ain't. Where ya goin'?"

"Wherever a hundred bucks will take me, I guess. Don't really have a plan, ya know."

"You'll figure it out." Aggie yawned. "I'm gonna try to get a little sleep, I think."

BEFORE DAWN THE next morning Maddie was awakened by loud voices outside her cell. She rolled over and saw half a dozen guards around Aggie's cell. The cell door was open and there was activity inside the small area. A guard stood up and shook his head. "She almost made it," he said. "Too bad."

The guards began to shuffle away. Maddie stood up and saw Aggie's sheet being pulled up to cover her head. She reached through the bars of her cell and grabbed one of the guards by the arm. "What happened?" she asked.

The guard jerked her arm away and pulled out her nightstick, hitting Maddie's forearm with it and pushing her farther back in her cell. "She's dead, dumbass."

"I...I was just talkin' to her a couple of hours ago. She's gettin' out today."

The guard looked over her shoulder at the covered body and smirked. "Looks like she didn't want to wait."

A second guard stepped between them. "I got this," she said to the other guard. "Put your baton away."

"This one's been a pain in my ass since the day she arrived," the first guard spat.

Maddie cradled her arm and bit back the pain as the guard left.

"You all right?" the second guard asked.

Maddie sniffed and tears ran down her cheeks. She glared at the second woman. "Who gives a shit?"

"I do. That's why I asked."

Maddie looked at her arm. "Prob'ly have a bruise, but it'll go away eventually." Her eyes strayed back to Aggie's body.

"She slit her wrists," the guard said matter-of-factly. "You see her with a shiv, James?"

Maddie shook her head. "She didn't want to die caged up in this place."

"She's free now, James."

"Will someone call her daughter in St. Louis and let her know?"

The guard stared at Maddie for a moment before speaking. "She doesn't have a daughter, James. Aggie killed the girl herself while she was high. That's why she was in here. Start packing your stuff. I'll come back when it's time to out-process you."

"Thanks," Maddie mumbled. Even in this place, people lied to cover their asses, and Aggie had been no exception. Aggie had saved Maddie's ass more than once and it was hard to reconcile that with a woman who had killed her own daughter. But it was easy for drugs to screw with your mind and lead anyone to do horrible things. Maddie would never know what caused Aggie to snap and murder her child or why the same woman had bothered to save her. Now it was no longer her problem and she stuffed her few belongings into a small canvas duffle bag.

Aggie's body was removed from her cell less than an hour before Maddie processed out. She stared at the hundred dollars cash in gate money and the bus ticket to the state line they'd handed her as she waited for a ride on the prison bus into town. That plus a set of worn-out civilian clothes and a few other small personal items were all she was leaving with. She breathed in a deep lung-full of air, but even it still smelled like the inside of the prison. She fell asleep during the twenty-minute ride into the closest town and was awakened when the bus jerked to a stop in a cloud of dust. She gathered her things and walked silently into the bus depot.

A couple of hours later, the bus rolled to a stop under a lighted canopy near the state border. She vaguely remembered performing somewhere in Texas a lifetime ago. She wiped drool from her mouth with the back of her hand and made her way down the narrow aisle between seats and stepped off into exhaust-filled night air. She waited until the other passengers picked up their suitcases before she picked up her small duffel bag and threw it over her shoulder. The shoes the prison had given her were uncomfortable, but she slowly began walking away from the bus station with her hands in her pockets. She had to find a place to crash until morning and the little food she'd purchased wore off hours ago.

She sauntered down the shoulder of the road, staying away from passing vehicles. A few hundred yards ahead of her she saw an old building. The neon sign said it was a restaurant, but it didn't look very busy. The building was built of cinderblock and the paint was peeling badly. Maddie looked through the front window at the menu hanging on the wall behind the counter before she opened the front door and stepped inside. She took a seat at the counter and placed her duffel on the stool next to her. A waitress with smooth auburn hair placed a menu and a glass of water in front of her and walked away.

Maddie tallied up how much cash she had left as she looked over the typed piece of paper that passed for a menu. The waitress returned a few minutes later and pulled a pen and pad from her apron. "What'll it be?" she asked. Maddie continued to peruse the menu, but could see the waitress was about medium height and slender. Her uniform was a little tight, but not revealing.

"Grilled cheese and soup," she said, setting the paper down.

"That it?" the waitress asked.

"And another glass of water." She could have ordered more, but had never been a big eater.

"Be right up," the waitress said. She turned and clipped the order over the service window. An old man grabbed it and read it. He stuck his head out and shifted a toothpick from one side of his mouth to the other. "Another big spender," he huffed. But Maddie ignored him as she sipped the water in front of her.

The lack of customers made Maddie a target for inane and unwanted conversation. "Passing through?" the waitress asked.

"Yeah."

"Where you headed?"

"Nowhere."

"Never heard of it." Suddenly a hand was stuck out and waited for a response. When Maddie looked up she was greeted with a smile that looked like it belonged on the woman's face. "Jan," she said.

Maddie rubbed her sweaty palms on the fabric of her pants. She took Jan's hand briefly, giving it a single pump. "Maddie."

"Good name."

"It's all I got I can call my own."

"Where you from?"

"Nowhere."

"Isn't that the same place you're goin'?"

"Yeah."

"Food up!" the cook called out. Jan walked to the service counter and picked up the plate and cup. She carried it back to Maddie and placed it in front of her. "Anything else you need?"

"No. Thanks," Maddie said, picking up half the sandwich and biting into it. She savored the taste as she chewed slowly. She dipped a spoon into the soup and blew on it to cool it. The soup mixed with her sandwich tasted good as she urged her taste buds to forget the taste of prison food. She couldn't keep a smile from crossing her lips when she finally sat back and took a relaxing breath. She reached into her pant pocket and pulled out a cigarette. She drew the smoke deeply into her lungs and held it a moment before expelling a long blue-gray stream of smoke. The perfect end to a perfect meal. She felt warmth surround her as she waited for Jan to bring her ticket. She pulled a dollar from her wallet and placed it on the counter after stacking her dishes and utensils, followed by her napkin. She brushed her sandwich crumbs into her hand and dropped them on top before pushing it away. She finished her glass of water and placed the glass neatly on top.

"You a college student?" Jan asked as she stuffed the dollar into her pocket and picked up the dishes.

Maddie shook her head.

"Never seen anyone but college kids stack their plates up this way. Less work for me. How about a little dessert? Maybe a piece of pie with a cup of coffee?"

"No, thanks."

"No charge," Jan hastened to say. "We'll just have to throw them away when we close anyway. The apple is pretty good."

"I gotta get on the road and find a place to sleep before it gets too late," Maddie said as she slid off the stool and picked up her duffel.

Jan placed the plates and silverware on the service counter and wiped her hands on a small towel as she followed Maddie to the cash register and rang up the sale. Maddie let her cigarette dangle from the corner of her mouth and reached for the wallet in her back pocket.

"Two-fifty," Jan said.

"Pretty cheap."

"The cook opened one can and toasted two pieces of bread," Jan shrugged with a smile.

Maddie stuck the two quarters of change into her front pocket and moved to the front door.

"See ya around," Jan said.

Maddie turned the doorknob and looked back at Jan. With a nod she said, "Doubt it."

Maddie stepped outside and took a deep breath before turning to her right and walking away, readjusting her duffel. The soup and sandwich had filled her stomach and made her drowsy. She'd need to find a place to hunker down for the night. She'd feel more alert in the morning. A sign on the main highway told her it was almost fifty miles to the next town, another place she'd never heard of. One step at a time, she thought. Wasn't that all life really was anyway. One step at a time. One decision at a time. Maddie heard a low rumble and looked at the sky and saw lightning in the distance. The clean scent of ozone reminded her of stormy days on her parents' farm in Nebraska and a light breeze ruffled her hair as she lowered her head to trudge on. A little water wouldn't kill her. At least it would be clean and fresh and smell like freedom.

The first fat drops of rain began sporadically two miles later. The access road she walked on had little traffic and few houses. She lowered her head and pressed forward. Off to her right lightning illuminated what looked like an abandoned shack. She made her way down a small slope and jumped over a ditch at the bottom. She could at least wait the storm out in the old shack.

Water was dripping from her head by the time she stepped onto the front porch and ran her hands through her hair. The front door stood partially open and she pushed it farther slowly.

The inside seemed dry and she dropped the duffel onto a dusty floor. She lit another cigarette and found an old milk crate to sit on. She carried it to the front porch and sat down to smoke as sheets of rain fell around her. When she finished her cigarette, she tossed it into a water puddle in front of the porch and stood up.

Once inside she prepared a place in the corner of the front room and lay down, curling her body into a fetal position to remain warm. It wasn't freezing, but the rain had managed to cool the air several degrees. She used the duffel as a pillow and was asleep within minutes. The usual noises she'd heard for the last ten years were gone. No screams in the night. No muffled talking. No grunts as women sought what pleasure they could get from a willing, or unwilling partner. Nothing other than the rain falling relentlessly on the old metal roof. She felt strangely safe and no dreams disturbed her sleep.

Chapter Three

THE SOUND OF birds chirping caused Maddie to blink her eyes open. Dust motes floated aimlessly in shafts of light that streamed into the old shack between cracks in the walls. She sat up and rubbed her hands over her face. There was no question that sleeping on the floor made her a little stiff, but she smiled when she realized no one had woke her up before she was ready to get up. She pulled the duffel into her lap and dug out a bottle of water. She took a long drink to get the taste of sleep out of her mouth, then dug out a granola bar she'd purchased the day before and opened it. She bit into it and walked onto the porch to eat it. That and maybe a cigarette would allow her to make it until lunch.

She squinted into the harsh sunlight reflecting off puddles of water left by the thunderstorm from the night before after igniting a match and lighting a cigarette. She relished the idea of being able to light up whenever she wanted instead of the times she was allowed. She drew in a lungful of air and smiled at the freshness, the cleanness of everything around her, the freedom.

Now all she had to do was find a way to pick up a few bucks so she could feed herself and put a roof over her head. Fleeting thoughts of lavish, five-star hotel rooms and seemingly unending buffets floated through her mind. She was so high or hungover most of the time she barely remembered them, but had once thought she was living the good life other people could only dream of. Too bad a probably good man had lost his life before Maddie woke up. The one thing prison taught her was that life was the cruelest bitch there was. You couldn't escape it, but with a little luck, you *might* endure it.

Halfway through her cigarette, Maddie watched several brightly painted tractor-trailers, followed by a line of vehicles towing trailers or campers, slow and turn onto a muddy road a few hundred yards from her temporary home. She flipped her cigarette into a puddle near the small porch and stood, stretched her arms over her five-eleven frame and interlocked her fingers, flexing her body back and from side-to-side to work the kinks from her muscles.

She walked back into the shack and threw her few belongings into her duffel. She sat on the floor to pull on her socks and shoes, which were thankfully dry now. She fumbled through the duffel to locate her toothbrush and a small tin of baking soda, then wandered out front and stepped off the porch toward the highway. The ditch she'd jumped over the night before had partially filled with water. She squatted down and dipped her hands into the run-off. She splashed the cold water on her face and wiped off the excess with her hand before pouring leftover water from her water bottle onto her toothbrush and dipping it into the tin of baking soda. The slightly salty taste of the baking soda tasted surprisingly refreshing. She rinsed out her mouth and swirled the toothbrush in the water again to clean off any excess soda. She thumped it against her thigh to remove the water as she turned back to the shack.

She decided to have another cigarette and take the time to further assess her situation. She leaned against a dry-rotting post that held up a portion of the roof that covered the porch and looked around.

She was near the outskirts of a mid-sized town. The road in front of the shack was four lanes and she was sure she would be able to hitch a ride. But to where? She knew she was still in Texas, probably near the Oklahoma border. If she went north, unless the geography had changed dramatically in the last ten years, there was nothing in Oklahoma for her. If she went west, eventually she might make it to New Mexico. Her options were limited at best.

The sunshine beat down on everything around her, turning the landscape into a sauna. No matter what, she'd need to find a way to put a little cash in her pockets before she did anything else. Maybe she'd hang around a few days. At least she temporarily had a roof over her head. Better than nothin', she thought with a shrug as she turned to walk into the old shack, address unknown.

Maddie didn't know how much time had passed when she heard voices yelling in the distance and the sound of hammers striking metal. She looked out a side window and spotted a group of small and medium trailers circled like a wagon train in a field just beyond the sagging barbed wire fence between her shack and the adjacent overgrown field and saw a small group of men swinging hand scythes to clear the underbrush away. Shortly, small campfires appeared, sending thin streams of smoke into the clear blue sky. Beyond the trailers, she saw what looked like a Ferris wheel rise gradually into the air, pulled erect by a couple of tractors.

Maddie shoved her duffel beneath a stack of debris in the corner of the shack and straightened her wrinkled clothing as best she could. She made her way toward the fence line and stepped on the bottom wire to hold it down so she could step between it and the middle strand without cutting herself on the rusty barbed wire. She hadn't gone far, but worked up a sweat due to the oppressive humidity that covered the area like a blanket. The group of shirtless men poked each other as she sauntered toward them, their skin glistining with sweat. They used an old towel to wipe down their heavily tanned bodies.

"You bring any water, *chica*?" one of the men called out with a smile that showed off sparkling white teeth.

"Nope," she answered. "Just came over to see what's goin' on."

One of the younger men laughed and grabbed his crotch. "If it wasn't so damn hot already, plenty might be goin' on, girl," he called out.

Maddie looked at the young man and grinned. "If you can't handle the heat, then I reckon you can't handle me neither," she said, setting off a round of laughter and hoots from the other men.

Finally, a muscular man with ebony skin said, "In a few more hours this'll be the Carson and Bailey Carnival. Got us a two-week gig during this little burg's rodeo, and some kind of fair."

"Sounds like fun," Maddie said. "You the boss?"

"We is still in Texas, ain't we?" he asked.

Maddie nodded. "A mile or two."

"Then it ain't likely this black boy is the boss, is it? If you's lookin' for a job," he said, "then try that big Airstream trailer over yonder." He pointed in the direction of the trailer. "Back to work, boys!" he called out. "It ain't gettin' no cooler."

Maddie started to walk away, but stopped. "Hey! What's your name?"

"Why?"

She shrugged. "Just like to know who I'm talkin' to is all."

"Apollo!" he called out with a laugh.

"Like the Greek god?"

"Fuck no. Like the theater in Harlem. My mama always wanted to go there."

Maddie trudged across the area that had been cleared by Apollo and his work crew and came to a stop at the door to the shiny Airstream trailer. She leaned against it to cool off for a minute before banging on the door with her fist. She heard scrambled movements inside and banged again. Finally, the door flew open and a red-faced man with thinning hair that had been badly combed over to cover his baldness stuck his head out. Cool air seeped out the door.

"Jesus H. Christ! It's hotter'n hell out here! What the hell you want?" the man snapped, running his hand down his hairy and suddenly perspiring chest. Red fingernails attached to slender fingers snaked their way over his shoulders and across his waist.

"Come on, sugar. I can't wait for you no longer," a woman's saccharine voice purred. Dark brown eyes met Maddie's and a smile cut across the man's face. Although he tried to hide it, Maddie clearly saw his body's arousal.

"I'm lookin' for a job," she blurted out as she tried to erase the sight of his erection from her mind.

"What can you do?" the man asked as he fidgeted.

"What do you need?" she asked, although she was pretty sure what he needed at that moment.

"Twenty-five a day. Take it or leave it," he snapped. "Plus food. No benefits. Find Buck. He'll do the paperwork." Immediately, the trailer door slammed shut in Maddie's face, followed by a growl and a woman's squealing laughter.

Unsure where she was supposed to find the mysterious Buck, Maddie wandered around the dirt grounds asking total strangers for his location. After three or four tries a busy, middle-aged woman with flighty, unnaturally blonde hair pointed across the carnival grounds. "Try the Midway. He's usually there somewhere. You can't miss him."

Before Maddie could ask why, the woman looked at her. "He's in one of them motorized wheelchairs."

"Thanks," Maddie said.

She strolled across the grounds, which were drying out enough to become dusty again, and looked around for the telltale wheelchair. On her second trip through the midway area she spotted pneumatic tires bumping over the entrance to one of the numerous booths that sat side by side.

"You Buck?" she asked, leaning her forearms on the booth's slightly sagging countertop.

"Who's askin'?" he answered brusquely.

"I...uh...just got hired by the guy in the Airstream and he told me to find you, so here I am."

"Did he finish fuckin' that girl yet?" Buck asked.

"Still workin' on it, I think," Maddie answered with a smile.

Buck pushed his Stetson back and glanced at his wristwatch. "Well, he better hurry the hell up before that damn pill wears off," he chuckled. He motioned over his shoulder with his thumb. "Drag that fuckin' box in here. I got a leak in the trailer and when we got caught in that downpour last night some of the prizes got a little damp, but they should be okay after a few hours in the fresh air and sunshine. God giveth and God taketh away, y'know."

"Amen, brother," Maddie muttered as she dragged the heavy box into the booth.

Buck maneuvered his wheelchair close to the box and flipped it open. The musty smell of damp stuffed animals wafted up and stung Maddie's nose slightly.

"Smells like my grandma's fuckin' attic," Buck groused as he attached a large panda to a hook and lifted it to the top row of hangers that filled three sides of the booth. "So, what did old man Carson hire ya to do?" he asked as he grabbed a second stuffed animal, staring at Maddie. "Your tits for sure ain't big enough for him to be interested in," he chuckled.

"Whatever needs to be done," Maddie answered. She stretched as far as she could to hang a stuffed alligator.

"Well, that's not very specific."

"I'm a trained mechanic and follow orders pretty well."

Buck stared at her, squinting one eye. "When did ya get out of the joint, kid?"

"What makes you think I was in prison?"

Buck fished a cigarette out of his shirt pocket and lit it. Then he held up one finger. "I know the state has a decent program for training inmates." A second finger went up. "Some inmates, the smart ones anyway, learn to follow orders and not ask too many questions." Third finger. "Inmates don't want much so they'll take the cheap-assed twenty-five a day plus food." Fourth finger. "Ya got that sort of haunted look about ya. Ya on probation?"

"Nope," Maddie said a little defiantly.

"Did your whole time, huh? Must not have been much."

"Ten fuckin' years!" Maddie snapped. "That long enough for you?"

"What were ya in for?"

"Vehicular manslaughter while under the influence." Maddie glared at Buck. "I paid my debt. Any more questions, smart-ass?"

"Maybe later. We need to finish hangin' this shit."

"What happened to you?" Maddie asked while they continued hanging the prizes in the box.

"Got stepped on by a horse...while under the influence," he chuckled. "Got a life sentence as a result. And believe me, kid, she wasn't worth it. Nobody fucks that good."

They worked the rest of the afternoon silently. By the time the last box was done, Buck said, "I don't know about you, kid, but I'm gettin' hungry. How do ya feel about fried pork chops and a mess of home fries?"

"Sounds good to me. You cookin'?"

"Hell no! Alice, one of the carnies, promised to cook for me if I set up her booth. It was her crap we just finished. She's always tryin' to fatten me up and cooks too much. Besides, since ya did more'n half the work, I reckon she owes ya too."

WHEN THEY ARRIVED at a faded blue and silver trailer, Maddie saw a middle-aged woman bending over an outdoor oven. A large, cast iron skillet rested on a rack about a foot above a low fire. Dough was wrapped around dowels stuck out at various angles along the edges of the glowing embers.

"Alice is the queen of campfire cookin'," Buck semi-whispered. "You'll want to kiss her after ya eat her cookin'."

Maddie hadn't eaten anything since the trail bar she'd called breakfast and the scent of real food caused her stomach to emit a low rumble.

"I brung ya a new customer, Alice," Buck said as he rolled up next to Alice and playfully swatted her ass.

Alice spun around and batted his hand away, but the look in her eyes didn't show any anger. "You better watch them hands, boy, or they might find their way onto my menu," she said. She raised her eyes and scanned Maddie's rangy body. "Who's this? Ya find another stray?"

"Carson hired her," Buck said. He grabbed Alice's wrist and pulled her down a little. "She helped me stock your booth. Figured ya owed her."

Alice straightened and stuck a hand out. "You're always welcome at Alice's Diner. Anyone who puts up with this worthless cowboy deserves a good meal." Alice smiled. "Alice," she added.

Maddie took the offered hand, but didn't smile. "Maddie. 'preciate it."

Alice was a bottle blonde, middle-aged, and had apparently enjoyed a little too much of her own cooking. Her round face was highlighted by friendly brown eyes.

"Why don't y'all wash up," Alice said. "The biscuits are about done."

Maddie caught the gleam in Buck's eyes when Alice patted him on the shoulder and squeezed it. She followed his chair to a nearby hose attached to a faucet sticking out of the ground. She turned it on and waited as the brownish water sputtered into a clear stream. She held the hose while Buck cupped his hands and splashed water on his face and neck. Someone had fashioned a towel rack out of heavy metal and stuck it in the ground nearby. Maddie tossed the towel to Buck. Once his face and hands were dried, he shoved his hat on and reached for the hose.

"I got it," Maddie said. She squeezed her knees together to hold the hose while she washed her face and hands.

"Still workin' on that trust thing?" Buck asked.

"Maybe," Maddie answered as she stood up straight and let the water drip off her face and run beneath her shirt. She ran the towel under her shirt and over her sweaty chest and stomach. She wondered if there was any way to return later and strip off her clothes to let the cool water sluice down her body. It would be her first free shower and she wouldn't have to look over her shoulder all the time for unwanted fingers.

"Alice has a shower in her trailer. I'm sure she'd let ya use it, but ya'd have to refill her tanks," Buck stated.

"What are you? A fuckin' mind reader?" Maddie snapped.

Buck shrugged. "Just a suggestion."

"She your woman?" Maddie asked as she turned the water off.

"From time to time," Buck said with a grin. "I don't mind a little bounce to the ounce and in my current situation, bounce works pretty damn good, if you catch my drift." He laughed as he started back to Alice's.

Maddie spent the next hour savoring the delicious meal Alice had prepared and watching the flirting going on between Buck and Alice. She was sure Buck would finish off the evening with a smile. In his own way, he was a kinda charming guy. The look on his face when Alice placed a hand on his thigh and slid it onto his inner leg as they chatted reminded Maddie of something she was forced to give up long ago, before she couldn't stand to be touched so intimately.

Maddie stood and stretched. "Thanks for the chow, Alice. I think I'll go to bed now. What's up for tomorrow, Buck?"

"I'm finishing the midway, but ya can probably help out Manuel. He's puttin' a couple of kiddie rides together and he don't read English so good." He glanced at Alice and worked his fingers into his jean pocket. He tossed a key to Maddie. "I'm gonna spend a little more time with Alice here. Go to my trailer, the red and white one, and grab a shower, kiddo. I got two big-assed water tanks and you'll sleep better after a shower." He looked back at Alice. "That okay with ya, baby?"

She waved a hand at Maddie, shooing her away. "If we run out of things to talk about, I know other ways to keep you occupied, cowboy," she promised with a smile.

"If I was standin' up, we'd be about the same height, give or take an inch. Borrow a pair of jeans and a T-shirt 'til payday. I got plenty," Buck added as Maddie walked away.

Although she tried to talk herself out of it, Maddie felt gritty and grimy after sweating all day. She retrieved her duffel from the shack and let herself into Buck's trailer. She rummaged around in his cabinets until she found an older, faded pair of jeans and a white T-shirt. They were obviously old, but looked better than the clothes she received before walking out the prison gates. She luxuriated beneath the warm water as she washed her hair and body. She borrowed Buck's straightedge razor to shave her legs and armpits. She knew she needed a haircut, too, but it would have to wait for payday. She only had sixty bucks left from her gate money and needed that to get through the next week.

She peeked out from behind the shower curtain of the small stall after drying off and sat down to pull on fresh underwear before wiggling into the jeans and T-shirt. By the time the carnival packed up and moved on, she might have enough money for a decent pair of shoes, ones that actually fit.

After she was cleaned up, combined with a full stomach, she felt drowsy. She fumbled around in her duffel and pulled out a hairbrush and a cigarette. Maddie took a deep drag and ran the brush through her hair. She styled both sides into a peak over the center of her head, disappointed when the hair was too long to stay up. She saw a small corkboard against the wall behind the table that served as a dining table and general catchall. She stood and leaned over it and glanced at the yellowed, old newspaper articles pinned to the cork while she finished her cigarette. A thin blue haze climbed over her and she slid a window open, watching the haze drift away as she read. Old Buck must have been quite a cowboy in his day, she thought as she tried to stifle a yawn. She stretched out on a padded bench that served as a couch behind the small dining table. She had no sooner lay down than she fell asleep.

THE SOUND OF a motor running shook her from her sleep. She rolled onto her side in time to see Buck's wheelchair being lifted into the trailer on a small platform. She sat up quickly and grabbed her duffel.

"Go back to sleep, kid," Buck said when he saw her. "I'll be asleep myself real soon."

"I didn't mean to fall asleep. You okay?"

"I reckon I'm finer'n peach fuzz," he said with a grin, spinning his chair around to face Maddie. He grinned and shook his head. "That woman rode me like a bronc buster tonight. Yee-haw!"

"Surprised to see you then."

"Her trailer's too small for me. I can stretch out better in my own bed. You find the clothes?"

"Yeah, thanks."

"I'll catch you on the flip-flop then, kid. I'm usually up kinda early," he said as he guided his chair along the narrow aisle that ran the length of the trailer and into the bedroom. He slid the door shut and Maddie lay back down. A moment later a pillow landed on her chest and she raised her head in time to see the bedroom door close again before the lights blinked off.

THE SMELL OF coffee and sizzling bacon roused Maddie from a sound, but dreamless sleep. There was a time when she slept like a rock, but many of those nights were induced by drugs, alcohol or exhaustion following sex. Ten years behind bars had changed that when she was forced to listen for the unwelcome intrusion of strangers in the night. A hand on her shoulder made her surge into defense mode and she swiftly wrapped her hand around a soft wrist, ready to hurt whoever dared to touch her.

"Ow!" a voice yelped as Maddie squeezed the straying arm tightly. She sat up and glared into wincing brown eyes. What the fuck was Alice doing there? Maddie released Alice's arm and rubbed her face.

"Bad dream," Maddie muttered. "Sorry."

Alice shook her arm and massaged her wrist. "Breakfast is ready, kid," she said.

Maddie nodded and sat up. "I didn't hurt you, did I?" she asked as she tried to calm her flare of anger.

"It'd take a heap more'n that," Alice grunted, still rubbing her wrist as she exited the trailer.

When Maddie stepped out, she saw Buck pouring a cup of coffee. A plate laden with bacon and fried eggs rested on a small folding table next to him. A second table near a camp stool waited across from him. Maddie picked up the empty cup next to her plate to fill it.

"Where's Alice?" she asked.

"Went back to her trailer to get ready for the day," Buck said as he stuffed his mouth full of eggs and bacon. "I don't know what happened when she went inside to fetch ya, girl, but if ya ever hurt her, I'll mess your skinny ass up good. Understand?"

"It won't happen again," Maddie said. "She startled me. I don't like bein' touched."

Buck swallowed the food in his mouth and washed it down with a gulp of coffee. He looked at Maddie for a moment. "Don't know what all you been through or really care, but you're back in the world now and can't treat everyone like the enemy. That's all I'm sayin'."

"I got it," Maddie said brusquely. She quickly stuffed the last bite of food into her mouth and stood to begin cleaning up. Water was already heating on the small cooker. She stuck her finger in and jerked it out quickly. She located a container filled with cooler water and a bottle of pink store-brand dishwashing liquid and began washing the dishes and pans.

"Ya got a place to stay?" Buck asked as he brought his dirty dishes to be cleaned.

"I'll find a place. There's an old shack over in the next field," she answered with a shrug.

"Ya can stay with me if ya want. I'm not around much and can use a little help from time to time."

"I don't mind workin, but I ain't wipin' your ass."

"I can still handle that myself," Buck said with a laugh. "But my ramp quits workin' the way it's s'posed to ever' now and then. Stuff like that."

"How much?"

"Nothin'." Buck shrugged. "It's only for a coupla weeks."

Chapter Four

MADDIE SPENT THE next couple of days setting up rides, repairing small problems that came up, and helping set up Midway booths. It was peaceful, uncomplicated work and she enjoyed it, for the most part. She liked walking down the Midway at night and seeing the thousands of bright lights that would draw customers to the booths to spend a few hard-earned bucks to win a cheap-ass, imported-from-Taiwan stuffed animal not worth a fucking quarter. Every carnie knew the tricks to winning the games, but, of course, they never divulged them to the customers.

Maddie didn't really trust adults who stopped at a booth she was working, but found an unexpected soft spot for young kids. The look of wonder on their faces when she handed them a prize made her smile. The winners spent three bucks and the booth operator lost fifty cents. It seemed like a fair trade.

The first Friday night the carnival was open, Maddie stopped to purchase a bottle of water. She gulped down half the bottle before leaning against the side of the drink stand to light a cigarette. A small boy trotted up to her and tugged on the hem of her T-shirt to get her attention. She smiled down at him as she exhaled a thin line of smoke before squatting down in front of him.

"What's up, Teddy?" she asked. "Wanna drink?" Teddy was the grandson of the carnie workers who offered pony rides for kids and was a familiar sight around the grounds. But he wasn't much of a talker.

Teddy shook his head and turned to point across the Midway toward the booths. She saw Alice wave in her direction and grinned. Maddie knew what he wanted, but enjoyed making a game of it with the boy.

"Does Gus need me?" she asked.

Teddy shook his head again and Maddie asked, "Larry?"

He grabbed her hand and began pulling her where she was needed. Halfway to Alice's booth, Maddie picked Teddy up and slung him in a circle around her shoulders, eliciting a giggle. When she set him down, she handed him a quarter and looked up at Alice. "You needed me?" Maddie asked, watching Teddy scamper away toward the sno-cone wagon.

"Yeah," Alice answered. "Can you take over my booth so I can go cook dinner for you and Buck before it gets too late?"

"Hot date later?" Maddie asked with a grin.

"There's always a chance that it'll get hot," Alice laughed. "Close down in another hour or so to come get your dinner."

"No problem," Maddie said, stepping behind the booth counter. Alice's booth was the simplest game on the Midway and even small kids, like Teddy, had a better than even chance of winning something. Throw the dart, break a balloon, win a cheesy prize. What could be easier?

Maddie leaned on the booth counter for a few minutes, then decided to replace several missing balloons. When she was attaching the last balloon to the backboard, a loud, belligerent voice behind her barked, "Hey, shithead! Gimme six damn darts!"

Maddie turned to find a tall, muscular boy, who appeared to be high school age. Next to him stood a blushing blonde girl. "What the fuck do you want, Brandi?" the boy said thickly, blinking incessantly.

She pointed to the largest panda in the booth. The young man scooped up a handful of darts, more than he'd paid for.

Maddie grabbed his forearm and said, "It's *three* for three dollars, buddy."

"What are they, fuckin' gold-plated?" the boy snapped, jerking his arm away. Maddie could smell the pungent odor of beer on his breath.

"No trouble, dude. I'll let you have four for three bucks since it looks like you're tryin' to impress your lady. Break four balloons and the bear's hers." Maddie winked at the girl.

Maddie stepped back, continuing to smile as she watched the boy wind up like Whitey Ford to throw his first dart. It slipped between two balloons and stuck into the board backing.

"Break three and you'll still win...just a smaller bear," Maddie said.

"Your sign says break three for the prize of your choice," the teen argued.

"*Not* when you start with *four* darts, pal," Maddie snarled.

"You offered me four damn darts. Now you're tryin' to screw me, you stupid bitch," he snapped.

"Look. I think you should leave," Maddie said, motioning to another carnie across the walkway. "You've apparently had too many drinks or are high on somethin'. Walk away, I'll give your three bucks back, and we'll call it even." She handed his money to him and he slapped her hand away.

The girl beside him grabbed his arm. "Let's come back later, Bobby Joe, when you feel better."

He jerked his arm back and it struck her in the face. "Leave me alone, Brandi!" he shouted as she cradled her cheek.

Maddie reached out and slapped the darts from his hand, pushing him backwards. "Go take care of your girlfriend," she yelled back, "before I call security."

"She's not my girlfriend! She's just a sure thing," he grumbled. He turned to leave, but spun around and shoved Maddie into the backboard holding the balloons. That pissed her off. She vaulted over the counter, grabbed his arm, ducked to avoid being punched as he swung his fist toward her, and landed a crushing blow to his chin that dropped him to the ground.

There were plenty of witnesses to the entire altercation who verified Maddie's version of events when two security guards arrived on the scene. A medic checked him out before he was escorted off the carnival grounds. Maddie figured it was a safe bet he probably wouldn't get laid that night. She closed Alice's booth and strolled toward Alice's trailer for dinner.

Over dinner, Maddie told Alice and Buck about the altercation she'd had with the drunken teenager, even though she didn't consider it a big deal.

THE GATES CLOSED after a successful opening night and workers were picking up trash as Maddie accompanied Alice and Buck back toward the Midway to make sure all the booths and rides were secured. Alice and Buck would replace prizes that were won while Maddie wandered off to check out the safety bars that held passengers in their seats on the Tilt-A-Whirl. Buck had heard that there were a couple that weren't locking correctly in place and empty seats meant less money.

She had just discovered a large plug of caramel some wise-ass had stuck in the first safety lock and removed it when she heard a noise behind her. As she turned her head, her arms were grabbed and pulled behind her by a huge teenaged boy. A second boy clamped his hand over her mouth as they dragged her off the ride platform. She fought to get away, as her memory of the shower room at Sand Ridge flooded her mind. At five-eleven, Maddie was bigger than the average woman, as well as stronger, but when she saw the teen she'd decked earlier, she knew she was outnumbered and in trouble. They wrestled her behind the ride while she kicked at them and twisted her head from side to side.

"I'll teach you to fuck with me, bitch," Bobby Joe said.

She managed to bite the hand covering her mouth and the boy jerked his hand quickly away.

"Guessin' you didn't get laid, huh, partner," she said with a grin.

The arms securing hers tightened. The boy holding her said, "Nope, but this might be more fun."

Bobby Joe drew his fist back and slammed it into the side of her face. "Damn, that felt good," he breathed as Maddie slumped slightly. "Next," he said and moved behind her to replace the large boy.

He stepped in front of Maddie and hit her solidly in the abdomen. Her head jerked back before falling onto her chest. The teen holding her released her and she fell to the ground on her hands and knees, gasping for breath.

"Your turn, man," one of them said to the third teen. "Don't chicken out. This bitch needs to learn she can't steal our money and get away with it. She's just another piece of carnie trash," he sneered. A hand grabbed her hair, lifting her head to meet another blow that knocked her flat. She tried to push herself up on wobbly arms, but a boot smashed into her side, followed by a flurry of other hits as they kicked her. She forced her arms up to protect her head and curled into a fetal position to wait for the beating to end.

"Back off!" a voice shouted from what seemed to be far away. She heard laughter and was barely able to make out someone coming toward her, in a wheelchair. Buck! she thought through a haze, struggling to remain conscious. "Find a deputy, Alice,"

Buck said. "And you boys just stand right where you are," he added. A second later, a gunshot split the air. "I told ya to stay right there, ya little pissants," Buck spat. "The next shot will kill any hope ya have of reproducin'. Now sit your fuckin' asses down!"

Maddie uncurled her body and managed to push herself up. *Never let 'em know they whupped ya,* she heard Aggie say through the haze in her mind. She staggered toward the three teens, blocking Buck's line of sight. The boy she'd hit at Alice's booth stood up and balled his fingers into tight fists. Despite the fact that her right eye was half closed due to swelling, Maddie grinned and brought her hands up to invite the bully to hit her again. "Just you and me, kid," she rasped. "This is your chance to show your buddies what a big man you are." It hurt to speak, but she was mad enough to ignore it temporarily.

The volume of her voice rose with each sentence. "You hit like a fuckin' girl, Bobby Joe! You're a fuckin' pussy who can't even get laid without payin' for it!" She could feel the rage rolling off the boy's body.

He looked at his friends as if trying to reassure himself they would back him up. He bounced slightly on the balls of his feet and Maddie watched the muscles coil along his arms. A second before he moved his arm to hit Maddie again, she swung her right arm up and smashed her fist solidly into his face, watching him fall at his friends' feet, unconscious.

"Next," Maddie croaked, but neither boy moved and just stared at the ground. "Good deci—," Maddie started before her knees buckled and she fell forward onto her stomach.

Less than a minute later, Alice returned with a sheriff's deputy and Apollo. They carefully rolled Maddie onto her back. The deputy pressed the button on the microphone attached to his shoulder and said, "Send a paramedic to the grounds behind the Tilt-A-Whirl." Then he turned to the boys and asked, "Who wants to be the first one to tell me what happened here? After your coach and I have a little talk, my guess is you three have played your last game. And considerin' how bad you played tonight, that's prob'ly a fine idea."

Apollo helped Maddie stand shakily and began washing the blood from her face while Maddie wrapped her arm around her ribs. "Looks like you gonna need a few stitches," he said. "And a few days off."

"No," Maddie rasped as she tried to breathe without hurting her ribs. "Need the money."

When the paramedic arrived, he advised Maddie to go to the hospital for stitches and an X-ray, but she refused, telling him to do what he could. He Steri-stripped a couple of bloody gashes on her forehead and cheek before wrapping her ribs with Ace bandages, cautioning her that while he thought her ribs were only bruised and not broken, it might take several weeks for the bruises to heal and she would be able to move normally again. Since she wouldn't have stitches, the cuts on her face would probably leave some degree of scarring once they healed.

On her way out of the back of the ambulance, the deputy stopped her to tell her she'd need to come in to file her statement. She shook her head. "Not pressin' charges," she said. "Tripped over somethin' and fell on some equipment. That's my statement."

"That's a damn lie!" Buck argued. "I saw them whalin' on ya, girl."

She tried to grin, but her jaw hurt too much to pull it off. "I've done worse to get laid myself, old man," she managed. "Let it go."

Maddie hobbled away, ready to swallow a handful of aspirin and get some rest. The two boys stood up and helped Bobby Joe, prepared to split, when the deputy stopped them. "I can't let you get away with bein' three cowards beatin' on a woman to prove you're real men, so for the remainder of this carnival's stay, you three will show up every night after closin' and pick up every fuckin' piece of trash on the grounds. Got it? Or I can let your coach know what you did so *he* can punish you. Any comments or questions, gentlemen? Now get on home and sober up," he ordered. "I'll be here every night to make sure you do what you're supposed to be doin'," he called out as they walked away.

SATURDAY MORNING, MADDIE woke up feeling as if she'd been run over by a tractor-trailer that then stopped and backed over her. She eventually was able to force herself up to use the bathroom — and she hesitated when she saw her face in the mirror. Her two black eyes vaguely reminded her of an uglier Alice Cooper. The cuts on her face had seeped during the night and made the skin around the cuts feel tight. Added to the bruise on her jaw, they gave her a somewhat Frankenstein-ish appearance. Alice Cooper would be proud, she thought, then covered her throbbing jaw that strongly rebelled against any attempt to grin. "Fuck," she muttered.

Buck brought her scrambled eggs for breakfast, but she couldn't chew normally and wound up simply swallowing them. She felt better when she swished hot coffee around in her sore mouth. It loosened her jaw muscles enough to allow her to talk softly to Buck. He only gave her light assignments for the morning and no lifting. Alice used warm, wet compresses to remove the original Steri-strips and replace them with antibiotic ointment and fresh strips.

By the afternoon, following a couple of prescription pain-killers Buck gave her, Maddie felt a little better. Good enough to relieve Alice at her booth for a while and get some fresh air. Food didn't appeal to her, but she was able to semi-suck a Slushie. Periodically, she gently pressed the frosty cup against her jaw to stop the swelling from getting any worse. As she rested her forearms on the booth counter to help her breathe a little easier, she spotted a familiar face wandering slowly down the Midway, accompanied by an attractive brunette. It was Jan, the waitress from the diner she'd stopped at the night she was released from Sand Ridge. When Jan looked toward Alice's booth, Maddie forced a half smile and raised an arm to cast her a wave. Jan frowned slightly and said something to the woman with her, hesitating before wandering toward the booth.

"Take a chance and win a prize," Maddie said, moving her jaw as little as possible.

"What the hell happened to you?" Jan asked. "Looks painful."

"Unhappy customer. Only hurts if I laugh, so don't tell me any jokes," Maddie said.

"Looks like he won that tussle," Jan observed as she lightly touched the strips on Maddie's face with her fingertips. "You do know you look like a raccoon, doncha, ya poor baby."

"I was kinda hoping ya wouldn't notice. Maybe if ya kissed 'em with them sweet lips, my boo-boos would go away. I have a few others further down, too, if you're interested," Maddie grinned crookedly. She glanced over Jan's shoulder at her friend and attempted a half-assed wink. She looked familiar and was studying Maddie like she was someone she should remember, but didn't. "Who's the shadow?" Maddie asked, returning her attention to Jan.

"Oh, I'm sorry. This is my friend, Dani. We went to high school together and she's visitin' me for the weekend."

"Cool," Maddie said, her eyes blatantly scanning the body of Jan's friend. "I'm not really into threesomes, but I'll try anythin' once," she continued, wincing as she forced a lascivious smile.

"Doesn't it hurt to smile?" Jan asked.

"Truthfully, it's a bitch, honey," Maddie answered. "Three high school punks beat the shit outta me last night, but I'll recover. Maybe after I do we can hook up and find a way to have a little fun," she added, waggling her eyebrows the best she could.

Out of nowhere, Alice stepped into the booth and chuckled. "Don't let Maddie kid ya, honey. Right now she can't even chew food, so fun's only a blip on the distant horizon."

Maddie noticed Dani's face pale suddenly as she glanced around as if she was looking for a hole to crawl into. "Your friend looks kinda sick. Maybe y'all should find some shade," Maddie said.

"I'm fine," Dani muttered. "Just a little tired."

"Stayed up too late last night yakkin'," Jan explained with a wink.

"Yeah, too much talkin' can wear ya out," Maddie said, looking at Dani. Turning her attention back to Jan, she said, "Personally, I prefer a little more action and a lot less talkin', know what I mean?"

"Absolutely, sweetie," Jan responded, running a finger over Maddie's forearm slowly. "Catch ya later," she added softly before walking away with Dani.

Alice slapped Maddie on the arm playfully. "What're ya gonna do if that gal shows up later expectin' 'a little action'?" she chuckled.

Maddie pivoted her head toward Alice. "I'll think of somethin'," she said with a crooked smile.

THE NEXT MORNING, Maddie was awakened by tapping on the trailer's aluminum door. She swung her legs over the side of her bunk and stood up, semi-straightening her tank top and boxers. It seemed too early for Buck to be bringing her lunch, but she was a little hungry. She took a cigarette from her pack and put it between her lips without lighting it. Then she pushed the trailer door open and returned to her bunk. She lit her cigarette and exhaled a cloud of blue smoke. "Just put it down on the table," she said. "I'll get it in a minute. Tell Alice I said thanks."

"Can ya feed yourself?" a woman's voice asked. "I'd be glad to help ya."

"Of course, I can—" Maddie started as she stood to slip into her jeans before glimpsing at the person who'd delivered her food. "Jan! What are ya doin' here?"

Jan shrugged coquettishly and smiled. "I brought your lunch. It's just chicken soup and a grilled cheese, but should be somethin' ya can chew without too much difficulty."

Maddie zipped her jeans, leaving the waist unbuttoned, and moved to the table slowly. She looked at Jan and grinned. "I haven't had home cookin' for a while. Thank you," she lied softly as she ran her hand slowly up Jan's back, lightly squeezing the muscle at the base of her neck. She grinned to herself when she felt Jan tremble involuntarily. "Join me," she rasped.

Jan met Maddie's eyes and searched them before answering. "I...uh...ate before I left my place," she said. "Wanted to get this to ya while it was still reasonably warm. Ya want somethin' to drink?"

"There's water in the fridge," Maddie said. "Get yourself somethin' if ya want it. Buck's probably got some wine coolers in there."

Jan placed a water bottle next to Maddie's food and sat down opposite her at the small kitchen table. Maddie ate slowly, taking small bites of the sandwich and chewing carefully. When she finished the sandwich, she reached over to the counter near her bunk and picked up a small bottle. She dumped a couple of pills into her hand and washed them down with the water.

"What're those? Pain-killers?" Jan asked.

Maddie shrugged. "Beats the fuck outta me, but whatever they are, they work pretty damn good."

"What're ya plannin' on doin' when the carnival moves on?"

Jan asked.

Maddie shrugged again. "Guess I could go with them, or I could set out on my own. Haven't really thought about it much. No real reason to stay around here."

"Can I ask ya a personal kinda question?" Jan asked.

"Depends," Maddie answered, leaning back on her padded seat and lighting another cigarette.

Jan cleared her throat and took a drink. Then she looked at Maddie and took a deep breath.

"Just spit it out, baby," Maddie forced out as she exhaled a stream of smoke.

"Where were ya before ya walked into the diner that night?" Jan finally asked.

Maddie blinked and gazed out the trailer window next to the table. "Incarcerated at Sand Ridge Women's Correctional Facility over by Big Spring for the last ten years," she finally answered with no emotion showing on her face. "As part of my rehabilitation, they even trained me to be a mechanic. Killed time, y'know."

"Do the people here know that?"

"Of course. It's a carnival. Most of them have done time and they don't care if they're workin' next to another ex-con." She looked at Jan and drew in another lungful of cigarette smoke. "Do you?"

"Not much."

"Why?"

"Because I think you're kinda cute, I guess," Jan shrugged. "And maybe I'd like to get to know ya a little better, if you're interested."

Maddie grinned. "I'm definitely interested, but ain't ready for nothin' permanent right now."

"I can live with that," Jan said as she got up and carried Maddie's soup bowl to the sink. Maddie stood up and stepped across the small space to rest her hands on Jan's waist. Jan covered Maddie's hands with her own. Maddie ran her hands over Jan's ass and pulled her close against her body, nibbling and biting along her neck, ignoring the pain in her ribs. Jan turned to face Maddie and took her face in her hands. Her tongue darted out to lick Maddie's lips. "That drives me crazy," she breathed.

"Good to know," Maddie said against Jan's lips before taking her hand and leading her to her bunk. Jan stretched out and scooted over to make room on the small space. "Tell me if I do anything you don't like, okay," Maddie whispered.

Jan nodded, as Maddie's hands started exploring her body, her lips covering Jan's deeply and possessively. Slowly Maddie removed Jan's clothes one piece at a time and hungrily lavished attention on newly exposed skin. However, every time Jan attempted to touch Maddie in the same way, Maddie pushed her hands away.

"What's wrong, baby?" Jan panted.

"Nothin'," Maddie grunted as her lips encircled a taut nipple and her thigh pushed between Jan's legs to be coated by her copious, slick wetness. "Don't worry about me. I'm just fine, baby."

Maddie slid down Jan's body and took her with her lips and tongue until she felt Jan arch and stiffen, her hands grasping Maddie's hair to pull her tighter against her pulsing sex. At the last moment, Maddie slipped her fingers inside and felt Jan explode. Then she pushed up to hungrily kiss her as she felt the proof of Jan's orgasm flow over her hand. A moment later, Maddie buried her head between Jan's breasts and curled up slightly, breathing heavily and shuddering uncontrollably, as her body, driven by the pleasure she knew she'd given the other woman, released. When she raised her head, Jan smiled and ran her fingers through Maddie's sweaty hair.

"Fuck, baby," Jan croaked. "I really wanted to touch ya while ya came."

"I'm good," Maddie said before resting her head on Jan's chest. "Thank you."

Jan looked at Maddie. "Hey, you're cheek's bleedin'. Are you okay?"

"I'm fine, just fine," Maddie sighed. "Might need a nap though. Those pain-killers make me drowsy. Sorry," she mumbled.

When Maddie awoke two hours later, Jan was gone, but Maddie found a note on the counter telling her about an auto repair shop in the next town that might hire her, if she was interested. And there was a boarding house not far away that didn't charge much until she could get on her feet again. Jan signed the note, *The one who got away.*

With no idea what that meant, Maddie took a quick shower to wake up completely, then looked around the small trailer and decided to do a little cleaning. In the process, she discovered a dusty old guitar case in the bedroom under Buck's bed. She flipped the silver latches open and lifted out an old Gibson ES 140. It was a vintage guitar and she wondered why Buck had it. Two of its steel strings were broken and although she hadn't played in ten years, she decided to give it a try.

She found a new package of strings in the bottom of the guitar case. After restringing the instrument and tuning it, she sat down and placed it across her thighs, smiling at the feel of it in her hands. It was comfortable as she ran her fingers down the strings and over the frets. She closed her eyes and slowly began to pick out a few simple tunes, remembering the feel and sound of the electric guitar she once used.

Gradually, the music began to come back to her as she lost herself in the chords. She had always loved playing, but now her fingers were tender as her callouses had faded away. Despite her sore fingers, she started to hum a song and eventually opened her mouth to sing softly. She was interrupted by the trailer door opening and the whirring sound of Buck's lift. A minute later, he backed into the trailer and turned his wheelchair to face Maddie.

"I'm guessin' your redheaded friend is gone," he said with a grin.

"Yeah. I took a couple of your pain-killers and the damn things put me to sleep," Maddie nodded. "But she left satisfied."

"She seemed real concerned about how ya was doin'," he chuckled.

Maddie glanced at him and simply grinned as she stroked the wooden veneer of the guitar. "When I woke up I decided to move around a little and cleaned up some," she said.

"Where'd ya find my guitar? Haven't seen it in a while."

"Under your bed. Ya play?" she asked.

"Used to. Give it up after my accident, but couldn't part with it. Good memories."

"It's a 140, isn't it? I haven't seen one in years. Still has a good tone," Maddie said.

"What did you play?"

"A custom-made Flyin' V. I liked its heavier tonal quality."

"Rocker, huh?"

"Nah, just a wannabe," Maddie said softly, standing to put the old guitar back in its case.

"Well, play somethin' for me while I eat one of these burritos Alice sent over in case ya was hungry," Buck said as he began unrolling a small aluminum-wrapped package in his lap. He took a big bite and said as he chewed, "Make it somethin' I know the words to in case I decide to sing along."

Maddie sat down and rubbed her sore fingers down her thigh before swinging the guitar back onto her lap. "How about this one?" she asked, hoping she would remember the chords. "First piece I ever learned, but it's kinda old," she said as she placed the fingers of her left hand on the strings and strummed the first chord of "Summertime" with her right thumb. She cleared her throat and sang the first words of the old song. Buck set his burrito on the counter and joined her. Their voices blended well together and Maddie smiled. Buck's voice was a mellow baritone that harmonized well with her lower range alto. They both laughed when they reached the end of the tune.

Singing with Buck and playing the old guitar had brought back bittersweet memories for Maddie—but filled her with a sense of calm she hadn't felt for years. But it was only a temporary feeling and she knew it.

"Hey, ya know what we should do?" Buck said.

"Get our asses back to work?" Maddie answered as she closed the old guitar case.

"Besides that. I should gather some of the guys and convince Carson to offer live music and a free dance our last weekend here," he said. "Go out with a bang, y'know."

Maddie shook her head. "You've got a decent voice, Buck, but count me out."

"Why, kid? I can tell by the way ya play, you'd be real good. Afraid you'd be successful?"

She turned and glared at her friend. "I've been successful, old man," she snapped. "It ain't all it's cracked up to be." She hadn't performed in public for years and was afraid her voice either wouldn't hold up or be as powerful as it once was.

"We'd be a carnie group and not likely to go beyond carnie gigs, but we might at least have a little fun," Buck grumbled. "Nothin' wrong with that, kid."

DESPITE MADDIE'S PROTESTS Buck rounded up a small group of amateur musicians, two guitarists, a drummer, a keyboard player, and a couple of back-up singers. After some confusion, they finally rehearsed after the carnival closed for the next five or six evenings and talked Maddie into at least giving it a try for one night, maybe a second if the first went well. She only agreed because she didn't want to disappoint the people who had befriended her when she had no one. She talked Alice into cutting her hair, which had grown down to her shoulders, back to its old familiar spiky length and style.

The last weekend of the carnival, Maddie walked onto the stage to perform during the free dance. When she finally stepped in front of the microphone, images from her past invaded her mind and she was transported to a time when she was fresh, and new, and hungry, just beginning her career. It was the most exciting time of her life and she'd loved it. Everything was fun and easy as they traveled from small club to small club, perfecting their own unique sound.

Until the night Shay and her entourage invaded the club where Maddie and her band were performing as a warm-up group. Maddie remembered feeling Shay's eyes follow her as she moved across the stage, sweat running down her hyped-up body as she raised her arms to acknowledge the cheers of the audience. Shortly after Maddie and her band left the stage, they were interrupted by a knock on their small dressing room door. When the door opened, Shay seemed to fill the opening with her magnetic presence. She was friendly, charming, and mildly flirtatious when she invited them to join her group for drinks and conversation. One drink turned into several fairly quickly until Maddie found herself being pressed closely against Shay's body as they danced on the small, intimate dancefloor. Maddie found Shay's dark eyes mesmerizing as they seemed to look deeply into her soul, wordlessly inviting her to let the older woman guide her on a stroll into the wild life. After that night, Maddie's life changed and everything gradually spiraled out of control.

As the carnie group warmed up, Maddie gazed out over the small crowd. A group of teenaged girls rested their arms on the front edge of the stage and stared up at Maddie. She hadn't been able to replicate the outfit she used to wear onstage but got as close as she could with tight black pants and a loose, flowing black shirt, trimmed with silver piping. Her light blonde hair stood out against the black outfit and seemed to glow under the hot lights over her.

Maddie closed her eyes for a moment and when she opened them again, for an instant, the faces of the girls at the apron of the stage were replaced by the faces of Shay and Courtney grinning up at her, tempting her. Maddie turned away quickly to face the other musicians and erase the ache of the pain the two faces brought back. She blinked several times and saw the members of the band staring at each other, waiting for Maddie to begin the first song. She swallowed and forced herself into automatic pilot, shutting down the painful past. She spun around and stomped her foot on the wooden platform three times before striking the first chord soundly and confidently.

The group played a variety of country-western songs with a few heavier rock tunes thrown in for the younger crowd. After the show Maddie was stopped by the attractive young woman, Dani, who had been with Jan on the Midway. She was shy and seemed somewhat reticent, but still looked vaguely familiar to Maddie.

While Maddie packed up at the end of the last dance set, Dani sat on a folding chair nearby. Maddie looked at her and nodded. "Somethin' I can do for you?" she asked.

Dani shook her head—but continued staring at Maddie. Finally, she said, "Your voice has changed, but I like it more now, I think. Somehow it seems mellower, richer." Dani shrugged. "Maybe it's just me."

"I'll have to work on that then. It's been a while since I sang," Maddie said.

"I know. Ten or eleven years. I was at your last performance," Dani said, fiddling with her fingers nervously.

"Yeah, that was a memorable night," Maddie commented. "Hope you enjoyed the show."

"I enjoyed tonight's more. It felt like it was the real you."

Maddie stood up straight and planted her hands on her hips with a grin. "Yeah, well, everyone's a fuckin' critic, but thanks."

"I don't expect you to remember me, but I wanted to thank you."

"For singin'?"

Dani shook her head again and looked frustrated. "No. I was with you when you were arrested that night and wanted to thank you for taking the blame for the accident."

Maddie didn't know what to say. Honestly, she hadn't believed she'd actually go to prison over it. It was just another bad decision in what now seemed like a lifetime of bad decisions. The girl with her was nothin' more than a vague memory. Maddie took the rap because if she hadn't been so blasted, the girl wouldn't have been driving. She had taken too many drugs and picked Dani up because she was angry with the woman with her, who minutes earlier had fucked her brains out.

At last, she said, "I was out of control. It wasn't your fault, kid."

Maddie picked up her guitar case and walked off. Dani followed her to the Midway. She approached Maddie again as she helped Alice close up her booth. Maddie lit a cigarette and lowered a plywood barrier to the front of the booth.

"Go home," Maddie said when she saw Dani. "I already said it wasn't your fault. Get over it."

"I can't. A man died and I...I was responsible."

Maddie scowled at her. "Look, kid, I'm not your priest, your preacher, or your rabbi. If you feel guilty, take it up with one of them. Just leave me alone. I can't do a fuckin' thing for you," she said as she tightened down the last screw holding the plywood and yanked on the board to assure herself it was secure.

"I only want to talk to you," Dani said. "That was all I wanted ten years ago. I didn't expect you to...to...."

"To fuck you?" Maddie grinned.

"Of course not! I want to apologize for being too young and too scared to take the blame myself."

Maddie leaned closer. "I was higher than a fuckin' kite that night. I had no idea what I was doin', but never believed it would cost me ten years of my life or my fuckin' career," she said with a bite in her voice. She tossed her cigarette away and looked at Dani. "Go home, kid."

"Stop calling me that. I'm not a kid anymore."

Maddie's eyes raked slowly up and down Dani's body and she smiled, licking her lips. "Yeah, I noticed that. Now get the hell outta here before I forget it. I need to finish this so I can get my beauty sleep."

THE NEXT NIGHT Dani returned to the carnival and dance. Maddie stared at Dani as she struck the strings of the guitar to begin the driving beat of a song about the pain of lust and desire.

Baby, baby, baby!
Kiss me,
Love me,
Tell me that you want me.

She moved as close to the microphone as possible, bent her knees slightly, and grabbed the microphone stand, giving the appearance she was making love to the microphone, her hands stroking the metal stand, all the while staring at Dani with hooded eyes. Although the song began with a heavy rock beat, it morphed into a slower rhythm that was easy to dance to, with plenty of room for periodic blissful groans or growls as Maddie swayed. She smiled as she watched Dani's face. She would make the young woman suffer in her own sweet way.

The beast inside me wants to feel your young body pressed against mine.
Needs to touch your soft skin,
Hungers for the heat of your lips on mine,
Driving me out of my mind with desire.
But somewhere deep in my soul
I knew you weren't ready.
Do you remember what I said
That night I set you free
From the beast raging inside of me?

During an instrumental interlude after the first stanza of the song, Maddie glanced down at the girls standing close to the stage, smiled, and reached down to one of them, who appeared to be thirteen or fourteen. She pulled the girl up onto the stage and whispered something to her before taking her into her arms and leading the girl into a slow dance.

Near the end of the interlude, Maddie returned to the edge of the stage and lowered the girl carefully to the floor again, pausing to throw her a kiss before picking her guitar up again to begin the second stanza.

Someday I'll find the one who'll take me away,

Someone who'll fill the hunger growing within me,
Clawing to be free.
I thought you were the one.
I thought I wanted you, I thought I needed you, baby.
But you were too young, so I moved on
Until you were ready to fill me with your desire.
Ready to come home where you belong, baby.
Until I was ready to lie safely in your arms and feel your tender
touch.

The band continued to play behind her. Maddie turned to face them for a moment, then pointed at the drummer who began pounding out a heavy beat that lasted a few seconds. Maddie faced the audience and struck the original chords that began the song, her voice crying out above the screams and whistles coming from the jumping crowd.

Then kiss me, baby,
Feel me, honey,
I know you want me
So let me make you mine.

The song ended with a loud scream and a joint guitar riff by Maddie and Buck. When the final chords faded away, Maddie grinned at Buck and saw Alice bouncing just off-stage as she clapped. Maddie leaned down and said, "I think you'll have a hot fan waiting for ya, Buck."

Buck nodded. "The music always makes 'em wet, kid. Good job tonight," he smiled.

While she was putting her guitar in its case after the show, Maddie asked Buck to bunk in with someone else. He looked around her at Dani and agreed.

Dani went with Maddie as she closed down Alice's Midway booth.

Maddie fired up a cigarette while working.

"When did you start smoking?" Dani asked.

"In prison while I was gettin' the drugs out of my system," Maddie responded as she wrapped a rope around her shoulder and elbow.

"Did it work?"

"Most of the time. As long as my hands stayed busy, I was okay." She wiggled her fingers at Dani and laughed at the flush that ran up her neck.

"Is there someplace we can talk privately?" Dani asked.

Maddie glanced around, squinting as the smoke from her cigarette floated up toward her eyes. "Nobody around here to hear anythin' you say." She grinned before adding, "Unless you have somethin' else *private* in mind." She moved closer to Dani and ran her fingers down her arm. "I can take care of that, too, baby," she whispered.

Maddie laughed as Dani pushed her away, glowering at her. She grabbed Dani's arm and said, "Follow me, kid."

MADDIE UNLOCKED THE door to the trailer she shared with Buck and stepped inside. She turned and held her hand out to Dani.

"Buck's stayin' with a friend. They found an all-night poker game somewhere. Come on in and make yourself comfortable," she invited.

When Dani ignored her, Maddie went inside and opened the fridge, grabbing a bottle of orange juice. She opened it and gulped down several swallows. When she looked up, Dani was standing in the doorway. "Close the fuckin' door if you're gonna stay. Can't afford to cool the great outdoors. Want somethin' to drink? We have beer, water, and some wine coolers."

"Water, please."

Maddie tossed her a bottle of water. Dani drank a couple of swallows as she looked around the dingy trailer.

"Sorry about the mess," Maddie said with a shrug. "It's the maid's year off." She cleared a spot on the small couch and waited for Dani to sit.

Dani looked at Maddie. "What happened to you? You had *everything*. Women, money, anything you wanted."

"*You* happened to me. I met you and, in a flash," she stopped to snap her fingers loudly, "everythin' I had worked so hard for was...gone," Maddie said, her voice heated.

"I was a *kid*, as you keep reminding me. I *trusted* you." Dani shook her head and laughed. "I only went with Jan so she wouldn't be alone. I had no idea what I was getting myself into. You should have chosen her."

Maddie plopped down next to Dani and propped her feet on an old milk carton. "Well, this is what you get after you finish payin' off the mother of all fuck-ups, baby. Impressive, huh?"

"Thanks for the drink, Maddie, but I think I should leave now."

"Leave? And miss all the fun?" She sat up and leaned closer to Dani. "I'm a lot more fun when I'm sober and actually *know* what I'm doing," she whispered. "Isn't this what you wanted ten years ago? To be alone with me like this?" Maddie nibbled at Dani's neck and placed her hand on her knee.

"Stop it," Dani said, shoving Maddie's hand away. "I was a confused kid back then and didn't realize what the hell I was getting into."

"Oh, come on, baby, don't be that way. After all, I never got to finish what I was doin' before you ran over that guy. You owe me just a little payback, doncha think?"

Maddie set her drink down and smiled lecherously at Dani, letting her eyes skim slowly down her body as she licked her lips. "So nice," she murmured as she brought a hand up and ran it to the back of Dani's neck, leaning closer to trail her tongue down her neck, stopping to suck softly at Dani's pulse point. Leaning farther over Dani, Maddie slowly maneuvered her lower on the small couch. But before Maddie could go any further, Dani grabbed the front of her shirt and pulled her into a mind-blowing kiss, drawing Maddie's tongue deeply into her hot mouth. Maddie felt her body respond as she returned the kiss just as fervently, her hand drifting up Dani's body and cupping her breast. Maddie pulled her close against her body, taking Dani's mouth hungrily and greedily while her hands explored her body freely.

"Is this what you wanted ten years ago?" she whispered into Dani's ear. "Because it's sure as hell what I wanted."

"I was a stupid kid and you were a drugged-out predator. I've learned a lot in ten years."

"True, but you've learned how to be a dynamite kisser." The feel of Dani's hand sliding beneath her shirt and down her muscled abdomen brought Maddie out of her temporary haze of unwanted desire and she sat up abruptly, moving away from Dani. "I think it's time for you to leave," Maddie said unexpectedly. "It's been a long fuckin' day." Maddie pushed her body up and ran a slightly shaking hand through her hair. She'd come too close to giving herself to someone else who had the power to hurt her. She stepped over Dani and went to the trailer door, pushing it open. She shook another cigarette from her pack and lit it, blowing a stream of smoke outside.

"So now you *don't* want me." Dani laughed.

"Don't you get it, baby, I *never* wanted you, but I would have happily taken you anyway and it would have been sweet, even if I didn't remember your fuckin' name the next day," Maddie snarled cruelly. "Hell, I barely remember you now," she laughed.

Dani stood and went to the door. She paused a moment before stepping out and looked at Maddie. "You've changed. And apparently not for the better."

"Yeah, well, life's a mean bitch, full of so much promise and so many cruel disappointments."

Maddie watched Dani walk away as she finished her cigarette and tossed it out the door. She lay down and threw her arm over her eyes. The carnival was suddenly becoming a minefield of unwanted emotions. She needed to escape before everything exploded around her. She reread Jan's note and got up, quickly shoving what little she owned into her duffel. She jotted a note for Buck, explaining her decision to leave, not sure yet where she would go.

She left the trailer, never pausing to look back and leaving the guitar behind. It would only serve as an unwelcome reminder of a past she was better off forgetting.

Chapter Five

MADDIE HITCHHIKED FOR a couple of hours before a truck stopped after midnight and agreed to drop her at a truck stop just outside of Wichita Falls, Texas. She ate enough food from a buffet at the truck stop to last her a while and began following the highway toward town until she found a sign for the turn-off to the Wichita County Civic Center.

Several miles later she located the Civic Center. Wichita Falls? Was this really the last town she and her band played before everything turned to shit? For them it had just been another nameless stop on a seemingly endless tour of nameless mid-American towns that all seemed to blend together after weeks, or had it been months, on the road. She wandered around the complex and finally saw the word "Auditorium" emblazoned on a section of the larger complex.

She didn't remember the venue they'd played being this large but didn't remember much after their arrival. She found the loading dock behind the auditorium and stared at a back entrance. They basically all looked alike, but in her mind, she could visualize grabbing the light green metal handrail down the back steps, Courtney draped all over her. Maddie was so fuckin' high she was lucky she remembered how to walk. All she wanted was to fall into a bed and sleep, but Courtney said something that pissed Maddie off and she'd waded into the knotted group of mostly teenage girls, screaming her name and reaching out for even the slightest touch on their hand or arm that they wouldn't wash for a week, until the next rocker came to town.

That was when Maddie saw her—a quiet, self-conscious looking girl trying to make herself invisible behind a pretty, and probably willing, young girl with shiny auburn hair. But Maddie liked a challenge. To the auburn-haired girl's disappointment, Maddie offered her hand and a roguish grin to the shy girl who said her name was Danielle. Honestly, Maddie didn't remember much after that until the damn accident.

A couple of blocks from the Civic Center, Maddie found a

pay phone that still had an intact phonebook attached. She flipped through it looking for an address for Oscar's Auto Repair Shop. The training she'd received at Sand Ridge qualified her as a certified mechanic. Somewhere in her stuff she carried a letter of recommendation from her instructor, David Larsen. She pulled the folded note Jan left in the trailer and looked up the address for Mama's Place. Sounded like a strip joint or something, but she needed a dry place to bunk. And luckily, it was on the same street as Oscar's. She turned to the front of the phonebook, looked around to see if anyone would see her, and ripped out the small street map.

By the time she walked to the street she wanted, the rooming house was closed. She spent the night on a porch swing and was awakened early the next morning by a shrill voice yelling, "Miz Flo, some stranger's asleep on your porch!" Maddie jumped up to see a buck-toothed, young black woman staring at her. A hand flew out and the young woman said, "Clorinda," shaking her hand in Maddie's face impatiently.

"Sorry, I must've dozed off," Maddie muttered, grabbing the hand to stop its continued annoying flailing. "Maddie," she said, eliciting a toothy grin. While she ran her hands over her face, a heavily tattooed, middle-aged woman with graying, crew cut hair, stepped onto the porch, wearing a black Harley-Davidson T-shirt, cut-offs and flip-flops.

"Whatcha need?" the woman asked in a low, whiskey smooth voice that sounded like it had spent too much time in too many bars over the years, her fists planted on her hips.

"Someone told me ya might have a room to rent at a reasonable rate," Maddie said, leery of the woman and the three women surrounding her, one of whom wore what appeared to be a police or sheriff's uniform.

"Trouble, honey?" the uniformed woman asked, resting her hand on the butt of the pistol on her hip. The woman was an inch or two taller than Maddie, with short ginger hair and piercing hazel eyes. Her face and arms were heavily covered with freckles.

"Nothin' I can't handle, Sal," the muscular woman replied with an affectionate smile. "Don't be late for work, baby." Turning back to Maddie, she extended her hand and said, "Flo. When did you get out?"

"Who said I'd been in," Maddie said defensively, ignoring the proffered hand. "Just lookin' for a place to sleep."

Flo grinned and said, "I ain't fuckin' blind, sugar. Regular people wouldn't be caught dead in them clothes. Besides, soon as I get your name, Sal here," she said, jerking her thumb at the taller woman behind her, "will run it to check out your background, won't ya, baby."

"In a fuckin' heartbeat," the woman in uniform growled menacingly.

"Maddie James," Maddie spat and stared at Sal. "Need me to spell that for you, *baby?*"

Flo's hand came up quickly and slapped Maddie's face. "Learn to show a little respect or get off our goddamn porch."

Maddie rubbed her jaw and fisted her other hand as she turned back to glare at Flo.

"I wouldn't," Sal threatened in a low voice. "Tell her when ya were released."

"Couple weeks ago," Maddie spat.

"Your probation officer send ya?" Flo asked.

"Don't have one. Did the whole dime," Maddie said.

"What were ya in for?" Sal asked.

"Vehicular manslaughter while under the influence."

"Where did ya do your time?" Sal asked

"Sand Ridge. Why all the damn questions if you're gonna run a background check anyway, Ranger Rick?" Maddie pointed at Flo. "And don't even think about smackin' me again. I don't like it. I'm just lookin' for a place to sleep."

Flo stuck out her hand again and Maddie took it without wincing from Flo's strong grip.

"I don't rent to troublemakers and ya got that look about ya. Obey the rules and we'll be cool. Rent's twenty a week. I provide breakfast and lunch. The girls, includin' you, fix dinner for everyone, except Sunday. Sal and me fix that, usually on the grill out back. No drugs, no liquor, no dates in the rooms. We share chores around the house. You'll need to sign up for those every Saturday morning. Do your own laundry. Weekly random room inspections. Questions?"

Maddie grinned. "Sounds kinda like being in prison, except for the food part. Do I need to make an appointment to breathe, too?"

"Watch it, hot shot," Sal growled as she poked Maddie in the chest.

Maddie slapped Sal's hand away.

"You're gonna have a problem with this one, Flo," Sal said.

"I got it, baby," Flo grinned. "Oh, and no smokin' inside. Go outside for that."

"Anything else ya *forgot*?" Maddie asked.

"I'll let ya know when I make up another rule just for you, princess," Flo chuckled.

Maddie picked up her duffel before following Flo into the older, but clean looking two-story house and up the stairs. Flo opened a door and stepped inside. Maddie looked around the room and dropped her meager belongings onto the bed.

"There's a Salvation Army Thrift store a couple of blocks away and a small Mom and Pop grocery. We grow most of our own vegetables out back."

"Bathroom?" Maddie inquired.

"End of the hall and another downstairs. You provide your own toilet paper and personal hygiene stuff. Dinner's usually around six. Elena's cookin' tonight, so it'll probably be tacos or some other Mexican delicacy," Flo said, making a face. "If you're hungry now, I'll whip up some eggs and gravy. We have chickens out back, too."

"Sounds good," Maddie said. "Any coffee?"

"There's a coffeemaker in the kitchen. Probably some left over. Ya can reheat it in the microwave. Don't cause no trouble and ya won't have none. Ya got off to a rocky start already, but livin' here ain't bad."

"Where were you?" Maddie asked.

"Percyville. A shithole, but I learned to keep my nose clean and my mouth shut. You're still workin' on that, I reckon."

"That where you met the Nazi?"

"Nope. This is her house. I met her doin' some renovation on it after I got out and we sorta clicked, y'know," Flo said with a smile. "Gonna be lookin' for a job?"

"I trained to be a mechanic while I was in and heard that Oscar's might be hirin', if he has an openin'," Maddie said.

"He usually has one if you're any good. Nice guy, but tough. Fair to the ex-cons who work for him. Retired probation officer. Don't put up with any shit."

"Great," Maddie mumbled.

"If ya have any money, ya might see if ya can pick up something a little better before ya ask Oscar for a try-out."

"Okay," Maddie nodded before pulling four wrinkled twenties out of her back pocket and handing it to Flo.

"Where'd ya get eighty bucks?"

"Been workin' at a carnival over in some burg near the border, repairin' machinery and workin' on the Midway. It's leavin' today, so I collected my pay and hitched over here last night."

Flo snorted. "Since there ain't a fuckin' thing here, I'd say ya made a piss poor choice there."

"Wouldn't be the first time," Maddie smirked. "It was a personal decision you don't need to understand."

THE FOLLOWING MORNING, Maddie was up before the sun, took a leisurely shower, and dressed in a pair of five-dollar jeans and a light gray T-shirt. She pulled on a cheap pair of work boots and clomped downstairs. While she was preparing a pot of coffee, Flo and Sal wandered into the kitchen, shocked to find anyone else awake before dawn. Sal's arm was wrapped loosely around Flo's neck and she held her affectionately.

"What're ya up so damn early for?" Sal growled.

"That against the rules, too?" Maddie quipped over her shoulder. "Just thought I'd check out the silverware in case I have a need to split quick-like."

"Learn that smart-ass crap in prison?" Sal sneered.

"I learned a lot of things in prison, chief," Maddie grinned. "You can give me a pop quiz later if ya feel the need, but right now I'm goin' out for a smoke. Coffee'll be ready in a few minutes."

Maddie strolled out the back door and lit a generic cigarette she'd purchased the evening before when she picked up her new clothes. She wandered casually around the well-tended back yard, stopping occasionally to examine the plants growing in the large garden. She smiled as she leaned against a fenced enclosure to watch the chickens pecking at the ground, accompanied by their chicks. Oddly, it reminded her of home, something she hadn't thought about in more years than she could count.

She closed her eyes and let the memories of growing up on her parents' Nebraska farm filter through her mind. All she could see at first was the smiling face of a young blonde woman. Seeing that face filled Maddie with a warm glow. Then she saw herself being suddenly lifted off the ground by strong, tanned arms a moment before she was tossed high into the blue sky, giggling as those strong arms caught her gently to toss her upward again, squealing with childish laughter. The memories fast-forwarded to a time when the childish laughter ended and she stared down at the peaceful, unsmiling faces of her parents, blurred by her tears.

Her parents had died unexpectedly, the farm was gone, and at sixteen, Maddie was considered too old for adoption and made a ward of the state. Funds from the sale of the farm were held in trust for Maddie until she turned eighteen and was on her own for the first time. That was when her journey down the road of poor choices started, slowly at first, then gathering speed until that night about eleven years ago. Maddie's hands were shaking by the time she opened her eyes and lit another cigarette to calm her nerves. She leaned down and picked up a chick, stroking it softly with her thumb. She set it down carefully before making her way back into the house. She filled a mug with coffee and took the plate Flo handed her. She joined Sal at the dining room table.

"You like chickens?" Sal asked.

Maddie shrugged. "They don't hurt nobody."

Sal shook her head and smiled. "Flo says they're calmin'."

"I s'pose," Maddie said.

"You grew up on a farm somewhere, didn't ya?" Sal asked over the top of her coffee mug.

"Nebraska, but since ya ran a background check on me, ya already know I did," Maddie glared. "What's it to ya?"

"Just curious," Sal shrugged.

"Curiosity killed the cat, y'know," Maddie muttered.

Sal stiffened. "Was that a threat, James?"

"An observation, but take it however ya want," Maddie said as she shoved the last of her breakfast into her mouth and stood to stack her dishes before carrying them into the kitchen.

SAL FOLLOWED MADDIE and leaned against a kitchen

counter, resting her hand on Flo's shoulder until Maddie left the room.

"I think you're makin' a mistake with that one, honey," Sal said.

"You interrogate her again?" Flo snorted. Turning her head to look at Sal, she smiled and said, "I wish you'd leave that cop attitude at work, baby. I can't get these women to trust us when you're always givin' 'em the third-degree because of that stick up your ass."

Sal leaned over and kissed Flo softly. "Sorry, baby. It's just a habit. Besides, I thought ya liked my ass."

Flo returned the kiss. "I do, but break that habit or ya might find yourself sleepin' on the damn couch."

Sal moved behind Flo and encircled her waist, nibbling at her neck. "I wouldn't like that, sugar, but neither would you," she mumbled as her hands began wandering.

Flo tried to shake her away unsuccessfully. "I was takin' care of my own...needs...long before I met you, y'know."

"But it's more fun when someone else does it for ya," Sal whispered as her hands covered Flo's breasts and squeezed lightly. "Damn. I love ya, Flo," she added. "And love takin' care of your...needs."

"Love ya, too, baby," Flo responded with a grin.

MADDIE WALKED DOWN the street until she spotted a large black and yellow sign above triple garage doors announcing Oscar's Auto Repair. She lit another cigarette and sat on the curb across the street from the well-kept looking business, her forearms resting on her knees. Fifteen minutes later, she fieldstripped her cigarette and stuffed the filter into the front pocket of her jeans as the doors were pulled up by chains. Three well-built, heavily tattooed muscular men who couldn't have been anything other than ex-cons, or three of the Village People, anchored the chains and strolled into the garage bays to begin working.

Maddie trotted across the street and sashayed slowly into the garage with her hands shoved into the back pockets of her jeans. She stopped beside the first man she saw and stood there silently, watching him as he worked under the hood of a fairly new

Chrysler 300. The man tossed a wrench onto a tool table next to him and straightened up, glancing at Maddie. "Hep ya, girlie?" he asked as his eyes drifted over her tall body.

"Oscar around?" she responded.

"Prob'ly in the office, but he don't need no Girl Scout cookies," the big man chuckled.

"Good thing because I ain't no fuckin' Girl Scout," Maddie said with a grin. "Even though I did manage to earn a merit badge for muff divin' at camp."

The big man grunted and stuck his head back under the Chrysler's hood.

Maddie glanced around and spotted a neon sign denoting the location of the business' office. She stepped over tools and auto parts to reach the office and rapped solidly three times on the door while looking over her shoulder at the three mechanics. The office door opened and a pleasant looking older Hispanic man motioned her inside, a telephone receiver against his ear. He pointed at an old vinyl covered chair in front of his desk. She sat down quietly while he continued his phone call.

A few minutes later, he slammed the receiver into its cradle and muttered, "*Bendejo.*" Then he smiled and looked at Maddie. "What can I do for you, ma'am?"

"I'm lookin' for a job and heard there might be one available here," Maddie said.

He leaned back and steepled his fingers against his lips. "What kind of job you lookin' for?" he asked.

"Mechanic. I have a letter of recommendation from Dave Larson, my instructor."

"Good man. You were at Sand Ridge then."

Maddie nodded. "Got out a couple of weeks ago."

Oscar pulled out a blank application and handed it to her. "Fill this out. Maybe a female mechanic won't be as intimidating to my female customers." He handed her a pen. "Be as specific as you can about what Dave taught you to do." As soon as she started to fill out the form, he stuck his hand out. "Oscar Melendez," he said.

Maddie choked involuntarily, setting off a coughing fit. "Madelyn," she finally managed as she took his hand briefly.

"Who's your probation officer? I'll need to contact him or her," Oscar said.

"Don't have one," Maddie said quietly. "Did my whole time."

"You find a place to stay?"

"Staying with Flo and Sal up the street."

"Good choice. They'll treat you right if you don't fuck up. Want a bottle of water?"

"Thank you, sir," Maddie answered.

After writing down everything she could think of, Maddie handed the form back to him and chugged half the bottle of cold water, not optimistic about being hired after he figured out who she was. While he looked over the form, she glanced around the office, stopping when her eyes landed on a photo of a handsome young man standing behind an attractive young woman. His hand rested easily on her shoulder and he held a girl who appeared to be around four- or five-years old. An older child, a boy around seven, stood next to his mother, smiling broadly.

Oscar noticed Maddie staring at the picture. "My son, Bryan, and his family. He's gone, but his wife and kids still live here."

"I'm sorry," Maddie muttered.

"Madelyn James," Oscar said, looking over her application. "I bet they called you Maddie...when you were little."

"Still do," Maddie admitted as she stood up to leave. Until that moment, she'd never truly faced the consequences of her actions. She hadn't been driving the vehicle, but her drug-induced actions had caused the accident that took Bryan Melendez's life in seconds, leaving behind a widow and two fatherless young children. "I'm sorry I wasted your time, Mr. Melendez," she said around a lump in her throat.

Melendez stood. "Come back in the morning. I have a kinda special project I think you'd be perfect for."

She shook her head. "I won't take this job because you feel sorry for me."

"I don't feel sorry for you. Hell, at least you're still suckin' air. My son is dead because of your recklessness and you have to live knowin' his wasn't the only life you affected," Oscar forced through gritted teeth. He took a deep breath to calm his emotions before continuing, "You paid your debt and I've forced myself to accept that. I have to believe you received the punishment you deserved, even though others don't. Come back tomorrow ready to work or I may have to get Sal to drag your sorry ass in. Pretty sure she'd enjoy doin' that. Now beat it."

"Yes, sir," Maddie muttered before leaving the small office. She nodded at the big man she'd spoken to earlier and stuffed her hand into her jean pocket to pull out a cigarette, lighting it after she stepped outside. She walked home, wondering why Oscar had even considered hiring the person responsible for the needless death of his son.

She sat on the porch swing to finish her cigarette and think, wondering where Buck, Alice, and the other carnies who'd taken her in and accepted her without question, were. She would miss them, their crass manners and humor. She was sure they were all trying to escape from something, but had never judged her. She fieldstripped her cigarette, rolling it between her thumb and middle finger and stuffed the filter in her pocket before entering the house. The sound of a deep bass throbbed through the front room of the house, bringing back the memory of her group's bass player, Thumper Mason, pounding out a driving beat that reminded Maddie of a pulsing heartbeat.

Flo came out of the kitchen wiping her hands on a towel tucked into the waist of her pants. "So when do ya start?" she asked.

"Tomorrow mornin'," Maddie answered. "Any coffee left?"

"Just made a fresh pot," Flo nodded. "I knew Oscar'd hire ya," she added.

"Why would he? He knows I did time for killin' his son," Maddie said.

"That was you?" Flo asked with surprise. "Don't mention that to Sal. She worked with Bryan."

"If she ran my background, she probably already knows," Maddie said as she filled a mug with coffee.

"Go out to the chicken coop for me and gather up any eggs ya find, will ya?"

"Okay. Got a basket?" Maddie asked, setting her mug down after taking a gulp.

"In the coop. Hey, did ya meet Crew while ya was at Oscar's?"

Maddie shrugged. "I dunno. What's he look like?"

"Big guy with lots of tattoos and a red beard."

"I saw him, but we didn't really talk," Maddie said. "Looked rough."

Flo laughed. "He does, but has a heart of gold. He protects his friends. Saved my ass."

THE NEXT MORNING, Maddie waited outside Oscar's, smoking a cigarette and sipping coffee from a travel mug Flo had loaned her for work, waiting for the metal garage doors to begin rising. She felt her stomach flutter with nerves when she heard the inside locks flip. She flicked her cigarette into the street and ducked under the first door when it was half open. The big man with the red beard said, "Eager beaver, huh?"

"Yeah. Workin' on my Eager Beaver Merit Badge," she smirked.

"Another smart-ass," he muttered as he hooked the first chain in place.

"Is there a merit badge for that, too? I need to add to my collection."

By the time the final door was open, Oscar came out of the office and walked to where Maddie was standing, examining a socket wrench. "Listen up, men," he started. "This is Maddie. Hired her yesterday. Just released from Sand Ridge recently and lookin' for a fresh start." Pointing to each man, he said, "The mountain there is Crew. You'll report to him for most of your problems. Then there's Freddie and Beau." He patted her on the shoulder and added softly, "Watch your back and don't fuck up."

"What's the special project you wanted me to work on?" Maddie asked, tying a navy-blue bandanna around her head.

"It's over in the last bay," Oscar answered. She followed him and stopped to stare at a rusting vehicle body whose axles were resting on four stacks of cinderblocks. The three men she'd just met, chuckled as they began working.

"What the hell is it, besides a car body?" she asked. "I'm not really trained for body work."

"It's the body for a sixty-eight Camaro, but needs a little work and a lot of love."

"Yeah," Maddie laughed. "Like an engine, transmission, and just about everthing else."

"Your job is to locate the parts you need to get the damn thing runnin'," Oscar said.

Maddie walked slowly around the body, bending over to

stick her head through a glassless side window. When she stood up, she said, straight-faced, "With a little work, a few cans of spray paint, and four roller skates, I might be able to get ya a really big pedal car. Otherwise, I'd say you're dreamin', *kimo sabe*."

Maddie glanced over at Crew who was chuckling and saw him lick his finger, mark an imaginary line in the air, and mouth *smart-ass*. She stifled a grin by rubbing her face and cleared her throat. "Any *imaginary* tools available for this *imaginary* vehicle?" she asked.

Oscar shoved a rolling tool chest toward her and walked into his office, returning a few minutes later with a small stack of books. "I assume you can read, so these should help," he said as he dropped them into her arms. She glanced at the book spines and found titles on bodywork, automotive painting, upholstery, and vehicle parts, plus two with schematics of the working parts of the original sixty-eight Camaro. "There's three or four decent salvage yards around here, but you might have to inquire at a few places in Dallas. They'll ship whatever you need here. Anything you can't locate, tell me and I'll find it somewhere."

She looked at Oscar and grinned. "Road trip?"

He shook his head. "Just let your fingers do the walking."

"Well, that sucks," she mumbled under her breath.

"This project belonged to my son so I figure you should be the one to restore it. My grandson wants to finish it and get it on the road. I had it hauled here a couple of years ago, but couldn't force myself to work on it."

Maddie watched the beginning of tears pool in Oscar's eyes and elected to keep her mouth shut. She rolled an adjustable work table closer, grabbed a stool, and sat down, piling the books on the table, and flipped open the manufacturer's book of schematics. "Got a pen?" she asked, holding out her hand. She found a pad of paper and began jotting down a list of part numbers.

The next time she looked up to stretch her shoulders, Oscar had disappeared. She picked up her now cold coffee and had just swallowed the last of it when Crew moseyed over and said, "Consider it job security, girlie. This one could last until you start drawin' Social Security," he chuckled roughly.

Maddie rubbed her eyes, tired from reading for what seemed

like forever. Crew handed her a cloth from his back pocket. When she used it, the cloth left grease smudges all over her face. "Give my regards to Flo," Crew grinned with another deep chuckle.

When she took a break for lunch, she was approached by a moderately handsome employee with long, dirty blond hair pulled back into a ponytail. His name was Beau and he sat beside her on a long bench and unwrapped his sandwich. He tore open a bag of chips and offered it to her.

"Got my own," Maddie said.

"What were you in for, honey?" he asked around his first bite.

Maddie stared at him coldly. "Manslaughter, even though it's none of your fuckin' business."

"A tough girl, huh?" he said with a smile. "Just tryin' to be friendly."

"Save it. I'm not interested in bein' your friend, so piss off," she said.

Beau gathered his lunch and stood up while Crew chuckled nearby. Beau leaned over and said softly, "You're kinda cute, but I ain't crazy about that smart mouth."

Maddie looked up and grinned. "You'll get used to it," she said as she unpacked her lunch. She glanced at her hands and stood. She walked into the restroom to wash her hands, glancing briefly in the mirror over the sink while soaping up her hands. "Sonofabitch," she mumbled when she saw the splotches of grease that crossed her forehead and cheeks. She tried scrubbing her face with soap, but all she achieved was smearing the grease over the rest of her face, leaving only her eyes and mouth clear. Her eyes blinked out at her like a minstrel performer and she grinned, then broke out with laughter. It felt good. She couldn't remember the last time she'd really had a good laugh.

She returned to the shop area and grabbed a bottle of degreaser, ignoring Crew and Beau's snickers and smiled, "Good one, big guy." Back in the restroom, she squirted a handful of degreaser into her hands and scrubbed her face until it was clean."

Chapter Six

MADDIE WAS CATALOGUING parts for her 'project' and looked up to see a tall, good looking teenaged boy with jet-black hair and curious brown eyes staring at her. Maddie noticed a guitar case resting against his jean-covered leg. She was in the middle of checking out an engine for the Camaro she'd located in Abilene that was delivered that morning. It was hanging on an engine lift and she was disassembling parts to see if they were still in good shape. The salvage owner guaranteed the engine, but Maddie was pretty sure it wasn't as advertised since it had been languishing in the salvage yard for a couple of years after being involved in a collision, not to mention being exposed to the elements. She'd already found several rusting parts that could compromise the ability of the engine to operate optimally.

"Need somethin', chief?" she asked as she wiped her hands on a shop towel and stared back at the boy, who looked about seventeen or eighteen.

He shook his head. "Just stopped by to visit Poppy...uh...my grandfather." He pointed at the auto body next to Maddie. "That's my car," he said.

"Right now, it's a POS that might grow up to be a car someday, but it's got a long way to go," Maddie said.

"Hey, Joel!" Crew called out. "How's it hangin', man?"

The boy smiled and blushed slightly. "No complaints, Crew."

"Cool," Crew nodded. "He's in the office."

"Yeah, thanks," the boy said. Then he looked back at Maddie. "That it's new engine?" he asked.

"Maybe," Maddie answered with a shrug.

"Uh...can I help?" he asked.

"I got it, kid," she said, picking up a wrench to remove the old spark plugs, which looked shot to shit, but you never knew. Shifting her eyes to the guitar case, she asked, "You play?"

"Yeah. Sometimes I come here to practice because it's pretty quiet," he answered with a smile.

"Maybe you can play while we're workin'. Anythin' beats

that country crap Crew always has on the radio," she grinned at Crew, who waved a hand dismissively.

"Maybe," he said before picking up his guitar case and walking to the office. Only a few minutes passed before the clear sounds of a guitar filtered into the bays from Oscar's office. Maddie listened for a minute and turned back to her work on the old engine.

She stopped long enough to grab her travel mug, tilting it up for a quick drink of her coffee. An instant later, the coffee spewed out of her mouth onto the floor of her bay. She jogged to the shop's water cooler and rinsed her mouth and throat repeatedly to remove the taste of oil and gasoline.

Beau was laughing hysterically, but stopped when she flew at him, hitting him solidly in the diaphragm with her shoulder, knocking the air out of his lungs mid-laugh. He sprawled on the cement next to the vehicle he was working on, gasping for a breath.

"You think that was funny, ya fuckin' moron?" Maddie yelled, standing over his prone body.

"It wasn't me, bitch," he finally rasped as he struggled to stand. He grabbed the side of his worktable and pulled it over, dumping tools on the floor. The sound of metal clattering on the cement brought Oscar rushing out of his office, followed by his grandson.

"What the hell's going on out here?" Oscar demanded.

"Just a disagreement, boss," Crew rumbled.

Oscar looked back and forth between Maddie and Beau. "Who started this?" he asked.

They quickly brought fingers up to point at one another.

"Then I guess you'll share the punishment," Oscar said, calming down. "I want this floor scrubbed down, so clean I can eat off it. And while you're at it, the toilets can use a good cleaning, too. Before you leave tonight!"

Finally, Maddie said, "It was my fault, boss. I hit Beau first."

"Why?"

"Someone put gas in my coffee and since he was laughin', I assumed it was Beau so I hit him," she explained.

"Did you put gas in her coffee?" Oscar asked Beau.

"I rinsed off a part I'd cleaned in gas, but didn't know she'd drink that shit. It was already fuckin' cold," Beau said.

"Just a misunderstandin', boss," Crew added. "Right, guys?" he asked.

Maddie glared at Crew, but stuck her hand out to Beau, mumbling, "Sorry, man."

Beau grabbed her hand and squeezed it so hard she could feel the bones in her hand rub together, but ignored it.

"That's real sweet," Oscar said insincerely, "but I still want this shit picked up and the floor cleaned."

"We got it, boss," Crew said before anyone could argue.

As soon as Oscar entered his office and shut the door, Crew stood between Maddie and Beau. Unexpectedly, he reached out and grabbed both of them by their shirts and jerked them close to his face. "I don't want any trouble here, got it?" he asked threateningly, shaking them slightly. "Pretty sure you put gas in Maddie's drink, Beau, and I'm pretty sure you overreacted, Maddie. We all gotta work here, so find a fuckin' way to get along." He shoved them away. "Or next time I won't do a damn thing to save your pathetic asses. Grow the fuck up," he snarled. "And clean this goddamn floor!"

Maddie set Beau's tool table upright and tossed his tools back on it, then grabbed a bottle of degreaser, and squirted it liberally on the floor before filling two rolling buckets with steaming water. She pushed one toward Beau and began scrubbing the floor. Within a few minutes, the back of her work shirt was soaked with sweat and she paused long enough to strip it off and toss it aside. Half an hour later, Joel left his grandfather's office and stopped to run a hand over the hood of the Camaro body, perhaps imagining what it could look like one day.

"Hey, kid," Maddie said. "I work better when there's good music in the background. Play somethin' for us."

Joel found an old milk crate and sat down, resting his guitar across his thigh, took a deep breath, and flexed his fingers before picking out a series of intricate notes that filled the garage with distinctively Spanish sounds that Maddie enjoyed, but was unfamiliar with.

"What is that?" she asked, wringing out her mop.

"Classical," Joel answered quietly.

Maddie nodded and swung her mop back to the floor. "Kinda soothin'," she said.

For the next hour Joel played a number of pieces Maddie

found interesting, and a departure from the heavy rock she knew. It was melodic and beautiful, unlike the hard, raucous pieces she'd played.

After that Joel showed up nearly every day, presumably to check on the progress of his car, always accompanied by his guitar. Occasionally, Maddie let him get his hands dirty by helping her tear down a section of the old motor or rebuilding an old part. She enjoyed talking to the boy and taught him the basics of how automobiles worked. During her breaks, she split her sandwich with him and she asked him about his guitar and how he learned to play. She confessed she played, but nothing as sophisticated as what he did.

One day she dragged in an old guitar she'd found at the thrift store, but set it aside while she worked. Joel showed up later than usual and swept up the shop while Maddie wrestled with a stubborn bolt on the engine. After her wrench slipped and she ripped the skin on her knuckles, followed by a string of curse words, she walked around trying to shake it off, her hand covered by a shop cloth.

"Are you bleeding?" Joel asked.

Maddie pulled the cloth back and looked at her hand. "A little. Not enough to get worked up over."

"That your guitar?" he asked looking toward her case.

"Yeah. Hearin' you play kinda made me wanna play again, but I'd rather try alone here before I force anyone else to suffer through it," she said with a smile.

"Want me to leave?" he asked.

"That's okay," she answered. "I really liked that one song you played a couple of days ago. It had a really drivin' back beat. Maybe we can work on a way to jazz it up a little, if you don't mind me joinin' you."

"*Caballero?*" Joel asked.

"Don't know the name," Maddie said. "Just play a few notes and I'll pick up the tune."

Joel settled the guitar on his lap and began plucking out the quick intro to the song. Maddie tapped her foot and jumped in, increasing the pace slightly and adding a couple of faster riffs, making the old guitar sing before ending on a sliding note. Joel followed in a slightly higher octave that blended with hers.

"Any lyrics?" Maddie asked.

"No. It's just something I wrote for my music class," Joel said. "But my teacher said it wasn't really classical guitar. Called it junk music."

"Because it's rock and roll, man. Really *good* rock and roll," she enthused, clapping him on the shoulder.

"Joel!" a woman's voice called out. An instant later, an attractive brunette walked through the back door of the shop. "Let's go, *mijo*, or we'll be late...again."

"Okay, Mom," Joel said as he packed up his guitar. He glanced at Maddie and grinned, mouthing, *My mother. Sorry.*

Maddie plucked out a few more notes before returning her guitar to its case and standing up.

"How's the car coming along?" the woman asked.

"Not too bad, considerin' it was only a body. It's a long process," Maddie answered. She saw the expression on the woman's face when she finally looked at Maddie and saw the recognition in her eyes.

"What are you doing here?" the woman snapped. Without pausing, the guttural sound of a wounded animal erupted from her throat and she stepped quickly toward Maddie, stopping in front of her, pulling her hand back, and slapping her with the full force of her rage. As she drew back to strike her again, Maddie grabbed the woman's wrist and held it. Maddie relaxed her grip, knowing her actions had caused the woman's grief and fury.

"Mom! What are you doing?" Joel asked, looking confused.

His mother jerked her arm away and spun around to face her son, her index finger in his face.

"I forbid you to come here again as long as *she's* here, do you hear me?" she demanded, pointing at Maddie.

"Why? What's wrong, Mom?"

She spun back around and stared hatred at Maddie. "Because your Poppy hired *her*, knowing who she was."

"So what?" Joel said. "She's working on dad's car."

"Not anymore," she spat. "She *murdered* your father."

Maddie couldn't blame her for her violent reaction and was sure her handprint remained on her face like a brand. In all honesty, she barely remembered the woman striking her at the end of her trial, but Maddie had snorted a line of coke before that appearance and was high. Her memory of the event was cloudy at best.

"W...what?" Joel stammered as he looked back at Maddie. When she saw the anguished look on Joel's face when his mother dragged him out of the garage, for an instant Maddie saw the teen as a seven-year-old boy, struggling to understand what happened to his father and closed her eyes to shut out the past. She wanted to say something, anything, to ease his grief and absolve herself, but this was the road she'd chosen. There was nothing she could say that wouldn't hurt someone else.

MADDIE WALKED TO work the next day, fully expecting to be fired. She straightened her work space and attached the list of parts the Camaro would need to a clipboard, and puttered around until Oscar arrived. He motioned silently for her to follow him into his office, then pointed to the chair in front of his desk.

"From the earful I got last night, I assume you've met my daughter-in-law, Natalie," Oscar said as he fiddled with things on his desk.

"Yes, sir," Maddie said. "I don't want to cause any more trouble, so I'll gather anythin' that belongs to me and be out of here within the hour. I appreciate the chance to work, sir." She stood to leave, but Oscar stood as well.

"Sit down, James," he ordered. "I don't take orders from my daughter-in-law. I already knew you were responsible for my son's death, but believe everyone deserves a second chance. Natalie needs to find a way to get over her bitterness."

"But you won't be able to see Joel if I stay," Maddie said. "I don't want to harm your family any further."

"I see the kids every weekend and that'll have to do."

"What about the car?" she asked.

"I bought it for Bryan, but never signed it over to him. Since I still hold the title, it technically belongs to me, and I'll have anyone I choose work on restoring it. Understand?"

"Yes, sir. Thank you," Maddie answered and offered her hand. Oscar took it firmly before sitting down again.

"Get back to work, James," he muttered.

"Yes, sir," she said softly as she left the office.

That evening after work, Maddie walked to a bar that advertised it was women-friendly. She needed a chance to unwind and relax before going home to Flo's. Maybe she'd get lucky and meet a friendly woman who wouldn't object to inviting her home for a little romp and wouldn't ask too many questions. Maddie straightened her work clothes and sauntered into a bar called The Kloset, looking through the dim smoky gray haze, pausing to allow her eyes and ears to adjust.

She had played dozens of clubs and bars similar to The Kloset when she was starting out and considered leaving because it reminded her of dancing with Shay, their bodies pressed together as Shay twisted Maddie's nipples painfully or left teeth marks on her neck. Maddie shook her head to throw off the memory.

She located the bar near the front and ordered a beer before finding a place in the shadows at the end of the bar to observe the pulsing dance floor full of gyrating patrons. On the far side of the dance floor, she saw a familiar face and smiled. Jan was attempting to coax her friend, Dani onto the dance floor, but Dani wasn't having it. Maddie finished her beer and walked around the edge of the dance floor until she quietly slid in behind Jan and encircled her waist, pulling Jan firmly against her body.

"Let's show 'em how it's done, baby," Maddie growled softly in Jan's ear.

Jan turned and stared at Maddie. Then a seductive grin split her face. "Well, if it isn't the wild child. I didn't think I'd ever see *you* again," Jan said as she wrapped her arms around Maddie. "Run away from the circus?"

"Somethin' like that," Maddie said with a shrug. "Dance?"

"You any good?" Jan flirted.

"Good enough, baby, but it's been a while," Maddie said, pulling Jan onto the dance floor as the DJ started a techno set. Maddie raised her arms over her head and thrust her hips against Jan, their thighs brushing.

"Ooo, careful, stud," Jan said with a smile.

"Or what, baby?" Maddie teased, her arm sliding around Jan's waist. "You gonna spank me?"

"I'll think of something, honey, but unfortunately, I'm staying with my friend for the weekend. We're celebrating her new job."

"Then why's she glued to the damn wall instead of celebratin'?" Maddie asked, looking over Jan's shoulder at Dani, who was trying very hard to blend in with the wallpaper.

Jan laughed. "She's afraid someone she knows from work will see her. Not really into the club scene, y'know? Only came here because I wanted to. She's a good kid, but a little socially awkward."

"Maybe we should loosen her up a little," Maddie suggested before dropping a firm kiss on Jan's lips and teasing her with her tongue, remembering the way Dani had kissed her in Buck's trailer the evening Maddie left the carnival.

Jan licked her lips when the kiss ended. "I, on the other hand, am already loosened up," she said invitingly.

"Yes, you certainly are, baby," Maddie agreed, her fingers working Jan's nipple into a tight knot as she nibbled at her neck.

Jan slipped her fingers into the front of Maddie's work shirt and pulled her into a darker area that smelled of old cigarettes and stale beer, accompanied by the muffled sounds of frantic, groping sex. Maddie grinned when Jan shoved her onto a love seat and covered her mouth in a blistering kiss. Her hands found their way beneath Jan's stretchy top as she returned the kiss as earnestly as she was receiving. She pushed her fingers under Jan's soft form-fitting bra and kneaded her generous breasts. Jan groaned as her hands began trailing their way up the inside of Maddie's thigh. Without realizing it, Maddie grabbed Jan's hand to stop its movement and inserted her thigh between Jan's legs, pressing it firmly against her crotch. Jan rocked against Maddie's muscular thigh, her breathing becoming more labored and her thrusts jerkier as she began to lose control of her body. Maddie kissed her and whispered, "Move up and let me taste you, baby." She pulled Jan up and pushed her panties aside, teasing her with her tongue until she felt the beginning of her orgasm trickle onto her tongue. "Sweet," Maddie mumbled as she sucked Jan hard into her mouth and traced her folds with her tongue. Jan slid down until she straddled Maddie's hips and collapsed into Maddie's arms. "I've missed you," Jan said softly, nuzzling a kiss against Maddie's chest. "Even though you don't remember me."

"It hasn't been that long, baby. Of course, I remember you," Maddie said.

"Before that, sweetie. We almost met ten years ago."

Maddie pushed her head back and stared at Jan. "Really?"

"I was waiting outside after your last concert, but you passed me up for Dani. Very disappointing," Jan pouted. "Dani and I were friends in high school and I forced her to go with me that night. That wasn't her thing either." She held her fingers up, slightly apart. "I was so jealous when you took her instead of me. Until her mother had to go pick her up at the police station," she laughed. "Served her right, but she never would tell me what happened." Suddenly, Jan pushed her body up and said, "Oh, my God! I left Dani alone out there. Sorry, sugar, but I need to go check on her."

"No problem," Maddie said as she helped Jan up. "This joint got a back door?"

"Back by the bathrooms, I think." Jan kissed Maddie lightly. "Thanks for another memorable evening, sweetie."

"Anytime, baby," Maddie said with a wicked smile. "My pleasure."

ON SATURDAY, MADDIE volunteered to work in order to catch up on a few simple jobs the guys hadn't been able to get to. She spent most of her time re-assembling the old Camaro while the other three did the other jobs. Oscar came in to work on the paperwork piling up on his desk. Maddie rolled beneath a vehicle on a mechanic's creeper to drain the oil before changing the filter and replacing the oil in a vehicle that came in late. She unscrewed the oil plug in the oil pan and pulled a bucket underneath the opening to catch the oil, which would be dumped into a recycling barrel behind the shop. As she watched the thick, dark liquid run out, she dipped her index finger into it. She checked the color of the oil and rubbed her index finger and thumb together to check the consistency. She sniffed it and touched her finger to her tongue lightly. The oil she was draining had been pumping through the engine too long and had turned nearly black and had a slightly burned taste and smell. It had a gritty feel and she would probably have to flush out the oil pan. It was a messy job, but at least the clean oil wouldn't pick up any old grit and carry it throughout the engine to gum up the pistons.

She sighed, thinking that the one-hour job had just turned into a three- or four-hour job. She should consider flushing the whole engine to clean everything up before running new oil through it. She would have to talk to Oscar though before she got too carried away so she didn't run up unnecessary labor costs for the customer. Over the last hour, she'd heard the three other mechanics leave one at a time, but was pretty sure Oscar was still in his office.

Maddie felt a tap on her work boot and glanced down to see a pair of low heels standing next to her feet. "We need to talk," a woman's voice said.

"If this is your car, it won't be ready for a few more hours," Maddie said as she began rolling from beneath the vehicle.

"I'm here on official business," the woman said, stepping back to allow room for Maddie to slide out.

"I haven't done anythin'," Maddie said. Once her head cleared the vehicle's undercarriage, she looked up to see Dani standing over her, unsmiling.

Dani waited as Maddie pushed up and stood, wiping her hands on a shop towel. "My office received this inquiry from the warden at Sand Ridge yesterday. I'll need to ask you a few questions, Ms. James, for my report."

"I haven't done anythin' illegal and I'm not on probation. I'm just your average non-voting, tax-paying former felon," Maddie said with a slight grin. "And I'm not sure the warden at Sand Ridge needs to know what the hell I'm doin' now."

"It's just a follow-up to keep track of recidivism rates."

"Sounds like a crock of bureaucratic crap to me to justify some request for more money that'll never find its way to the inmates," Maddie chuckled.

Dani glared at her for a moment, then asked, "You do know that having sex in public is against the law, don't you?"

"I haven't," Maddie stated. "I haven't done anythin' non-consensual and, as far as I know, that little club is private property. There were at least three or four other couples in the same room enjoyin' one another's company. What's this bullshit really about? I'm busy and have work to do before I reach retirement. I don't get paid to keep bureaucrats employed by worryin' about how I choose to spend my free time."

"Leave my friends alone!" Dani blurted out heatedly.

"Then tell your *friend* to stop comin' on to *me*," Maddie snapped back.

Dani glowered and glanced at the form in her hand. She cleared her throat and asked, "How long have you been employed here?"

"Two or three months. Ask Oscar." Maddie shrugged. Then she added," If it matters, you can tell the warden I got this job partly because of the trainin' I got from Dave Larsen at Sand Ridge. Good man."

"Where are you residing?"

"Boardin' house a few blocks from here since I don't have a driver's license yet."

"Any problems since your release?"

"They weren't problems for me. Any other questions or can I get back to work?"

"Do you regret having committed the crime you were convicted of?"

"What's the difference? It was a learnin' experience."

"What did you learn?"

"To trust no one. Everyone's got an angle. What's yours?"

"To be at peace with myself someday."

"Good luck with that, but you can start by gettin' the hell out of my life and leavin' me the fuck alone, knowin' I would have fucked you eleven years ago if I'd had the chance, whether you wanted it or not, and wouldn't have thought twice about it. If we hadn't hit that other car, your ass would have been mine. It took me years to admit that to myself and wake up."

"I'm sorry," Dani said quietly before reaching out and wrapping a hand around Maddie's arm. Maddie pulled her arm away and angrily spun Dani against the car she was working on.

"I don't need you to feel sorry for me. You have no fuckin' idea who I am or what I could have done to you. What I could still do," Maddie seethed.

"Then why don't you do it?" Dani snapped. "You keep threatening to, but never do. Maybe I wanted it then. Maybe I still do."

"Then you're either out of your mind or just a fuckin' tease," Maddie spat. "Get the fuck out of here. I don't do rape. Been there, done that, got the scars to prove it."

"Have you ever let anyone see the real you?" Dani asked softly.

"I don't even know who the real me is anymore," Maddie admitted. "Now get out of here," she sneered.

Dani reached out and touched Maddie's face. Maddie shook her head, then took Dani's lips in a crushing kiss. When Dani didn't try to resist, Maddie lessened the force behind the kiss. Dani slid her hands into the waist of Maddie's sweatpants to touch her, but Maddie stopped the movement of her hands, holding them as she deepened the kiss.

"Let me touch you," Dani breathed as the kiss ended and Maddie began kissing her neck.

"No. I'm not finished with you yet," Maddie said. "I'm in control here." Dani squirmed to get away, but Maddie only grinned and held her in place.

"Is that what you need? To be in control?" Dani asked as Maddie pressed against her roughly.

"Control is the only damn thing I've got left," Maddie grunted. "It's mine."

"Then fuck me if that's what you want and get it over with," Dani challenged her.

Maddie continued to hold Dani's wrists as she lavished her with kisses, sliding one hand down to cup Dani's crotch. "God, you're so hot," Maddie breathed as Dani stopped struggling against her. Finally, Maddie pushed away, breathing hard, her eyes closed. "Get out of here. Just go!" she said harshly.

When Dani hesitated, Maddie's eyes flew open, filled with barely controlled rage. "Go! Now! And don't come back!"

"Mad—" Dani started.

Maddie held her hand up to stop her from saying anything else. "I have work to do. Get out!" Maddie picked up a tool and returned to the creeper and rolled beneath the car she had been working on. When she heard Dani's footsteps walking away, she suddenly had an overpowering urge for a hit of cocaine. Drugs, like making love to a woman, were a habit she thought she'd kicked years before. Certain Dani was gone, Maddie grabbed her jacket and headed for the door.

Oscar stepped out of his office and stopped her. "You finished with that car yet?" he asked.

"I'll be back," Maddie scowled over her shoulder, shrugging her jacket on.

"You don't need it, you know," Melendez said.

"What?"

"Whatever it is you're after."

"Leave me alone, old man. I don't owe you anythin'. I've paid my debt."

"But was it really yours to pay?"

Maddie stared at him and continued walking away. "I'll be back, boss. Just need some fresh coffee," she said.

Chapter Seven

MADDIE HUNCHED HER shoulders against the blast of an early freezing Canadian wind that had worked its way into north Texas and buried her gloveless hands deep in the thinly lined pockets of her denim jacket. Should've looked for a pair of gloves, she thought. She looked up at the heavy gray sky and hoped the weatherman was wrong when he predicted possible snow flurries the next few days.

She semi-remembered playing in deep snow as a child. She couldn't wait for winter to fly down hills riding her sled on her father's Nebraska farm. Zooming down the gently rolling hills took her breath away, but pulling the sled uphill again wasn't as exhilarating. Occasionally, one of her parents would tow her back up behind the farm tractor. When the cold got to her, she would push through snow up to her knees, change into dry sweatpants and her favorite flannel shirt and down a bowl of hot soup next to a roaring fire, unable to imagine anything better.

She squinted as icy pellets flew against her face and shivered. When had this ever been fun, she wondered as she approached Flo's and paused only to stomp debris off her work boots before entering. She walked into the living room and looked at Sal, kneeling in front of the fireplace, stacking various-sized pieces of tender in the firebox. Sal glanced over her shoulder and stared at Maddie. "Chilly?" she asked.

"Fuckin' freezin'," Maddie said. "Think you can get that fire goin' any more slowly?"

"Keep smartin' off and it'll never get done," Sal muttered.

"Any coffee still in the kitchen?" Maddie asked.

"Do I look like your damn maid? Go look for yourself, smart-ass," Sal retorted.

"Somethin' smells pretty good," Maddie took a deep breath and commented off-handedly.

"After all the shit you snorted back in the day, I'm shocked you can smell anything," Sal said with a smile.

"Me, too," Maddie responded without rancor. "You want a

mug, in case there is any coffee?" she asked.

"I wouldn't turn it down."

Maddie smiled as she pushed open the swinging door into the kitchen and headed to the coffeemaker. It had taken her a while to get used to the abrasive Sal, but now she sort of enjoyed the barbs they tossed at each other on a daily basis. She was never sure how serious Sal was about what she said, but it gave Maddie a chance to work on controlling her sometimes volatile temper, if not her smart-ass remarks.

"See Sal?" Flo asked.

"Of course. Kinda hard to miss the six-hundred-pound gorilla in the room," Maddie chuckled as she prepared two mugs of coffee. She hadn't quite managed to develop an amicable relationship with Flo yet, but respected what the gruff woman did for the women who rented rooms from her.

"You won't always get away with comments like that, y'know?" Flo said.

"But it's fun while it lasts," Maddie answered. Before she took a mug to Sal, she opened the oven door and looked inside. "Good-looking brisket," she noted, pinching off a bite and stuffing it in her mouth. "Tastes good, too."

"Get your damn paws off the meat, bitch," Flo said, delivering a smack to Maddie's butt. "Should be good. Been cookin' for over twelve hours."

"What's the occasion?" Maddie asked.

"I invited a friend over for dinner, so hang any attitude outside or I might have Sal shoot you." Flo laughed. "She'd like that."

"Yeah, yeah," Maddie muttered, carrying coffee into the living room.

She set Sal's mug on the hearth and asked, "Who's comin' over that's special enough for brisket?"

"A friend of Flo's," Sal answered.

"I got that part already," Maddie said.

"Just a sweet girl who helped Flo get out of Percyville. Only met her once or twice myself. Kinda quiet, so try not to scare her to death," Sal said, sitting in front of the fire she'd finally lit and sipping from her mug. "Grew up around here, I think. The new Assistant County Attorney. In other words, she puts people like you in prison when you fuck up."

"That s'posed to scare me, Deputy Dog?"

"Just a friendly warnin' to mind your p's and q's around Flo," Sal said with a shrug. "Otherwise Flo *might* rip your head off and I *might* not stop her."

Maddie frowned. "I've been home fifteen minutes and have been threatened that you might shoot me and Flo might rip my head off. Seem to be battin' a thousand today. I don't get that many threats from the three felons I work with."

"What can I say? Must be your sparklin' personality," Sal said with a grin. "Guess I should go clean my gun in case I need it later," she added with a laugh.

MADDIE REMOVED HER work boots and began stripping her work clothes off. She tossed them in the hamper and stepped in the shower to scrub the day's grime from her body, taking time to get the oil and grease from under her short fingernails. While in prison, she refused to go into the shower room unless she was alone or was certain Aggie's girls were the only ones already in the shower. Now, it felt wonderful to not be looking over her shoulder all the time and she felt great as the hot water ran over her head and down her body. She toweled off and returned to her room to dress. Obviously, Flo was eagerly anticipating her guest's arrival and Maddie was determined to try to put her best foot forward. She'd used a part of her paychecks to purchased cheap but decent clothing and comfortable shoes.

She found a seat in the living room after offering to help Flo set the table for dinner and attempted to chat up a limited conversation with a couple of the other boarders. Everything smelled wonderful and Maddie was starving. Finally, Flo asked her to open a bottle of wine to go with dinner. The doorbell rang while Maddie was working on opening the bottle. As Flo went to the door, Maddie took the bottle into the dining room and set it on the table. She looked up in time to watch Flo hug her guest and take her coat, handing it to Sal to hang in the front closet. Then her guest looked into the dining room and smiled at the flickering candles on the table. A couple of wrapped packages sat next to a place setting obviously reserved for Flo's guest.

"You didn't have to go to so much trouble, Flo," Dani said, "but it's beautiful and smells delicious." She briefly hugged Flo and Sal. "Thank you," she said, her eyes twinkling in the light from the candles, reflecting her barely contained excitement. For an instant, she looked like the girl Maddie had picked up after leaving her final show, innocent and curious. Maddie shrank back into the shadows as much as possible, watching Dani surreptitiously, liking what she saw more than she knew she should. Dani's cheeks were still slightly ruddy from the cold outside, giving her cheeks a rosy blush. Her hair fell loosely around her face and strands shimmered in the available light. It had been a couple of months since Maddie had seen Dani, but she vividly remembered the heat of her body as she pressed against it, and the way Dani's body fit against hers.

Unable to hide in the shadows any longer Maddie asked, "Want me to pour the wine now, Flo?" She worked at not letting her eyes meet Dani's.

"Sure," Flo nodded before turning to Dani again. "Danielle, this is our newest boarder, Maddie James." Pointing at Dani, she continued, "This is my friend, Danielle Hunter, the new Assistant County Attorney."

"Pleasure, ma'am," Maddie muttered as she poured half a glass of red wine into each goblet.

Throughout dinner, Maddie ate silently, occasionally picking up a partial string of the non-stop conversation between Flo, Sal, and Dani, but no matter how hard she tried, Maddie couldn't seem to tear her eyes away from Dani. If they had met under different circumstances, she might see a future worth pursuing, but that time had passed long ago. From time to time, Dani shifted her eyes to glance in Maddie's direction and Maddie saw her discomfort.

After dinner, Maddie and the other girls cleared the table and straightened up everything in the kitchen. By the time they joined the others in the living room, Sal had turned on their stereo system and soft music drifted through the front room.

Maddie found a place to sit alone and watch the others. Periodically, a couple of the boarders danced together and Maddie couldn't help but smile as more experienced dancers attempted to teach a younger woman how to waltz or two-step correctly. Dani laughed and clapped her hands, enjoying the antics of the other women.

Maddie wasn't sure what time it was, but knew she was tired.

While she was sipping her wine, Dani stood and moved closer to where Maddie was sitting.

"We haven't had much of a chance to talk this evening," Dani said. "Mind if I join you?"

Maddie stared up at her and shrugged. "It's a free country," she said.

"How are you?" Dani asked, settling next to Maddie and turning slightly to face her.

"Makin' it," Maddie mumbled so softly that Dani had to lean closer to hear her.

"I don't think we got off to a very good start and—" Dani started.

"Oh, I don't know," Maddie smirked. "Since you've already kissed me twice, I think we started out pretty good."

Dani blushed slightly before responding. "I seem to recall that *you* kissed *me* the last time. Wouldn't that make us even?" Dani parried.

Maddie shook her head slowly. "I admit you surprised me the first time, but I think you *wanted* me to kiss you the second time," she grinned.

"I did not!" Dani hissed.

"We could tell the others what happened and let them decide," Maddie suggested.

"Does it really matter since it's no one else's business?" Dani asked.

"Is that a concession?" Maddie answered.

"A statement," Dani smiled. "Would you care to dance?"

"I'm not a great dancer, but I'm willing to give it a try if you are," Maddie said, setting her glass down and standing to offer Dani her hand.

An involuntary chill ran through Maddie's body when Dani's warm hand took hers. She slipped a hand around Dani's waist and drew her closer, resting her hand in the middle of Dani's back before stepping off to the beat of the music. Dani slid her hand across Maddie's shoulder and onto the back of her neck. Maddie closed her eyes to feel the warmth of Dani's body lightly touching hers, breathing in the sweet scent of her shampoo, feeling her soft breath against her cheek.

"Would you like to come to my place for dinner some evening?" Dani whispered.

"I...uh...never turn down a free meal," Maddie managed.

"I have a lot on my calendar this week. I'll contact you."

"I'll be lookin' forward to it," Maddie smiled.

When the song ended, Maddie returned to her seat alone and Dani returned to her conversation with Flo and Sal. Maddie finished her wine and asked a bored-looking Clorinda for a dance to something a little more upbeat. Everyone laughed at their wild gyrations when they finished the dance with a flourish as Maddie flung the young woman the length of her arm and pulled her back again to dip Clorinda with a smile. Clorinda jumped up and hugged Maddie, throwing her arm around her shoulders as they panted their way back to their seats and plopped down. Not long afterward, Dani stood and waited for Sal to get her coat from the closet, leaving a few minutes later following hugs and kisses to most of those present.

Maddie went upstairs to get ready for bed. It had been a long day and the partying downstairs lasted longer than she anticipated. She was ready to doze off peacefully on a full stomach. She stripped down to her T-shirt and boxers and started to turn the bed down when a knock on her room door stopped her. She opened the door to find Flo looking at her.

"What's up?" Maddie asked.

"We need to talk," Flo said. She walked into the neat room and looked around before closing the door.

"Little late for a room inspection," Maddie said lightly.

"What the hell were you doin' tonight?" Flo asked. "I saw you flirtin' with Dani."

"I wasn't flirtin'." Maddie shrugged. "I knew you wanted to impress your guest and just wanted to make her feel welcome in your home. That's all. I swear, Flo."

"I saw the way you looked at her all evenin'," Flo frowned.

"How was I lookin' at her?" Maddie asked.

"Like you was sizin' her up for dessert," Flo answered, her voice hard and cold. "I wouldn't be happy if you did anythin' to hurt her. She's a nice lady and that makes her strictly off-limits to you."

When Maddie started to say something, Flo mashed her finger against Maddie's lips and growled, "All I want to hear from you is that you understand what I'm sayin'."

Maddie managed to nod. "I'm sorry you feel that way, Flo,

but I wouldn't do anything to hurt or upset you or your friends." But Dani had already invited Maddie to dinner at her place and Maddie really wanted more than the impulsive kisses they'd already shared. She'd carefully avoided a hug or kiss from Dani as she prepared to go home, which left Maddie hungry and mildly frustrated.

Flo took a step closer and poked Maddie in the chest. "Keep it that way. Dani deserves someone better'n any of us."

"Agreed," Maddie admitted. "Can I get some sleep now, Warden?"

THREE DAYS LATER, Maddie received a phone call at work from Dani inviting her to dinner Saturday evening. Maddie hesitated before accepting, hoping Flo wouldn't find out she would be alone with Dani.

Late Saturday afternoon, Maddie told Flo not to save dinner for her because she was meeting the guys for pizza and beer. She walked to Oscar's, opened the rear door, and changed into the better clothes she'd stashed there the day before. She killed a little time before calling a taxi to drive her to Dani's address on the other side of town. It was a one-story duplex a few blocks from the central downtown area. It was located in a well-kept part of town, that appeared to be inhabited by mostly upwardly mobile young professionals. Maddie liked the area, but felt a little out of place. As she walked up the brick sidewalk, she checked her clothes. She rang the doorbell and quickly rubbed the toe of her shoes on the calf of her leg to dislodge anything she's picked up at the shop. She was examining the shine on her shoes when the front door opened and she looked up to see a pleasant-looking older woman with graying hair staring at her. Maddie's first thought was she was at the wrong address. She glanced at the numbers next to the door and then back at the woman. "Uh—" she started.

"If you're looking for my daughter, Danielle, you're at the right place," the woman said with a smile. "She told me we were having company for dinner. I'm Gladys Hunter."

"Madelyn James," Maddie responded, stepping cautiously inside and surveying the homey-looking interior as she removed her jacket.

"I live next door, but eat with Danielle most evenings," Gladys volunteered. She reached out and touched Maddie's forearm lightly. "She's an excellent cook," she said in a low voice. "Girl always liked to cook, but she didn't get it from me," she added with a wink. "Where did you and my Danielle meet?"

"Through work," Maddie answered. Technically, it wasn't a lie.

"Are you a lawyer, too?" Gladys inquired.

"No, ma'am. I...uh...fix things," Maddie hedged, wondering where Dani might be.

"I'll let Danielle know her guest has arrived," Gladys said cheerfully. After a step or two, she turned back toward Maddie and said, "Please have a seat, dear. Make yourself comfortable."

"Thank you, Mrs. Hunter," Maddie acknowledged with a smile. Spending an evening with Dani and *her mother* wasn't what she'd envisioned, but the not-so-subtle warning she'd gotten from Flo still niggled in her mind. With her mother there, Dani would be relatively safe from Maddie's evil clutches. Maddie spent a few minutes examining the pictures on the walls, smiling at a couple depicting Dani acting like a goofy child playing in the snow with a strange-looking, large dog.

"That was my father's Airedale, Kaiser. He was my playmate and protector," Dani's voice said from behind Maddie.

"Looks like you kept him busy," Maddie said.

"We loved wrestling in the snow," Dani said with a trace of sadness. "I miss him." In a happier voice, she said, "We're eating at the kitchen table. This place isn't big enough for a real dining room, but it's big enough for me."

"That's all you need then," Maddie said.

"I'm sorry my mother dropped over. I wasn't really expecting her this evening."

"She told me she ate here most nights. I hope I'm not intrudin' on your time together," Maddie said.

"You're not. I'm glad you could make it," Dani said with a faint blush.

Maddie held out a chair for Gladys and waited for everything to be placed on the table before holding a chair for Dani and taking a seat herself.

"This looks great," Maddie commented.

Gladys leaned over and semi-whispered, "I told you she was

a good cook, but didn't learn it from me."

"You were a good cook, Mom," Dani said. "You just didn't enjoy it that much."

"That's true," Gladys nodded. Then she looked up suddenly and smiled broadly. "Maybe your friend can come back in December and I won't have to help you bake all those damn cookies you insist on making every year. No one needs that many cookies, Danielle," she huffed. "Do you like cookies, Madelyn?" she asked.

"I do. Very much, ma'am," Maddie nodded.

"Danielle makes a million every Christmas and after baking that many, I don't have the damn stomach to eat them," Gladys said, nudging Maddie's arm.

"I give them away as gifts, Mom. You know that," Dani said.

Maddie looked at Dani and grinned. "I'd be happy to help. I'm not much of a cook, but follow directions pretty well," she offered.

"It's still a way off, so we'll see," Dani mumbled. "Another biscuit?" she offered.

"I'm glad Danielle has made a new friend," Gladys said while Maddie chewed a bite of meat.

"I have friends, Mother," Dani said.

"I know you do, dear, but you can't ever have too many friends. Don't you agree, Madelyn?"

Thinking briefly about the women who protected her at Sand Ridge, Maddie answered, "Generally, that's true, but there are times friends can't always be trusted, ma'am. Even very close friends." In the end, even Aggie had built their friendship on a lie. Maddie had trusted women who claimed to love her, but in the long run they had never done anything but hurt her.

"You might be right," Gladys nodded. "The only time my Danielle was ever in trouble was because of a friend."

Maddie noticed Dani pale slightly. "That wasn't Jan's fault, Mother," she said.

"She talked you into going to that damn concert with her," Gladys blustered.

"I chose to go so she wouldn't have to go alone. It was my decision," Dani shot back.

"And I was the one who had to pick you up from the police station in the middle of the damn night," Gladys reminded her daughter. "I didn't see Jan there to rescue you."

Maddie's eyes widened slightly and to bring the minor disagreement to an end she asked, "Did you enjoy the concert?"

Dani looked at Maddie for a moment and cleared her throat. "Yes. It was very...stimulating," she answered quietly.

Maddie grinned. She'd never heard anyone call one of her high-energy performances "stimulating" before and it amused her, although in a strange way it was also slightly insulting.

After dinner, Maddie helped Dani clear the table, while her mother wandered into the living room to select a video. Maddie set a stack of dishes on the counter and looked at Dani.

"Stimulating?" she questioned. "Really?"

"I could have said 'interesting', I suppose," Dani smiled as she placed a large bag of popcorn in the microwave.

"*Not* an improvement," Maddie sulked.

"I'm sorry, but at that time in my life, heavy rock wasn't my thing. I didn't want to go, but let Jan talk me into it," Dani explained.

"Well, I feel *so* much better now," Maddie said. "What kind of music did you prefer, at that time in your life? Just curious."

"Joan Baez, Simon and Garfunkel, Carole King, and a few others," Dani answered.

"You weren't even born when they were big on the charts," Maddie said, astounded.

"They were my father's favorites. After he died, my mom played them all the time, so I sort of grew up listening to them. I didn't keep up with much else. Sorry," Dani apologized with a shrug. "Ready to watch a probably old movie now?" she asked as she dumped the popcorn into two medium bowls.

Dani set a bowl on an end table next to Gladys and the second on the couch between Maddie and herself. Once the film began, Maddie stretched her arm along the back of the couch, slowly running her fingers into the soft, feathery hair along Dani's nape and massaged the muscles that ran down the back of her neck. Maddie felt Dani relax and shiver slightly.

Halfway through the movie, Gladys fell asleep, snoring softly. Dani woke her gently and walked her to her side of the duplex. "She'll sleep all night now," Dani said when she returned. "Would you care for a cup of coffee?" she offered.

"Sounds good," Maddie answered. When Dani went into the

kitchen to prepare the coffee, Maddie followed her. She stood behind Dani as she poured water into the coffeemaker and pushed the button. Before Dani could turn around, Maddie began massaging her shoulders softly. She brought her mouth close to Dani's ear and whispered quietly, "I'd have to be dead to forget the way you kissed me the last time I saw you. You were so hungry." When Dani finally turned around, Maddie caught her lips for a brief kiss.

"That the best you got?" Dani asked with a smile when Maddie pulled away.

"I don't know what you like," Maddie said. "And I don't want to scare you."

"I'm not sure either, but I know I'm not afraid of you. Maybe I'm more afraid of myself."

Maddie's mouth hovered close to Dani's. "That's good, very good," Maddie breathed. She traced Dani's upper lip with the tip of her tongue. Dani's tongue slid out to touch Maddie's for a moment before slowly sucking it into her mouth where she continued to suck it gently, stroking and circling it with her own tongue. Maddie relaxed into the sweet feelings she was experiencing and ran her hands into Dani's hair.

When the tender kiss ended, Maddie mumbled, "It's gettin' late. I should go. Thanks for a great meal," she said with a smile.

"Now?" Dani asked unbelievingly, her eyes slightly unfocused. She stopped Maddie as she turned to leave. "Why?"

"To stop you from makin' a horrible mistake you'd regret later," Maddie answered, her voice oddly sad-sounding. "I've been known to get carried away. You're not ready for that."

"But Jan was?" Dani retorted.

"She just wanted to fuck," Maddie said with a shrug.

"Did you let her touch you?" Dani asked.

"No one touches me," Maddie ground out tightly.

"Why? Were you sexually abused as a child?"

Quickly, Maddie stepped closer and took a moment to gather her emotions before speaking. "No!" she spat. "Don't try to fuckin' analyze me. Better trained people than you have tried."

"I'm sorry," Dani said softly, reaching up to stroke over Maddie's lips with her fingertips.

Maddie shook the touch off and walked out the front door of the small duplex without another word. Yes, she was abused, but not by her father. The only people who had ever abused her were other women who sought to control her. The only way she regarded sex now, was as a struggle for control over another woman. Danielle Hunter wasn't prepared for that type of interaction and Maddie couldn't force herself to hurt the young woman.

THE NEXT MORNING, Maddie blinked her eyes open, stretched, and swung her legs out of bed. Collecting her bathrobe, toothbrush, shampoo, and other toiletries, she opened the door to her room and made her way toward the upstairs bathroom, hoping a shower would make her feel better. When she returned to her room twenty minutes later, still drying her hair with a towel, she found a piece of paper taped to the door. She glanced at it quickly before tossing it on her dresser and getting dressed.

After breakfast and cleaning the kitchen, Maddie wandered outside to smoke a cigarette, volunteering to feed the chickens and clean out their coop. She rested her arms on the fenced enclosure and reached into her pocket to withdraw the paper taped to her door. All it really was was a phone number, but there was no name attached. There wasn't anyone Maddie could think of who might be calling her. It wasn't the shop number, but she didn't know Oscar's home or cell number. She'd call after taking care of the chickens.

Nearly an hour later, Maddie paused to clean the bottom of her boots before stepping into the warm kitchen again. She washed her hands and picked up the receiver on the wall phone, dialing the mystery number. After several rings, a voice finally answered with a soft, "Hello."

"Uh, yeah, this is Maddie James. I had a call from this number earlier and – " she began.

"Maddie! It's Dani. Are you doing anything important today?" Dani asked.

"Not unless you consider cleanin' out a chicken coop important," Maddie answered.

"Well, I need to get out of the house and enjoy the mild weather for a while. So, I thought I might go fishing and was wondering if you'd like to keep me company," Dani explained.

Maddie looked around to make sure she was still alone. "I

don't know. Hadn't really thought about it."

"There's a pretty nice lake not too far from town where my dad used to take me. It was stocked last spring, so we should be able to catch enough for dinner, if you like fish, that is. If nothing else, it would give us a little time to just talk. I didn't mean to upset you last night and fishing seemed like a good way to make it up to you," Dani said fairly rapidly.

"I don't have a fishin' license or any equipment," Maddie hesitated.

"I have extra rods and stuff and you can just hand me your rod if a game warden comes by. It'll be fun, I promise," Dani said. "Dress warm in case there's a breeze off the water and I'll swing by to pick you up in about an hour, okay?"

"Yeah, I guess," Maddie finally agreed. "But can I just meet you at your place?"

"I drive right past Flo's on my way out of town, plus you won't have to pay for another cab ride. See ya soon," Dani said cheerfully as she disconnected and left Maddie listening to an annoying dial tone.

Flo would shit a fuckin' brick if she thought that Maddie would be going anywhere alone with Dani. Maddie envisioned coming back to Flo's later and finding her stuff packed up and sitting on the front porch with Sal waiting for her with a rifle across her knees. She rushed up the stairs and threw on her jacket. She stuffed a toboggan in her pocket and strolled nonchalantly down the stairs, deciding to wait outside for Dani, hoping Flo or Sal wouldn't see Dani's vehicle pull up in front of the house. She threw her hand up and said, "Goin' for a walk. Be back later," before stepping out of the house.

An old, beat-up, weathered Chevy truck swung to the curb and before Maddie could get off the porch, Dani jumped out and started walking toward her, smiling broadly.

"You're early," Maddie managed, her eyes taking in Dani's tight, faded light blue jeans that were ripped at the knees and her warm-looking sweatshirt.

"I know," Dani acknowledged. "But the weather was so great, I couldn't wait. Glad you're ready."

Glancing back at the front door, Maddie said, "Then let's get out of here."

The door opened quickly and Flo glared at Maddie. "Enjoy

your walk?" she asked.

"Hey, Flo! I invited Maddie to go fishing with me today," Dani said cheerfully.

"Oh, really," Flo frowned, knowing Maddie had lied to her.

Unexpectedly, Dani asked, "Why don't you and Sal go with us? It'll be a blast!"

"Yeah, probably a shotgun blast," Maddie mumbled under her breath.

"If we catch enough fish we can fry them over a fire. Nothing beats fish cooked outside over a fire, right Sal?" Dani said as Sal joined Flo at the front door.

"What about the other girls?" Sal asked.

"They can heat up the leftovers from last night," Flo said. "That your daddy's truck?"

"Yeah, I haven't driven it in a while, but it fired right up. The only minor problem is that you and Sal will have to follow us in your car. There isn't enough room for all of us in the cab. Is that a problem?" Dani asked.

"Not for us," Flo said. She looked at Maddie and asked, "Is that a problem for you, James?"

"Nope. The more the merrier," Maddie muttered, pulling her toboggan out of her jacket pocket and onto her head.

Dani laughed. "It's not that cold out, Maddie."

"Colder than you think," Maddie said, trying to avoid the icy look in Flo's glare.

"Give us a few minutes to change and get everythin' loaded," Sal said.

Dani reached out and took Maddie's hand to lead her to her truck. "The heater still works pretty good," she said as they stepped off the porch. Maddie noticed Flo's stare shift down to their hands for a moment before she went inside to help Sal.

"I have a confession," Maddie said as she settled into the cab of Dani's truck.

"What's that?" Dani smiled, starting the old truck and flipping on the heater.

"I've...uh...never really been fishin' in my entire life," Maddie admitted, a little embarrassed at her confession.

"Not even when you were a kid?" Dani asked, looking amazed. "Who hasn't ever been fishing?"

"I haven't, okay!" Maddie snapped. "I grew up on a farm, but all we had was a stock pond. It wasn't a way we entertained ourselves. Too much real work to do with the land and animals," she said sullenly. "Besides, I've never been the outdoorsy type."

Dani patted her on the thigh and said, "Don't worry about it, Maddie. We'll get you set up. Then all you'll have to do is sit and wait for something to try to steal your bait. For me, it's just a chance to relax away from work," she smiled.

Thirty minutes later, they located a secluded spot on an inlet on the bank of the small lake and unloaded their equipment. Dani spotted a fallen tree that was partially sticking above the water. She handed Maddie a rod and reel and picked up a small cooler. She threaded her arm through Maddie's and pulled her toward the semi-submerged tree. Sal and Flo carried a couple of folding chairs to a small pier someone had constructed off the shoreline and began preparing their rods and reels.

Dani stopped near the downed tree and said, "This is a good spot."

"Why?" Maddie asked.

"Because the fish like feeding around the rotting branches of a tree like this one. The only problem might be throwing your line too close and getting it tangled in the branches," Dani explained. "Get a worm out of the cooler and put it on your hook."

"What?" Maddie exclaimed, making a face.

Dani laughed. "They don't bite, silly," she said. "But they wiggle a lot."

"It's a slimy fuckin' worm," Mattie grumbled.

"Yeah, but fish really like them, especially if they're a little lively," Dani grinned, watching Maddie slowly poke a finger into the worm container and make a face when a worm wiggled past her finger to get away.

"They don't seem all that crazy about bein' a meal for the fish," Maddie commented.

Dani took the container from Maddie, reached in, and grabbed a worm. "Just have to let 'em know who's boss," she said as she began attaching her worm to her hook. "Now you bait your hook," she grinned, "unless you want me to do it for you."

"I got it," Maddie huffed. While Maddie worked the worm onto her hook, Dani placed her hand on Maddie's back and rubbed it with her thumb, lending encouragement. After a brief instruction about how to cast her line, the two women sat on the exposed tree trunk. From time to time, a breeze blew in off the water and Dani shivered a little, scooting slightly closer to Maddie's body. Eventually Maddie slid her arm around Dani's waist to share her body heat.

"LOOK AT THAT," Flo fumed. "She can't keep her damn hands off Dani. I'm gonna go over there and break that shit up," she added, setting her rod down.

Sal's hand stopped her. "They ain't doin' nothin', Flo. Maddie ain't dumb enough to do anythin' with you starin' at her...unless she's got a death wish or somethin'."

"I can't just sit here and do nothin', Sal. It's like watching a snake slither up to its next victim," Flo argued.

"I told ya that takin' her in was a bad idea, sweetie," Sal said. "Now look where givin' her a second chance got you."

"I'll find a chance to talk to Dani if you find a way to get Maddie off somewhere," Flo smiled.

DANI GLANCED AT Maddie and noticed she looked cold and bored. Maybe the fishing trip wasn't the best idea after all. She'd hoped she and Maddie would be alone to talk and get to know each other better. Looking out over the calm water, Dani asked, "Where's your bobber?"

"What?" Maddie responded. "Must've dozed off. Sorry."

"Where's your bobber?" Dani repeated.

"I don't even know what a fuckin' bobber is," Maddie answered irritably.

"It's that red-and-white plastic thing on your line. If it jerks or disappears, it lets you know you caught a fish," Dani explained excitedly, standing up. "Pull your line in, Maddie."

"How?" Maddie asked.

"Get up and I'll help you," Dani said.

Standing next to Maddie, Dani wrapped her arm around Maddie's waist and pointed to the handle of Maddie's reel. Maddie nodded and began reeling something in until a large, wriggling fish appeared above the water.

"Bring the fish closer and grab it," Dani instructed.

"Why?" Maddie asked.

"Unless you're planning to cook it on that line, you have to get your fish off the hook," Dani explained.

"Nuh-uh," Maddie said, shaking her head. "I already had to touch a disgustin' worm, but I ain't touchin' a damn fish too."

"You big baby," Dani teased, slapping Maddie's arm playfully before wrapping a hand around the fish and removing the hook from its mouth.

While celebrating Maddie's first fish, Dani had leaned her rod and reel against the tree trunk to assist Maddie. Suddenly, her tackle fell over and was being dragged into the water. While Dani held Maddie's catch, she pointed at her steadily disappearing rod and reel. "Grab my rod and reel, Maddie," she yelled.

"Shit!" Maddie said, dropping her rod and reel on the bank, jumping to the edge of the water and wading in to grab the rod before it disappeared. She backed up, but tripped over a submerged root. Now soaking wet from head-to-toe, Maddie finally got her feet beneath her and continued backing up until the bank became steeper and her feet slipped out from under her. But Maddie held on to the rod stubbornly and reeled Dana's fish to shore, lifting the rod to bring the fish out of the water and swinging it around for Dani to remove from the line. Dani tossed Maddie's catch farther up the bank and wiped her hands down the sides of her jeans before reaching out to remove hers.

At the end of the great fish fight, Dani smiled and Maddie laughed as Dani offered her a hand up. Dani rubbed a hand over her butt to brush off some of the mud from her fall, squeezing her butt cheek firmly.

"Sorry. Just couldn't pass up that little opportunity," Dani said with a smile. "Hope you brought a change of clothes."

"I did. You gonna volunteer to help me undress now, too?" Maddie grinned, waggling her eyebrows. Maddie laughed at Dani's sudden blush.

Despite the blatant innuendo, it was probably the first time Dani had seen a genuine smile on Maddie's face that didn't look either predatory or lecherous. Even though Maddie hadn't been thrilled with the fishing idea, she was having a good time.

"We've got our dinner!" Dani hollered. "How're y'all doin'?"

"Just waitin' on Flo," Sal called back. "Apparently she ain't holdin' her mouth right. Hey, Maddie! Let's clean our fish and get a fire goin' while we wait on slowpoke here," she added, patting Flo on the back and leaning down for a quick kiss. Flo shoved her away, half-heartedly, and cast her line into the water again, a little farther out.

"I'll go up and see if I can help Flo while you change and you and Sal do your thing, okay?" Dani said, patting Maddie lightly on the abdomen. "You okay with taking our fish up there to clean them? Hopefully, we won't be long. The sun's going down and it could get colder later."

"Yeah, I think I can handle that," Maddie said. "But I'll let Sal clean the fish."

Dani noticed Maddie's face had returned to its usual demeanor. She leaned in and dropped a light kiss on her cheek. "Thanks, Maddie."

"No problem," Maddie muttered as she picked up the stringer holding their two fish and wandered up the bank to where Sal was setting up a table.

"Round up some rocks and make a circle over there for our fire while I gut these fish," Sal directed, but without her usual rancor. "Unless you wanna clean the fish."

"Pass," Maddie said, making a face. "But I'm gonna get on some clean clothes first."

"Bet today isn't quite what you expected, is it?" Sal commented as Maddie started to walk away.

"What do you and Flo think I expected, to drag Dani out here alone in the fuckin' middle of nowhere and rape her ass? I'm not a fuckin' animal!" Maddie seethed angrily, shoving Sal backward.

More quickly than Maddie thought possible, Sal grabbed her arm and held it while she swept Maddie's legs from under her. Maddie landed on her back, but before she could jump up to strike back, Sal pointed a finger at her. "Calm the fuck down," Sal spat. "Flo just don't want Dani to get hurt."

"I got it, okay?" Maddie said, staring up at Sal. Sal stuck a hand out to help Maddie up.

Maddie grabbed the hand and pulled her body off the ground with no indication she would attempt anything. "I don't want any more trouble than I already have, so tell Flo if she wants me out of the house, just say so. I'm tired of bein' watched all the time with y'all waitin' for me to do somethin' *you* think is wrong," Maddie said, brushing leaves and other debris from her wet clothes. She stomped away to change clothes. A few minutes later, she returned and began moving rocks around the fire pit someone had already started. Then she headed off to gather wood.

DANI SAT IN Sal's folding chair and threw her line into the water. "Not having much luck, huh?" she said.

"I can share Sal's if I have to," Flo shrugged.

Following a few minutes of silence, Dani looked over at her friend. "What's wrong, Flo? You and Sal have a disagreement about something?"

"Nope. We're fine," Flo answered curtly.

"Well, something's wrong and I'll just keep nagging at you until you spill it," Dani said with a mischievous smile. "You know I will," she teased.

Flo shifted her body to look at Dani. "I'm just not sure it's smart for you to be spendin' time with Maddie. Sal don't trust her and I don't want you to get hurt."

Dani shrugged. "I like her, Flo. I enjoy spending time with her. Can't help it," she sighed. "When we've been alone, she's never done anything inappropriate."

Flo's eyes widened. "When have you been alone with her?"

"I invited her to dinner at my place last night and, honestly, although I don't care, I thought we might be alone today. She did me a favor, so just call it repaying a debt."

"What favor?"

"It's personal, Flo, and I'm not prepared to discuss it. Just give her a break, okay? For me." Dani had no sooner finished speaking when something jerked at her line. She traded rods with Flo and laughed, "It's your dinner, so bring it in. Then we can start cooking."

Flo plopped her fish on the worktable in front of Sal. It was the largest one. "Damn, baby! You must be starvin'!" Sal said with a smile.

Dani wandered off to help Maddie collect firewood. She sneaked up behind Maddie and threw her arms around the unsuspecting woman's upper body, trapping her arms against her sides. Maddie brought her arms up to break the hold and spun around with an arm cocked back, her eyes wild, ready to deliver a blow to her attacker, but stopped short of hitting Dani.

"Ya shouldn't sneak up on people like that," She reached out and ran a shaking hand down Dani's arm. "I coulda hurt ya," she said softly.

"But you didn't," Dani grinned.

ONCE EVERYTHING WAS packed up and they were ready to return home, Dani hesitated to fall in right behind Sal and Flo. She drove well below the speed limit and let Sal get far ahead of them so she and Maddie could have a chance to talk during the drive. But Maddie didn't seem to be in the mood to talk.

"Did you enjoy your first fishing trip?" Dani asked.

"Yeah. Thanks for invitin' me," Maddie answered as she continued staring out the side window.

"What did you enjoy the most?" Dani tried again.

Maddie thought for a minute before answering. "Sounds stupid, but I really liked the quiet, only interrupted by the steady rhythm of the little waves as they ran to the shore. It was peaceful and calmin'. Reminded me of walkin' on the beach in California. The waves were bigger, but just as steady. Almost like the heartbeat of the ocean, y'know."

Dani pursed her lips and nodded. "I've never thought about it that way, but you're right. The heartbeat of the ocean, huh? That would make a great song," she said.

"It would," Maddie agreed. "Maybe some day someone will write it."

"You could," Dani smiled at her.

"Packie could, but I'm not much of a songwriter. I just sang 'em," Maddie said.

During their brief conversation, Dani turned off the main road and brought the truck to a stop, switching the lights off. She took Maddie's hand and entwined their fingers. "I've been wanting to do this all afternoon," she sighed.

"Do what?" a confused Maddie asked.

"This," Dani breathed as she moved closer to Maddie and pressed her lips against Maddie's.

Maddie deepened the kiss eagerly, her body moving against Dani's. She lifted Dani up to straddle her thighs as Dani's hands found their way into Maddie's hair. Maddie was breathing hard as her tongue made its way into Dani's mouth. Dani groaned when Maddie found her breast and arched against her to increase their contact. Unexpectedly, Maddie pushed away, worked to catch her breath, and said, "We should stop."

"Why?" Dani grinned and moved to kiss Maddie again. "I'm not sixteen anymore."

Dani stared at her as Maddie moved her off her lap.

"Because...because..." Maddie tried, looking around. "We should...uh...get back to Flo's. She'll be worried about where you are," Maddie said, refusing to look at Dani.

"Flo's my friend, not my *mother*," Dani responded, running her fingernails up the inside of Maddie's thigh.

"Please stop...don't," Maddie forced herself to say as tears began shimmering in her eyes.

Dani felt more frustrated than she had the night before. She didn't understand why Maddie had first seemed so passionate, then suddenly become so distant. It was hard for her not to lash out at Maddie's rejection again. She forced herself to turn the key in the ignition and back out of the secluded area. "Okay. Home it is then," she managed.

Chapter Eight

SABREENA DOUGLAS WATCHED the comings and goings at Oscar's Auto Repair from behind a tinted porthole window in an old blue-over-blue cargo van parked in the public parking lot across the street from the shop. She never believed Maddie had the guts to fight her without Aggie standing behind her and Bree would like nothing more than to get even. The month before her release, she was handed an anonymous, typed note by another inmate she barely knew, telling her where Maddie James was living and where she worked. She pulled the note from her coat pocket as she watched Maddie arrive at the shop and reread it with great interest.

After waiting all day, dreaming of the things she would do to that cunt, Sabreena watched her pull down the last bay door after the other workers left. Certain Maddie was alone in the cinderblock building, Bree stepped out of the van and sauntered casually down the small alley to the back door of the shop. One of the men with her jimmied the door open and they slipped inside.

"WHAT'D YOU FORGET this time?" Maddie laughed, pulling her head from under the hood of a vehicle and wiping her hands on a shop towel. The smile fell from her face when she saw Sabreena Douglas, followed by three thick-necked men, move into the light. It had been over a year since Maddie had seen Bree Douglas and she hadn't planned to ever see her again. Maddie, with Aggie's help, had fought back against Bree and her prison trafficking ring and even though Maddie suffered numerous cuts and bruises and survived being shanked, she never became one of Bree's bitches following the shower incident after her arrival at Sand Ridge. Bree looked a little rougher around the edges than Maddie remembered, but she was pleased to still see the scars she put on Bree's face.

"What the fuck do you want?" Maddie demanded.

Bree shrugged. "Just thought I'd see how you was doin' out

in the free world."

"Well, you saw, so leave."

"Or what? You gonna beat me up again?" Bree laughed. "You cost me a fortune," she said. "You owe me for refusin' to put your goods out there."

"I don't owe you shit! I wasn't a whore and wasn't gonna let you turn me into one," Maddie snapped.

"We'll see," Bree smiled. She closed her eyes and took a deep breath. "It's a shame really. I still remember that tight little pussy of yours. It would feel real good about now. And Aggie ain't here to save your ass this time." Her tongue swiped around her lips. "We can do this the hard way or the easy way. What's it gonna be, James? Either one works for me," Bree said nonchalantly with a shrug before hiking her hip onto a stool with a smile.

Maddie's fist tightened around a large Phillips screwdriver and she flipped it over leaving the handle exposed.

"Okey dokey," Bree said. "The hard way then." She looked at the men with her and said with a cold smile, "She's mine, so don't damage the goods...too much."

Out of the corner of her eye Maddie saw one of the men moving closer. When he was within range, she swung the screwdriver handle and caught him on the jaw. A second man grabbed her and tried to wrestle the screwdriver away from her. She managed to pull it up, then released it as he jerked it down. The point drove into his upper thigh. He screamed and fell to the floor, bleeding badly.

"Well, so much for the beginners," Bree huffed. "Doncha hate weak men who think women are as weak as they are?" she asked conversationally.

Maddie turned quickly to face the last man, but wasn't fast enough to dodge a fist aimed at her abdomen. The hit doubled her over. The man stopped advancing toward her and she managed to catch a breath and stand.

"Give it up," he rumbled.

"She won't," Bree said casually, examining her fingernails.

While Maddie was preparing herself for round two, something struck the back of her head. She pitched forward, wrapping her hands around the area where she'd been hit. She curled her body up tightly waiting for the pain to pass and the synapses in her brain to begin working again. The last thing she vaguely remembered was a glancing blow to her face by a solid fist.

"Take your friends and I'll meet y'all back at the bar in about an hour or so," Bree said. Sure they were gone, she knelt next to Maddie and took her chin between her thumb and index finger, shaking it back and forth. "Don't worry, sugar. I won't do anything until I know you can feel everythin' I'm gonna do to you, bitch."

Then Maddie felt her work coveralls being unzipped and her legs being shoved apart as Bree pushed her hand toward Maddie's crotch.

"No-o-o-o," Maddie groaned before her body jerked and she sank into darkness.

MADDIE AWAKENED, HER head thudding dully, lying on the old cracked couch in Oscar's office and covered by a scratchy wool blanket. She slowly opened one eye and found Crew sitting behind Melendez's desk, reading and drinking a cup of coffee. She grunted as she tried to sit up.

"Finally awake, huh?" Crew asked.

"What time is it?" Maddie managed.

"Found you around seven. Thought I was gonna have to call the paramedics."

"What happened?" Maddie asked, shaking her head and wishing she hadn't.

"Looks like a half-assed attempt at a burglary. Prob'ly kids. We're missin' a few tools, but somethin' musta scared 'em away. You finish that car you was workin' on?"

"Almost. Needs new plugs."

"Take the day off and clean house or somethin'. We'll survive without you. I'll explain it to the boss and finish that car for ya. Need a ride home?"

"I can walk. It's not far."

"Well, if you get to feelin' bad, call your girlfriend or—" Crew started.

"Ain't got no fuckin' girlfriend," Maddie managed to growl.

"Then get Flo or Sal to haul your ass to the hospital and let a doc check out that knot on your head."

"Okay, Mom," she said as she stood and wobbled around for

a moment before she placed one foot in front of the other and concentrated on moving forward. After walking the two blocks to Flo's, Maddie wasn't sure what had happened, but didn't think Bree had done what she had planned, but didn't know why. She didn't remember anything after being clocked on the jaw. She took a long, hot shower and collapsed onto her bed, naked.

Chapter Nine

A SCRUFFY-LOOKING middle-aged man, covered by an old rain poncho and a droopy wide-brimmed hat wandered down an alleyway between a local furniture store and a second-hand appliance store. He poked through piles of debris with the long wooden handle from a discarded broom that he was using as a walking stick, looking for a new box to call home, at least for one night. It had rained off and on over the past three days and the boxes he'd already found were either too wet or not tall enough for him to stretch out in. He scratched at the beard that covered the lower part of his face and looked around the alley. Pretty slim pickin's, he thought until his eyes landed on an intact refrigerator box stuffed with the plastic the refrigerator had probably been wrapped in. If the plastic sheeting was large enough, he might be able to cover the box enough to stay reasonably dry.

He dragged the box off a pile of other broken down boxes and had it half folded back into its original shape when he noticed the corner of an oil-stained, heavy-duty blue tarp sticking from a stack of bulging garbage bags. The tarp had metal eyelets he could use to tie it securely around his new home. If nothing else, it might become a new poncho to protect him from the rain. But whatever was in the garbage bags was heavy and prevented him from pulling the tarp free. Finally, he grabbed a bag and slung it off the tarp, followed by three additional bags. At last he grabbed the edge of the tarp and jerked it with all his strength. It moved a little. Confidant that his efforts were paying off at last, he set his feet and tugged at the tarp. Suddenly whatever was holding it in place released its grip and something inside the tarp rolled free as he pulled it across the alley. He turned triumphantly to gaze down at the bloody, beaten body of a woman, her skirt pushed up around her chunky buttocks. He spotted a purse lying next to the body and reached down to grab it, finding a few dollars in cash and a credit card. He quickly stuffed the credit card and cash into his pocket and tossed the purse back near the body. He didn't want to get involved with the police, and chose to abandon the box, walking to a pay phone a block away to dial the 9-1-1 operator, and split, long gone before the first police car arrived on the scene.

Within an hour, the alley was swarming with police officers, detectives, and forensic investigators. They searched the alley and went through the victim's clothing, searching for anything that might give them a clue to her identity. Detectives Bart Nolan and Jorge Suarez, arrived on the scene not long after lunch. Nolan hadn't been happy when they had been called away from their meal because their names were at the top of the call-out list. He had gulped down the remainder of his pot roast and mashed potato dinner, smothered in gravy too quickly and wished he had a shot of Pepto to settle his roiling stomach. He looked at his partner and expelled a healthy belch.

"Feel better now?" Suarez grinned.

"Remind me not to get the pot roast next time," Nolan complained. "Didn't taste any better the second time around."

"I told you to get the burger, man. That joint isn't called a greasy spoon for nothin', you know," Suarez chuckled.

"Hey!" Nolan called out to a nearby officer. "When did the Medical Examiner take the body?"

"'Bout half an hour ago. Sistrunk was afraid it would start rainin' again and didn't want it to wash away anything useful," the officer responded. "How much longer, Detective?" he asked.

"Got a hot date or somethin'?" Nolan asked.

"Prob'ly just some junkie who had a disagreement with her dealer or a pro holdin' out on her pimp," the officer muttered.

"Prob'ly right. Now look for somethin' to support either of those theories," Nolan called out. "Is there a list somewhere of everything the forensics guys collected?" he asked.

"At the lab," the officer said.

"Tomorrow let's pay a visit to the ME and the lab first thing," Nolan said. "We can't do shit until we ID the vic and look over the lab reports anyway. Stop someplace on our way back to the house so I can pick up some Pepto, will ya?" he said, pressing his hand against his abdomen.

Chapter Ten

"HOMICIDE, NOLAN," THE detective snapped as he grabbed the ringing phone on his desk.

"Bart, it's Natalie," a woman's voice said.

Nolan smiled, remembering his best friend's pretty wife. "How are you, Nat? How're the kids doin'?"

"We're all pretty good, Bart. Have you talked to Oscar lately?" she asked.

"Not for a while. Why? Is he okay?"

"He's lost his damn mind!" Natalie exclaimed. "Someone's got to talk to him. The old fool won't listen to me."

"What are you talkin' about, Nat?"

"He hired that woman and I can't let Joel or Marissa near the shop as long as she's there," Natalie sniffed.

"Calm down, sweetie. What woman?" Nolan asked, running a hand through his hair in frustration.

"The one who killed Bryan!" Natalie said, frantically. "I was supposed to be notified when she had a parole hearing."

"Maddie James?" he asked.

"Yes! I went to the shop to pick up Joel and she was there. I slapped her and dragged Joel out of there. I called Oscar later and he gave me some bullshit about her deserving a second chance. I reminded him that she didn't give Bryan a second chance. He's dead!" she cried. "Maybe he'll listen to you, Bart. Please."

"I'll stop by and talk to him, but I can't promise he'll listen. I'll keep an eye on James, too. Felons like her always fuck up eventually, Nat. Try to take it easy, okay," he said softly.

"Thanks, Bart. I knew since you were Bryan's best friend you'd understand," Natalie said.

The next day, Nolan begged off his usual lunch with Suarez and picked up a couple of Mexican lunches from a little mom-and-pop food truck he knew Oscar liked. On the drive to Oscar's shop, he tried to organize his thoughts about how to best approach the retired probation officer. He knew Oscar could be a stubborn cuss, but hoped he'd realize how much his decision to hire Maddie James was affecting his family.

He parked along the side of the small business and leaned into his car to pick up the two lunches. He opened the side door of the shop and strolled to Oscar's office, taking in the shop's interior, including the employees. He knew them all personally, except Maddie, because he'd made it his business to make sure none of them fucked up.

He tapped on the office door as he looked around. When the door opened, Oscar smiled broadly and embraced Nolan, inviting him into the office.

"Whatcha doing, Mr. Detective?" Oscar asked.

Nolan pulled a Styrofoam container from a bag and set it on Oscar's desk along with a plastic knife and fork. He sat down and took out a second container, pulling a chair closer to the desk. "Haven't seen you in a while and Delgado's sounded good," Nolan shrugged.

Oscar smiled and opened the small refrigerator behind him. "Corona or Dos Equis?" he asked.

"I'm still on duty, but what the hell? Corona. Got any lime?" Nolan asked.

"Not like you to ask stupid questions, Bart," Oscar chuckled as he stuck a slice of lime into Nolan's bottle. "So what brings you here, besides lunch?" he asked as he put the first bite of his enchilada meal into his mouth and chewed slowly.

"Can't I just stop by to see an old friend?"

"Highly unlikely," Oscar smiled.

Nolan cleared his throat with a drink of his beer. "Actually, Oscar, Natalie called me yesterday and was pretty upset."

Oscar muttered what Nolan recognized as a string of Spanish expletives under his breath. "I'm sorry about that, Bart, but I'll tell you exactly what I told her. This business isn't hers and I don't take orders from my daughter-in-law. I don't have to consult her before I hire a new employee."

"But you *knew* who she was when you hired her, right?" Nolan asked.

"Of course I did! I'm not as senile as Natalie believes," Oscar retorted. "The woman served every fucking day of her sentence and never asked to be considered for early release. If Natalie has a problem with that, I suggest she take it up with Judge Whitaker who assigned her punishment. It's not my job, yours, or hers to extend the sentence imposed by the court."

"So, how's the angel doin'?" Nolan asked snidely.

Oscar shrugged as he continued to eat. "Works hard, good mechanic, has only had one minor problem since being hired. Dependable employee."

"What minor problem?"

"She got into a scuffle with Beau because he found a way to 'accidentally' put gas into her coffee. Both at fault. Beau pushed his luck and she over-reacted, so I had to punish them both," Oscar explained. "They get along fine now. No big deal."

"She ever mouth off?"

"They all do that occasionally, but it doesn't mean nothing. I'd appreciate it if you didn't lean on them, Bart, and tell Natalie to back off."

"You know she won't, Oscar, and I can't say I blame her," Nolan said.

"She needs to find a way to move on. Bryan would hate how bitter she's become," Oscar noted.

"She lost the love of her life, Oscar. The father of her children, for God's sake!"

"And *I* lost my only son, but there is no honor in not being able to forgive. My biggest fear is that Natalie will become a bitter, unhappy woman and make Joel and Marissa the same way," Oscar said wearily.

It was obvious that Nolan wouldn't be able to convince Oscar he'd made a mistake and the conversation swung around to a general discussion about what was going on in the Wichita Falls Police Department. Nolan finished his lunch and glanced at his wristwatch. "Well, I better get back to work. It was good to see you again, Oscar," he said.

Oscar stood and offered his hand to Nolan. "Thanks for the meal, Bart. Tell Natalie you tried, but my decision hasn't changed."

Nolan shook Oscar's hand and nodded before walking out of the small office. He paused a moment, then wandered over to the bay where Maddie was working. Leaning closely over her shoulder, he asked, "Whatcha workin' on?"

"Looks suspiciously like a car to me," she said.

Nolan smacked her on the back of the head and growled, "It was a simple question and didn't require a smart-mouthed answer, smart-ass."

"Hey, James!" Beau hollered, "let me borrow your ratchet for a minute. Can't find mine right now."

Maddie's head jerked toward Beau and the fist gripping the ratchet in her hand relaxed as she tossed it to him.

"Thanks, kid," he said as he caught it.

"No problem, chief. You're welcome," she said with a smile.

"Whose vehicle is this?" Nolan prodded.

"Oscar's," Maddie responded through clenched teeth.

"I've known Oscar twenty years and have never seen this damn car," Nolan needled.

Maddie spun around and stood chest-to-chest with the big man, refusing to move an inch. "Then I guess you don't know him as well as you claim, *officer*," she said with a smirk. "Otherwise you'd know he bought it for his son."

Nolan brought his hands up and grabbed Maddie's coveralls, jerking her up and even closer until they were nose-to-nose, glaring at one another. "I don't have a fuckin' problem with that. My fuckin' problem is with *you*, smart-ass!" he hissed.

"Hey!" usually quiet Freddie shouted, taking a step closer. "Let her go, man!"

"Butt out!" Nolan snapped, still glaring at Maddie. "This ain't your business."

The door to Oscar's office flew open and Oscar stepped out, red-faced and angry. "What the fuck do you think you're doing, Bart? Get your hands off my employee and get the hell out of here before I call a cop and press charges for assault!" he threatened.

Still angry, Nolan roughly shoved Maddie away and into the car behind her. She stepped sideways and reached behind her to rub her back where it had struck the vehicle. She looked over her shoulder at Crew and said with a grin, "He called me a smart-ass twice, Crew. Do I get double credit for that?"

"Prob'ly," Crew grinned back with a thumb up.

"Shut up!" Oscar and Nolan yelled simultaneously.

STILL ANGRY, NOLAN stomped back into the squad room and dropped heavily into his rolling chair.

"Bad lunch?" Suarez asked.

"I've had better," Nolan grumbled.

"Well, this should cheer you up," Suarez grinned as he floated a sheet of paper onto Nolan's desk.

Nolan snatched the paper up and glanced over it quickly. Finally, he nodded and said, "It's a start. Anything else?"

"She just got out on an early release from Sand Ridge about two months ago. Supposed to be in Houston, but missed her last couple of meetin's with her parole officer. They're lookin' for her happy self."

"Got a number? I'll let her PO know we found her," Nolan said.

FOLLOWING A LENGTHY conversation with Sabreena Douglas's parole officer, Nolan grinned and muttered, "I gotcha now, bitch." He pulled the paperwork for an arrest warrant out of his desk drawer and wrote in a list of his findings as part of his sworn affidavit before telling his partner he'd be out of the office for a few minutes. Two hours later Nolan brought a department-issued sedan to a stop in the parking area next to Oscar's Auto Repair again, pushed his door open, and got out. He readjusted his pants, surveyed the area around the shop and took a deep breath. It hadn't taken him long to convince the judge that he had substantial probable cause to place his suspect under arrest.

"How far are we from the crime scene?" Nolan asked.

"Couple of blocks maybe," Suarez responded, glancing around.

"Wonder if there's a more or less straight shot from here to there. Too much risk of bein' seen if you tried to push a body down the sidewalk out front," Nolan said.

"There's a back alley where the dumpsters and stuff are," Suarez said.

"Call forensics to scour the whole area so we can tie up this case," Nolan smiled, slamming his car door. "Let's do it," he said as he pulled his weapon from his holster and approached the side door of the business.

When the two detectives entered the shop area with their weapons drawn, Beau nudged the person working on an engine in the bay next to him on the shoulder. When Maddie looked up, Beau nodded toward the approaching men. She pulled her earbuds from her ears and frowned. She glanced at Beau and he muttered, "Cops are back."

"Looks like," Maddie muttered in response while she wiped oil from her hands.

"Hands up!" Nolan ordered loudly.

"What the hell's going on out here?" Oscar demanded with a frown as he stepped out of his office a moment later and saw his employees standing with their hands raised.

Beau wrapped his fingers around Maddie's arm and leaned closer. "Stay cool," he said.

Maddie shrugged. "I ain't done nothin'," she said, unconcerned.

Nolan reached into the inside pocket of his jacket and pulled out the warrant, handing it to Oscar. Oscar read the paperwork and stared at Nolan. "This has to be a mistake, Bart," he said.

"Not according to my evidence," Nolan said before approaching Maddie. "Turn around and put your hands behind you back," Nolan ordered. "Madelyn James, you're under arrest as a suspect in the murder of Sabreena Douglas," he said, glaring at her as he reached for his handcuffs.

For a split-second, Maddie looked shocked, but quickly recovered. "I'm not all that worked up about her bein' dead, but I didn't kill the stupid bitch," she spat, taking a step back. She slapped his hand away when he reached for her. "I didn't do nothin'! I ain't goin' to jail again for somethin' I didn't do, motherfucker!"

As Nolan pulled Maddie's right arm back to cuff it, he glanced at her damaged knuckles. "How'd you mess up your knuckles, James?" he snapped as she tried to jerk her hand away. He pressed his weight against her and asked, "Do that while you were busy rapin' and beatin' Sabreena Douglas to death?"

"Chill, Dudley," she seethed as she tried to suck in a breath to calm down while being mashed against a car body. "I barked 'em on an engine."

Nolan spun her around and jabbed her in the chest. "What did you call me?" he asked.

"Take it easy, Maddie," Oscar warned.

"Nothin'," Maddie responded through clinched teeth, staring coldly into Nolan's eyes.

"Y'know," he continued, his eyes locked on Maddie's, "I didn't like that mouth eleven years ago and don't like it much now either, smart-ass."

"Cool down, Nolan," Suarez said.

Nolan glared at his partner. "Don't tell me to cool off, Suarez. This bitch killed my best friend," Nolan ground out. "I arrested her punk ass myself."

Nolan grabbed her left arm while she continued to resist. Maddie swung her foot back and struck Nolan hard on the shin. Enraged, he grabbed her by the back of the neck and slammed her face down on the edge of the Camaro engine compartment. He finally finished cuffing her and jerked her up by her shirt collar, smiling when he saw blood running over her lips and dripping from her chin. Despite the injury, she continued to kick and jerk, attempting to wrestle out of Nolan's grip as he pulled her arms farther up her back in order to keep control of his prisoner as he recited her Miranda rights.

Nolan dragged Maddie to their car and shoved her into the back seat. In a last act of defiance, she raised her legs and kicked the side window with all the strength she had left, cracking the glass. The beginning of a headache pulsed through her head and she stared sullenly at the floorboard under her feet as the car backed up and drove away.

NOLAN SHOVED MADDIE into a holding cell, not bothering to wipe the blood from her face or remove the handcuffs. Suarez hung back when Nolan walked away. "Turn around," he said. He removed her cuffs and grabbed a package of wet wipes from a nearby desk, shoving them between the bars of the cell.

"Thanks," Maddie said when she sat down and blew her nose, then began running wet wipes over her face, wincing as she reached the area around her nose. She gingerly fingered the skin between her eyes and felt the lump from where she hit the Camaro starting to swell. She laid back and closed her eyes to wait for her headache to pass.

Nearly an hour later, Maddie opened her eyes when she heard the holding cell being unlocked. Her headache had disappeared, but the moment her eyes opened, it came roaring back, strong enough to make her slightly nauseated.

"Let's go, James," Nolan said. "Time for your close-up."

Maddie pushed her body up and walked slowly toward him.

He took her by the arm and led her down a flight of stairs into the booking area. An officer took her to a counter and pressed her fingers against an ink pad before taking each of her fingers and rolling them onto a cardboard form. Then he slapped a wet wipe against her chest to clean off the ink before handing her off to a female officer.

"Hold this in front of your chest and face the camera," she ordered. Maddie looked stoically into the lens and then turned left and right for her profile mug shots. "Go behind the curtain and remove your clothes," the female officer said with no inflection.

"For what?" Maddie asked suspiciously.

"So we can photograph any identifying tattoos or scars and get you into a jumpsuit so the lab can examine your clothes," the officer answered. "I'll also need to get a shot of your knuckles. After that, the detectives will be waiting to ask you a few questions upstairs."

Maddie stripped and waited patiently while the officer photographed a tattoo on the back of her neck and the scars down her side where she'd been shanked at Sand Ridge. Her tattoo was a Celtic infinity symbol she'd gotten as a gift to herself on her eighteenth birthday.

Once she was dressed again, a male officer handcuffed her and escorted her to interrogation. When she was seated, he released the handcuffs, leaving her to wait. She smiled to herself, figuring no one would appear for a while, hoping to make her "sweat" while she waited. Instead, she crossed her arms in front of her on the table and rested her head on her forearms. She hadn't done anything.

Flo believed Maddie was a sexual predator, biding her time until she could molest an innocent girl like Dani. But Dani wasn't the innocent woman Flo thought she was. She had practically been asking Maddie to take her, but she hadn't. If she had, at least there would be a reason for her ass to be sittin' in another cell.

The door opened finally and Maddie was awakened as it slammed shut. The noise plus the lights striking her eyes again also roused her temporarily slumbering headache back to life. Nolan leaned against the wall behind her as Suarez sat across the table from her. He pulled a stack of photos from a file and began laying them down in front of Maddie. The last picture was of a bloody and beaten Sabreena Douglas, who was obviously dead. "You told us you knew Sabreena Douglas, Maddie. How did you know her?" Suarez asked.

"From Sand Ridge. We were there around the same time," Maddie answered with a shrug. "Along with about fifteen-hundred other women. You gonna question all of them, too?" she smirked.

"None of them were in Wichita Falls when she was killed," Suarez said. "Only you were."

"Lucky me," Maddie said, crossing her arms over her chest. "But timin' is everythin' and mine sucks," she grinned.

Nolan smacked Maddie solidly on the back of the head, not helping her headache. "You think this is funny, James?" he growled, leaning close to her ear.

"I think you could use a chill pill, chief," she mumbled.

"Rumor from Sand Ridge was that Douglas led a prostitution ring inside," Nolan said. "She recruit you as one of her bitches?"

Maddie stood up and turned to face Nolan. "I was *never* anyone's bitch, you stupid pig," she ground out, ignoring her headache.

"That why she shanked you?" Suarez asked.

"Don't know who did that," she said to Suarez.

"The hell you didn't," Nolan laughed. "You found out she was in Wichita Falls, you lured her to Oscar's, and you raped her until she bled to death, then you hid her body. But, unfortunately, you dumb fuck, you left behind enough evidence that even Mister Magoo could follow it back to you. That gives you motive and opportunity."

"These your tools?" Suarez asked.

"Could be. We all have the same tools."

Pointing at the screwdriver and creeper, he said, "These two have your prints on them."

"Then, I guess they're mine unless someone borrowed them," Maddie admitted.

"Bam!" Nolan shouted, pounding a fist on the table. "This is just too damn easy!"

Maddie's head was killing her and she pressed the heels of her hands against her eyelids to relieve the pressure in her head. Suddenly, she jumped up and ran to the garbage can in the corner and vomited.

Nolan continued to laugh. "Knowin' you just got nailed for murder should make you sick, James. Not everyone believed you killed Bryan on purpose, like that soft-hearted judge, but now you're really gonna pay." He grabbed her by the arm and dragged her out of the interrogation room, back to the holding cell, where she fell onto the cot to wait for her stomach to settle.

That gave her plenty of time to think, trying to figure out what had gone wrong. There wasn't much to do in an eight-by-ten cell except sleep and think. She felt like everyone she'd started to trust lied to her, given her false hope that she could finally have a life. Dani led her to believe there could be something between them one day, but she'd lied. Had she only been playing with Maddie? Tempting her to do something she wasn't ready for? Maddie squeezed her eyelids shut, forcing her headache away. She rolled onto her side, hoping sleep would make her feel better. While anything was possible, having Maddie arrested seemed a little over-the-top.

A FEW DAYS later, the County Attorney dropped a file on Danielle Hunter's desk, along with a note that there was a possibility it would be brought before a jury as a capital case due to the circumstances and viciousness of the crime. When Dani flipped open the file, she was stunned that a case had actually been brought against Madelyn James. Even though she had to admit that Maddie was a complex and distrustful woman, she couldn't force herself to believe Maddie was a killer.

Going over the material a second time, Dani noticed that Maddie never asked for an attorney even though it was her right. She never refused to answer questions, essentially admitted the tools were hers, and she acknowledged knowing the victim. Dani considered not accepting the case, but if she could help Maddie in any way, she had to be in a position to know what was going on. The first thing she needed to do was speak to Maddie.

Late that evening she walked into the county jail and presented her credentials to the night jailer. Dressed in jeans and a sweatshirt she didn't look like a county attorney, but claimed there were a few questions she needed to have answered before proceeding.

"I'll ask her," the jailer said, "but she's refusin' to talk to anyone. Just lays there, starin' at the ceilin'."

"Tell her I insist," Dani said in her most official-sounding voice, even though she was shaking inside.

"County Attorney's here to ask you a few questions, James," the jailer said after he entered her cell block. "Get up!"

"I'm not talkin' to anyone and you can't make me, Goober. Tell him to go away," Maddie said, rolling toward the wall.

"Then you can just listen," Dani said from behind the jailer.

Maddie turned her head toward the door to her cell and then rolled back to stare at the wall. "Go away," she said.

Dani patted the jailer on the shoulder. "I need to speak to her alone," she said. Certain the jailer was gone, Dani wrapped her hands around the cell bars and said, "The police believe you raped the victim with a foreign object and, as a result, she bled to death from internal hemorrhaging due to being repeatedly penetrated by that object, which they have identified as yours. Help me refute that, Maddie. Please," she begged.

In the middle of Dani's description of how Bree died, Maddie leaped off her cot, and rushed at the bars of her cell, "*You're* prosecuting me? I would *never* rape a woman because I know what it's like and how much it fucks with your mind. You should know that after all the times you've tried to tempt me." Maddie grabbed her head and mumbled, "I couldn't. I...wouldn't. You betrayed me, just like...everyone...else," she forced out as Dani watched the light and rage disappear from her eyes before she collapsed to the floor next to her cot.

"Jailer!" Dani called out. "Call an ambulance!"

Paramedics arrived and examined Maddie, noticing the pronounced lump between her eyes and the fact that her pupils were not dilating equally. At the hospital she was rushed in for a CAT scan, which revealed a moderate concussion. She was admitted for observation and handcuffed to her hospital bed.

Dani stayed with her a few minutes, leaving orders that Maddie was to have no visitors without the consent of the County Attorney's Office, regardless of who wanted to see her or the reason.

When she finally got home that night, she made two phone calls, one to a private investigator she worked with during her time with the Innocence Project; the second to an attorney who was her mentor with the project. She hoped she could convince him to represent Maddie, even though she hadn't requested an attorney. Without representation, the County Attorney's case could be thrown out on a constitutional violation. In the meantime, she planned to do everything she could, legally, to prevent the case against Maddie from going before a judge and jury.

EARLY THE NEXT morning, Dani flashed her credentials at the officer behind the main desk of the Wichita Falls Police Department and asked for directions to the Homicide Unit. She had the preliminary reports concerning the death of Sabreena Douglas, but wanted to see their evidence against Maddie first-hand and get answers to any questions she might be able to come up with. She tried to take deep breaths to calm down and appear non-threatening.

Then she almost laughed out loud at the idea anyone might find her threatening. After all, she was a twenty-seven-year-old woman who was just embarking on her legal career and certainly didn't appear very intimidating. Even her mentor, Saul Orbach, advised her she might not be tough enough for defense work and being successful as a prosecutor would depend on her win-loss record. However, from the time she was a little girl, Dani had wanted to follow in her father's footsteps. Glenn Hunter was a successful and sought-after defense attorney, a lion in the courtroom. Although she wasn't as flamboyant as her father, Dani's mind was just as sharp and she believed others probably underestimated her ability based on her reticent, girlish demeanor.

She walked into the squad room and spotted Detective Nolan quickly. She marched to his desk and dropped her briefcase on it to get his attention.

Nolan glanced up and grinned at her. "What can I do for ya, Counselor?" he asked, sounding slightly bored.

"I hope you're aware that, according to witnesses to Maddie James' arrest, *you* came dangerously close to crossing the line," Dani said quietly.

"I was defending myself during the apprehension of a suspect," Nolan said, leaning back in his chair. "Wanna see my bruises to prove it?" he sneered.

"No, but I do want to see the file on the Sabreena Douglas murder," Dani said. "There've been some questions raised by her attorney about the information you provided on the affidavit for the arrest warrant. I'll need to double-check the information personally."

"Is the County Attorney requesting the file?"

"As the Assistant County Attorney and the Counsel of Record assigned the Douglas case, it is my job to verify all information, Detective. The County Attorney doesn't want this case to cross his desk again due to a constitutional issue on appeal," Dani explained matter-of-factly. Then her voice hardened. "Do I need to go over your head about this matter, Detective Nolan?" she asked.

He patted his hand on the wooden top of his desk and stood up. "Grab a chair and I'll go get the file," he relented.

"Thank you," Dani said. "Is there a room where I can examine the file without being disturbed?"

"Suarez, show Assistant CA Hunter where the conference room is located," Nolan huffed.

"And I need to see the *whole* file," Dani called out to Nolan's back. "Even if it's something you considered not pertinent, in case it becomes an issue at a later time."

"Yeah, yeah," Nolan mumbled as he shuffled away.

Chapter Eleven

SAUL ORBACH, A distinguished-looking gentleman in his sixties, walked into the Wichita County Memorial Hospital ward where injured or ill detained persons were held. He stopped at a desk manned by a uniformed officer and presented his credentials. The officer examined his identification and searched Saul's briefcase and person. It reminded him of what most prisoners were subjected to and why he chose to work on their behalf. He was finally escorted by another armed officer to Maddie's locked room. When he entered, he found her handcuffed to a hospital bed, lying on her side, staring at the wall. He cleared his throat and she glanced over her shoulder at him for a moment before resuming her examination of the wall.

"What the hell do you want?" she asked. "I didn't ask for a fuckin' lawyer."

"What makes you think I'm a lawyer," Saul asked with a smile.

"You look like one, Matlock," she snorted. "I don't want a lawyer."

"Why?"

"They just take your money and you never see them again. Get out!"

"I'm Saul Orbach and I'm here to help you, Miss James," Saul said coolly. "*Pro bono*, which means..."

"I know what it means," Maddie snapped. "I'm not a moron! And I don't give a shit who you are. So leave before I have the guard remove you. I have a headache," Maddie growled. "No one can help my ass, so leave me alone!"

"I spoke to the Assistant County Attorney yesterday on your behalf and she will make arrangements for me to examine the evidence the police have collected," Saul pressed on.

"You can't trust that bitch," Maddie growled. "She'll tell you one thing to make you believe her, then turn around and stab you in the fuckin' back. Just go away. You're fired!" she shouted.

DANI BEGAN A new daily routine. She went in to work early every morning, worked through lunch, and left promptly about six each evening. When she arrived home, she changed into comfortable clothes, prepared dinner for herself and her mother, and began working on finding information that would be helpful in Maddie's case. Some information she forwarded to her investigator, Liam Sullivan. She spoke to her mentor, Saul Orbach, who informed her he hadn't been able to persuade Maddie to talk to him. In fact, Maddie had fired him. As a result, he planned to send her letters filled with questions, hoping she might write back eventually. It wasn't ideal, considering someone at the jail opened and read all incoming mail before the inmate saw it, but he needed to establish some kind of contact.

One evening, two weeks after Maddie's arrest, Dani was putting dishes in the dishwasher when her doorbell rang. She dried her hands quickly and walked to her front door. She swung it open and greeted Oscar Melendez.

"Can I speak to you for a moment, Miss Hunter?" he asked.

"Of course. Please come in. Would you care for a cup of coffee? I just made a fresh pot," Dani offered.

Oscar rubbed his hands together to warm them. "Thank you, Miss Hunter."

"Cream and sugar?"

"Black is fine," he said. He took his cup and sat down at the kitchen table. Dani stirred a little cream and sugar into her cup and joined him.

"How can I help you, Mr. Melendez?" she asked.

"You're prosecuting Maddie James' case, aren't you?"

Dani stared into her cup for a moment. "Yes, I am," she sighed.

"Maddie worked for me and I was there when she was arrested. You should check into that," Oscar said.

"Why?" Dani asked.

"I spent my whole career in law enforcement, Miss Hunter, and there was something about her arrest that bothered me, but it took me a while to reconcile it in my mind. I like Maddie. She works hard, don't cause no trouble, never objects to working overtime, and is a damn fine mechanic."

"Sounds like a good employee to have," Dani commented. "What in particular bothered you about the arrest?"

"Bart Nolan is a good cop, but he let his personal feelings get in his way. You see, he was my son's best friend and took Bryan's death pretty hard. In fact, he was the motorcycle officer who responded to the accident that killed Bryan," Oscar explained.

"He arrested her back then?" Dani asked.

"Yes, and now he sees this arrest as his revenge for Bryan's death. He was one of those who disagreed with Maddie's sentence back then," Oscar said shaking his head.

"Did you disagree with her sentence, too?" Dani asked.

"Probably at first, but I'd told Bryan to get his damn seatbelt fixed. It never locked right and could have been replaced for twenty lousy bucks, but he thought he was a safe driver, so what could happen?" Oscar admitted. "He died because he wouldn't spend twenty fuckin' bucks," he muttered. "I'm sorry. Please pardon my language," he added sheepishly.

"No problem, Mr. Melendez," Dani said.

"Anyway, I'm convinced Bart stepped over the line and used excessive force when he arrested her. He slammed her head onto the hood of that vehicle hard and I was surprised he didn't dislocate her shoulder," he continued. "She was bleedin' when they took her out."

"She was diagnosed with a concussion a couple of days later," Dani said.

"Is she alright?" Oscar asked.

"She will be in time," Dani answered.

"If you have any questions, you can talk to any of my employees. They were all there," Oscar volunteered. "Probably will want to talk to Crew anyway. He came to work one morning and found Maddie unconscious the day after we were robbed."

"What's his full name? I'll have it checked out," Dani nodded as she wrote.

"Crew Faulkner," Oscar said with a smile. "He looks scarier than he is. Kind of a rough-looking cuddly type, but he likes Maddie. We all do."

"You do know that I'm not Miss James' attorney, right?" Dani asked. "It's not my job to get her off."

Oscar smiled. "I know, but I asked around and know you worked for the Innocence Project. Just because you're a prosecutor now doesn't mean you want to convict the wrong person."

"No," Dani said. "I wouldn't want to do that, but I can't represent the State *and* the defendant."

"I understand," Oscar said, finishing his coffee and standing up. "Just do the best you can."

"Oh, before I forget, when did you file your burglary report?" Dani asked. "I didn't see it in the case file when I looked through it."

"The day Crew found Maddie. The police stamped it when I turned it in. Should be in the file unless it wound up a burglary file." Oscar extended his hand and said, "Thanks for your time...and the coffee."

"No, thank you, Mr. Melendez," Dani smiled as she took his hand before escorting him to the front door.

Oscar turned as he stepped onto the small porch. "Maddie said something a little strange while Nolan was trying to handcuff her. Maybe she'll tell someone what that meant."

"What did you hear, Mr. Melendez?"

"She said she wasn't going to prison *again* for something she didn't do. Odd remark, don't you think? Well, good night, Miss Hunter," Oscar shrugged. "Probably nothing."

Dani closed her door and leaned heavily against it, covering her eyes and allowing her tears to flow freely. She didn't know how, but was certain Oscar Melendez believed Maddie had not been responsible for his son's death. Once she gathered herself, she called Liam and gave him Crew Faulkner's name, as well as Jorge Suarez's, suggesting he question both men and briefly told him Melendez's concerns, minus his final comment.

Liam told her he had an appointment to interview the warden at Sand Ridge for more information regarding the disagreement between Maddie and Sabreena Douglas. He'd contact her afterward with his report of anything pertinent.

While Dani tried to gather herself, she dialed the number for Flo and Sal's home. After two or three rings, an irritated voice answered, "Yeah, what?"

"Sal? It's Dani. Is Flo there?"

"Yeah. Hang on, Counselor. And by the way, your timing sucks," Sal said.

"Sorry, Sal. Next time take the phone off the hook," Dani chuckled.

"Hello, Dani," Flo's happier-sounding voice said.

"Guess y'all are home alone this evening. Sorry, Flo," Dani apologized.

"Don't worry about it, hun. She'll recover. We sent all the kiddies to a double feature at the drive-in," Flo laughed. "I swear Sal's the horniest woman I ever met."

"Sorry I disturbed your time alone then," Dani smiled. "I was just wondering if you'd been to see Maddie yet?"

"Went a couple of days ago, but she wouldn't see me. Thought I'd give it another shot tomorrow. She still in the hospital?" Flo asked.

"As far as I know. I asked a friend who's an attorney to talk to her, but she threw him out yesterday," Dani told Flo. "Sooner or later she has to talk to someone."

"I'll do what I can, but she don't really trust me yet."

"Let me know how it goes if she does say something, Flo," Dani said.

After saying good-bye to Flo, Dani sat on an easy chair and called Directory Assistance to locate a California phone number for Maddie's former agent. Maddie had a number of unusual peculiarities and Dani decided to contact a few people who might be able to provide some insight into her past to give Dani a feel for who Maddie James was and how to get her to open up.

ANXIOUS TO LEARN more about Maddie, Dani walked into her duplex a little earlier than usual, after dropping off take-out chicken at her mother's, telling her she had work she'd had to bring home from her office. Dani took her coat off and dropped her briefcase on the couch, stopping only to grab a legal pad and pen and toe-off her shoes before punching a number into her cell phone.

"Yeah," a gruff voice answered following four or five rings.

"Hello," Dani responded. "My name is Danielle Hunter and I'm—" she got out before the party on the other end disconnected. Annoyed, Dani punched in the number a second time.

"Yeah," the same male voice finally growled. "Not takin' any new clients at the moment, babe."

"Don't you dare hang up on me again," Dani said quickly. "I'm looking for Jackson Carville."

"For what?" the man asked.

"Are you Jackson Carville?"

"Last time I looked in the mirror. Did someone kick off and leave me a few bucks?" Carville chuckled.

"Afraid not. I'm calling about Maddie James," Dani said.

"Who?" Carville asked, sounding confused.

"Maddie James and the James Gang," Dani repeated slowly. "You were their agent eleven or twelve years ago," she added to shake his memory.

"Maddie's in jail someplace. Texas, I think. Haven't spoken to her in at least a decade," Carville said.

"What can you tell me about her?" Dani asked.

Carville harrumphed and said, "I can tell you that bitch cost me a fortune in attorney and cancellation fees when she got her ass arrested."

"Go on, please," Dani encouraged.

"She was a promising singer who could've made it big, but snorted too much junk up her nose. Just beginning to get noticed when she fucked up and went to jail. In this business, honey, if you ain't workin', you ain't even the flicker of a memory," Carville said with a bite in his voice. "She was a smart-ass, especially when she was high, which was most of the time."

"Did her drug use affect her music?" Dani asked.

After a moment, Carville said, "Funny thing about that. She always performed when she was high, but, if anything, her performances were solid and high-energy. Told me her girlfriend provided her with drugs to overcome her stage fright. Must have worked, because they seemed to ramp up her personality and performance until the show ended," he reminisced before adding, "but then she had a tendency to crash pretty hard."

"Did you know who her girlfriend was?"

"Never met her. Some old rocker. Must have been a pedophile though because Maddie was still in her teens when they hooked up, I think. If Maddie hadn't been such a blatant dyke, I might have given her a whirl myself. She got a kick out of yankin' my chain when she was flyin' high. Bitch," he muttered.

"Do you know what happened to the members of the James Gang?" Dani inquired.

"I know they disbanded after Maddie was arrested and, as far as I know, none of them ever achieved the popular success they had before that. But they're still hangin' around the fringes of the music industry."

"Are you still in contact with any of them?" Dani asked hopefully.

"I ran into Thumper at a talent search a few months back. I have a number for her around here somewhere," Carville said. In the background it sounded like he was rifling through a bunch of papers and opening and closing drawers. After what seemed like an interminable time, Carville came back on the line. "Yeah, I think this is it. Huh. Margaret Mason, was that really Thumper's name? I'd rather be called Thumper, too," he laughed. "So Middle American, y'know."

"The number?" Dani prodded.

"Yeah, yeah," he huffed.

Dani wrote down the number and read it back to him to make sure she had it right. "I appreciate your help, Mr. Carville. Thanks for the information," she said before disconnecting. She glanced at her clock on the wall and smiled. Considering the two-hour time difference between Texas and California, she still had time to contact Thumper, the bass player with the James Gang. Praying she'd be able to reach her, Dani punched in the number and waited. She was wishing she had a cup of coffee when the other end of the line was picked up. A young girl's voice said, "Dennis residence. Trina speaking."

"How are you, Trina? My name is Dani. May I speak to your mother, please?" Dani asked pleasantly.

Something muffled the receiver and Dani heard a voice yell, "Mom!"

A moment later, a woman's mild voice said, "This is Peg Dennis."

"I hope I'm not disturbing you, Mrs. Dennis. My name is Danielle Hunter and if you have the time, I'm calling because I have a few questions about Maddie James. You were Thumper Mason of the James Gang, weren't you?"

"Well, that's certainly a blast from the past and I was Thumper for a couple of years, but there probably isn't anything I can tell you about Maddie that you don't already know. It was a relatively short run, unfortunately," Thumper said. "But not without its memorable moments."

"Jackson Carville told me you're still involved with the music industry," Dani said.

"Really only peripherally," Thumper said. "I'm living in Monterrey and occasionally book Indy groups trying to break in at small clubs along the West Coast."

"What can you tell me about Maddie?" Dani asked.

"In the beginning, I liked her. We were about the same age, but were never what I'd call besties. She was just a nice young woman, an above average guitarist, and a killer singer who really knew how to sell a song. An unusual mix of Joplin and Etheridge with a little raspy Chapman thrown in," Thumper said.

"When did you begin to *not* like her?" Dani asked.

"It didn't happen all at once. Probably after her girlfriend, Shay, dumped her for a younger model."

"But Maddie would have only been...what? Twenty, twenty-one?" Dani gasped.

"Probably closer to twenty, honey. If I remember correctly, I think they broke it off right after Maddie's twentieth birthday. You had to be around Shay to understand. She was a control freak, among other things, and Maddie would do just about anything for her. She needed the affection, such as it was, for some reason," Thumper explained.

"Was she the one who introduced Maddie to drugs?" Dani asked.

"Yeah, but we couldn't complain too much. Back then we were all tweakin' something off and on to take the edge off," Thumper said.

"Do you remember Shay's last name?"

"Didn't have one as far as I know. I heard she oded a couple of years ago anyway. When Maddie started picking up a groupie after every concert for sex and staying stoned until we moved on to the next venue, I sort of began keeping my distance from her. She threw it all away for sex and drugs. Pathetic," she sighed.

"Do you know where the other members of the James Gang are now?" Dani asked.

"I know they're all here in California. Hang on and I'll get on my laptop and give you the most recent numbers I have. Can't promise the numbers are still good though," Thumper offered.

"Anything will help," Dani said.

"Can't you get this stuff from Maddie?" Thumper asked.

"She refuses to talk to me or anyone else," Dani answered.

"Always was stubborn," Thumper chuckled.

Thumper returned in a few minutes and gave Dani the most recent contact number she had for the remaining three band members and wished Dani well before hanging up. Dani set her cell phone down and ran her fingers through her hair, pushing it back. Then she went into the kitchen to prepare a pot of coffee.

While she watched the coffee drip into the carafe, she thought back to the things she'd learned from Carville and Thumper without reaching any conclusions. So far, she only had puzzle pieces that didn't make a picture. Her quest was personal and maybe Liam and Saul would find something more factual. Liam could coax information out of a sphinx and Saul was phenomenal at finding breadcrumbs that led to a different path.

She carried a large mug of coffee into the living room and sat down again, looking at the three names on his list. She finally punched in the number for Catherine Krupke, the drummer for Maddie's band, known as "Cat". The final two band members, Packie and Pidge, would have to wait until the next evening. Dani put her mug down and shoved her fingers into her hair and waited. Tomorrow, she would make a list of specific questions to ask the final two musicians.

Following several rings, she was preparing to hang up and try another name when a breathy, female voice finally answered, "Dr. Krupke."

"Catherine Krupke?" Dani asked.

"Yes. Sorry, but I dozed off in my hot tub and didn't hear the phone ring for a while," the woman said. "How may I help you?"

"Were you once the drummer for the James Gang?" Dani asked to assure herself she had the right person.

"Once upon a time, just like any good fairy tale," Cat laughed. "Don't tell anyone though. I don't want to ruin my reputation."

"I won't," Dani smiled. "I was wondering if you'd be willing to answer a few questions about Maddie James."

"I'm not really associated with that world any longer. I've moved on to a better place. What's this really about?" Cat asked suspiciously.

"I'm an attorney and am assisting her with a legal matter. I think I will be more help if I understand where she's coming from, so to speak, and she's not very forthcoming," Dani lied smoothly.

"What do you want to know?" Cat huffed.

"What kind of person was she?" Dani asked.

"Nice enough, but confused from time to time. Personally, I thought she was looking for someone to replace her mother, but I'm not a shrink. Otherwise, why the hell would she hang around with that pervert, Shay No-Last-Name?"

"Why do you think she was a pervert?" Dani challenged.

"Because she was hanging all over a 'girl' twenty years her junior and pumping her full of drugs so she could control her and introduce her to all that kinky S&M bullshit she was into. I know Maddie didn't like it, but allowed herself to be abused rather than lose Shay's affection. Bitch dumped her anyway for a twelve-year-old who was a little more malleable. But the damage had already been done," Cat said. "Maddie hopefully doesn't still have all those disgusting piercings Shay insisted she get supposedly to heighten her pleasure," she added sarcastically.

"What damage?" Dani asked, jotting down notes furiously. "What piercings?"

"The idea that real love wasn't love unless it was...painful," Cat sniffed. "Maddie was extremely confused and grew distrustful, even of her own band members, almost to the level of paranoia. I never saw her piercings, but she told me she had a couple of slave rings that were connected by a chain that Shay could jerk to make sure she had Maddie's complete attention any time. Some seriously sick shit. Probably where the phrase about yanking someone's chain came from. After Shay's departure back to middle school, Maddie was always looking for someone who'd hurt her to prove they really, truly loved her. Finally, she picked up a roadie in Baton Rouge who turned out to be a younger version of Shay, only probably sicker."

"Do you remember her name?" Dani asked.

"Courtney something. Pidge might know. Pretty sure Courtney hit on her when Maddie was sleeping off her last high."

"How did they hook up?"

"Courtney started following us in Mobile, I think. Maddie didn't notice her until after our Baton Rouge show. Pretty blonde roadie who was up for anything, damn promiscuous, and had access to a seemingly endless supply of drugs," Cat told her.

"Sounds like the perfect groupie," Dani said.

"She was a pushy and demanding bitch," Cat said bitingly. "Demanded all of Maddie's off-stage time. We couldn't even find time to rehearse decently. From the way Maddie looked, I thought Courtney must have been a pretty rough lover, too, like Shay. I saw bruises and bite marks on Maddie's body more than once. One time, at the beginning of a performance, Maddie could barely manage to get on stage. In my opinion, Courtney would get Maddie drugged up and sexually abuse her while she was too high to resist whatever was happening to her. But then again, I couldn't prove anything and Maddie wouldn't listen to anyone. We all thought it, but couldn't really do anything to help her," Cat said, ending her story.

It was more than Dani wanted to know and she wasn't sure she would be able to do anything to convince Maddie to trust her.

"Do you know what happened to Courtney after Maddie dumped her?" Dani continued.

"If we're lucky, she walked in front of a bus," Cat laughed. "Otherwise, I have no idea and don't really care. She was a nobody. Probably still out there somewhere ruining someone else's life."

"I appreciate the information. Thank you for speaking to me, Dr. Krupke," Dani said.

"You're welcome. It was a turbulent time, but eventually led me to a more stable life," Cat said. "Good luck with Maddie's legal problem," she added before disconnecting.

EARLY THE NEXT morning while Dani was dressing for work, her cell phone buzzed.

"Danielle Hunter," she answered.

"Morning," a voice said. "Got a minute?"

Dani smiled as she recognized the voice. "Good morning, Liam. How are you?"

"Not bad, kid," he answered. "I've got a little information for you. Can we meet for lunch?"

"That shouldn't be a problem. Will your information be helpful?" she asked.

"If you're the prosecution," he said cryptically. "I'll see you about twelve-thirty at the Longhorn Grill."

"Okay. Have a good day, Liam," she said as the call ended.

She spent most of the morning going through the evidence file for the case against Maddie, searching for any weaknesses and going over the newest lab reports from the examination of items collected at Oscar's business. She should be able to introduce the tools, which were identified as Maddie's. However, her fingerprints on the items were only partial prints. A decent defense attorney could certainly question them as rock-solid evidence. Because the items were listed as stolen items, whoever took them managed to rub off everything except a couple of partial prints. Plus the defense should have Oscar's burglary report, which made it likely whoever took the tools was also a killer. She hoped Liam found something useful because so far the evidence seemed plausible. However, in her gut, Dani still couldn't convince herself that Maddie was a ruthless killer.

By twelve-thirty she was sitting at a table in the Longhorn Grill, anxiously watching for Liam's arrival, her hands wrapped around a cup of hot coffee to warm them. Five minutes later, Liam strolled in and wove between the tables to join her. A waiter appeared quickly and offered him a cup of coffee as Liam removed his coat and hung it on the back of his chair after depositing a file on the table.

"It's pretty chilly out today," he commented blandly as he sat.

"It's mostly because of the wind. Knife's right through you," Dani said. "Welcome to winter in Wichita Falls, Texas."

Liam flipped open the file folder as he sipped his coffee. Then he launched into his report, "I've interviewed the employees at the repair shop. The most potentially useful information came from Crew Faulkner, but a lot of what he told me amounted to speculation he thought would help the accused. Unclear how helpful it will actually be in the long run. Also had a guarded conversation with Jorge Suarez. He obviously didn't want to accuse his partner of doing anything that might have been out-of-bounds legally, but might admit it if pressed when called to testify. Claims the accused was uncooperative and combative, which could have justified Detective Nolan's actions. In my opinion, the helpfulness of Faulkner or Suarez is questionable at best. However, the information from Sand Ridge could be better for the accused," he said with a slight smile.

"I spoke to the warden, Christina Nolan," he continued, holding a hand up to stop Dani from asking any questions. "I'll answer your questions after I tell you everything."

"Okay," Dani agreed softly.

"By the way, Warden Nolan is the ex-wife of Detective Bart Nolan. From what I could gather, it was a somewhat contentious divorce and she admitted he has a very short temper. She voluntarily gave me a list of women her staff believed were involved, either voluntarily or coerced, into being in an inmate prostitution ring run by the decedent. Most are still incarcerated at Sand Ridge. Douglas and James were involved in an ongoing dispute, apparently caused by Douglas's attempts to force James into her little ring. James aligned herself with another group of very undesirable women for protection. James still took a few knocks over it. Warden Nolan believed, but couldn't prove, that Douglas was responsible for the stabbing of James during an altercation on the rec yard. The warden also rather reluctantly believed that some of her guards used Douglas's group as enforcers occasionally against other inmates. One of those enforcers was a Selena Gutierrez. She became Douglas's heir-apparent and took over the prostitution ring after Douglas was released. I requested an interview with Gutierrez and she agreed, if I could promise to get her sentence reduced. I told her I would look into it, but couldn't promise anything. After that, the only thing she would admit was being involved in an assault on James ordered by Douglas as retaliation for her assault on a guard in which the guard was injured. No other specifics. Now, questions?"

Dani exhaled loudly. "That's a lot, but not really that much, Liam," she said. "What did Crew actually tell you?"

"He found James unconscious on the floor of her work bay when he came to work, but couldn't remember the day. When she came to, he sent her home. We could check her time card to see when she left, I suppose. He thought she was preparing to leave because her coveralls were partially unzipped, fought with the burglars and lost, but believed that was how she could have injured her knuckles. Then the burglars probably grabbed what they could and ran, leaving her unconscious. Again, mostly speculation," Liam answered.

"We have the burglary report Melendez filed which was the

same day Crew found Maddie. I'll look it up," Dani said. "I need to know more about the retaliation assault."

"Doubt you'll get it from Gutierrez. She's doing life for beating a man to death during a robbery. No deals to be made there and she won't talk without a deal," Liam said. "Maybe James will tell you."

"Unlikely," Dani sighed. "Even if she did, it would only bolster her motive."

"Unless something unexpected turns up, James is pretty much screwed," Liam admitted.

"Can I get the records for these inmate prostitutes?" Dani asked, waving the list.

"Probably, but unless any of them were released, it probably won't do much good," Liam shrugged.

"When you have them, let me know," Dani said.

Liam nodded. "It'll take a week or so. That okay?"

"It'll have to be, I guess. Thanks, Liam. Ready to order? I'm buying."

"Then let me check what kind of steaks are on the menu," he said. "Why are you so interested in this case anyway? Looks like a loser to me, kiddo."

"I know the accused and find it hard to believe she would commit this crime, Liam," Dani answered.

"Why? The police have some pretty convincing evidence."

"It's mostly circumstantial," Dani rebutted.

"Well, realistically, your suspect has already done ten years for another felony. It's not too difficult to believe she might do it again," Liam shrugged. "Prison changes people in ways you can't imagine, Dani. This one may be a loser."

BY SEVEN THAT evening, Dani settled into her comfortable easy chair and glanced at her legal pad. She wasn't sure the members of Maddie's band were being very helpful other than helping her understand Maddie's background. So far they'd all admitted they should have done something to keep Maddie from destroying her life, but hadn't. But hadn't she done the same thing? She should have confessed to being the driver when Bryan Melendez was killed. But she hadn't, just like everyone else who'd let Maddie down. The least she could do now was not be too afraid to stand up for her.

She picked up her phone and punched in the number for the James Gang's back-up singer and keyboard player. Three rings later, a laughing woman answered, "Joe's Pool Hall. You rack 'em, we sink 'em."

Dani smiled. "Is Patricia Davis there, please?" she asked.

"Pidge! It's some woman for you. Should I be jealous, baby?" the woman called out.

"This is Pidge," another woman said. "Stop it, Lynn. It's your shot."

"Miss Davis, my name is Danielle Hunter. Were you a member of the James Gang?"

"Wow! I haven't heard that in forever, but I was back in the day."

Repeating her lie from the evening before, Dani said, "I'm an attorney and am helping Maddie James with a legal matter. Would you mind answering a few questions?"

"I guess. Did she get out of jail?"

"Yes. Her current situation is unrelated to her previous legal problem," Dani said. "I've already spoken to Cat and Thumper and just need to verify a couple of things with you, if I could."

"No problem. How are they?" Pidge asked.

"Fine apparently. And you?"

"Workin' every damn day in the studio band over at Paramount. Pay's steady and covers the rent," Pidge answered.

"Do you remember a young woman associated with Maddie, named Courtney?" Dani asked.

"Oh, hell," Pidge muttered. "Unfortunately, I do. There were a few times I wanted to beat her to death."

"Who're you talkin' about?" a voice in the distance asked.

"That bitch, Courtney, that Maddie picked up when we were on tour," Pidge said.

"Fuck her!" the voice yelled back.

"What can you tell me about her?" Dani asked.

"Came on to me a few times when Maddie was sleepin' off her partyin' from the night before. Claimed she was more woman than Maddie could handle or some bullshit like that, but I think Maddie was too nice for her. Maddie was a good kid, but not that worldly. When she wasn't high, she thought every place we went was fascinatin'," Pidge laughed. "Besides, I already had a good woman waitin' for me at home and wasn't gonna waste my time with a loser like Courtney."

"Do you happen to remember her last name?" Dani asked, crossing her fingers.

"It was something weird, but started with a C. Wanted us to call her CeeCee, but no one did. I'll think about it. Any other questions?"

"Cat thought Courtney might have abused Maddie. Know anything about that?" Dani tried.

"Chalayne. C-H-A-L-A-Y-N-E," Pidge spelled out.

"What?" Dani asked, confused

"That was Courtney's last name. Chalayne. Not sure about the abuse thing, but one time I had to help Maddie onto the stage. She whimpered somethin' about Courtney bitin' her on a very sensitive part of her body. I thought she was gonna pass out, but she pulled it together when the show started," Pidge said. "You talk to Packie yet?"

"She's my next call," Dani said.

"Good luck. I heard she was teeterin' close to the edge, doin' a pretty good imitation of Maddie with the drugs and wild child life now. She was only around nineteen when she joined us, but a helluva guitarist. Couldn't sing for shit though," she chuckled. "Still managed to write our best songs. Hope she doesn't throw her talent away like Maddie did. Okay, my wife is gettin' antsy. It's my shot," Pidge said quickly.

"Thanks for your—" Dani began as the call suddenly disconnected. "—help," she finished to dead air.

Chapter Twelve

NEARLY A MONTH passed without much movement on Maddie's case. She was released from the hospital and taken back to the county jail. The County Attorney began dropping not-so-subtle hints that the case should go to court no later than the beginning of January. While he appreciated the idea that Dani wanted to present a case that left zero wiggle room for the defense to sneak through, it wasn't every day the State was handed a case where they could prove probable motive, means, *and* opportunity. It was a gift, for God's sake and the taxpayers of Wichita County had every right to demand swift justice.

"Just one more thing I need to check, Chief, to be thorough," Dani promised, stalling as she waited for the files Liam had promised in a week, three weeks earlier. The minute the County Attorney left her office, she punched Liam's number into her cell phone and nervously tapped her foot beneath her desk waiting for him to answer. "Pick up, pick up," she hissed under her breath.

"Hello," Liam's weak-sounding voice finally came on the line.

"Hi, Liam. Where's that file you promised to send me?" she asked hurriedly. "You told me it would be a week and now it's three weeks later."

"I sent it. Didn't you get it?" he coughed.

"Obviously not," she answered impatiently.

"Check your spam," he said.

Dani clicked on her spam folder and said, "Not there."

"Let me check my sent folder." A few seconds later, he said, "Damn, looks like I goofed up the address. I came down with the flu and substituted a comma for a period. Must have been because I had a fever. Let me re-send it. I'll stay on the line until I know you got it. Sorry about that, kid."

"Are you feeling better now, Liam?" she asked, feeling bad that she'd jumped on him. She should have checked sooner. As soon as the mail icon popped up, she clicked to make sure the file had arrived intact. "I got it. Go to bed and rest now, Liam, and thanks," she said. "Sorry if I sounded irritable."

"Surprised you weren't totally pissed. I would've been." He tried to laugh, but broke into a coughing fit.

"Get well soon," Dani said before ending the call. She transferred the file onto a thumb drive and dropped it into her briefcase to print out at home.

AS SOON AS her mother left after dinner, Dani took her legal pad and a pen from her briefcase and scanned the notes she'd made concerning the evidence against Maddie and her interviews with others who'd known her before her imprisonment. She circled a few things and scribbled a new set of notes about those particular items. Although there were no usable fingerprints, she was curious about a typed note found in the victim's pocket.

Other than confirming that blood on the paper belonged to the victim, the paper was generic notepaper available at any five-and-dime. The only significant thing was the lab technician's opinion that the note was typed on a 1960's model IBM Selectric with a changeable font. Without the machine, he couldn't deduce more. But it definitely hadn't been computer generated.

Dani doubted that "Packie" Packard, the James Gang's acoustical guitarist, would be able to tell her much more than the other band members already had. The only other person of interest was Courtney Chalayne. Cat said Maddie picked her up in Baton Rouge and they remained together until the Texas portion of the band's tour ended in Wichita Falls. No matter how hard Dani tried, she barely remembered the young woman who walked out of the theater with Maddie that night. Only that she'd been wrapped around Maddie like a boa constrictor before Maddie suddenly shoved her away and walked into her throng of screaming fans.

Dani clearly remembered Maddie's lean, slender body, hugged by formfitting black leather pants that outlined her provocatively swaying hips and buttocks as she moved. Even though she hadn't wanted to go to the concert with Jan, she had to admit that, at that moment, when Maddie embraced her fans, Dani was fascinated and drawn in just like all the others. Maddie demanded their undivided attention and adoration, and Dani didn't know, or care, what became of the boa constrictor once Maddie approached her. Now, a decade later, Dani needed to locate Courtney Chalayne.

Courtney could be anywhere, but all Dani really had was what Cat told her, so she clicked her Google icon and typed Courtney Chalayne into the search line. A brief bio popped up, but only said she had attended LSU and listed her hometown in Louisiana. On a hunch, Dani looked up the number for the Registrar's Office at Louisiana State University. She would call the next day during her lunch break.

Dani was tired and decided to relax in a nice hot bubble bath with a glass of wine.

DURING HER LUNCH break the next afternoon, Dani called the LSU Registrar's Office. After a little fast talking and a couple of white lies about trying to track down Courtney Chalayne as part of an estate settlement, Dani was given a number listed for Claude Chalayne in Ceour d'Mer, Louisiana. When she dialed the number, a woman answered, "Chalayne Charters."

"Is Claude Chalayne there, please?" Dani asked.

"Out ona fishin' trip. Won't be back for a coupla days. I'm his wife. I kin answer any questions ya got," the woman said.

"Okay. I'm trying to reach Courtney Chalayne on a legal matter. Is she there?" Dani tried.

"She don't live here. What kinda trouble that 'ho got herself into dis time," the woman laughed. "We ain't bailin' her skanky ass out agin."

"She's not in trouble, Mrs. Chalayne. I just need to locate her," Dani said.

"Last we heard, she was in Nawlins, prob'ly hookin' agin," Mrs. Chalayne chuckled.

"Do you happen to have a contact number for her, ma'am?" Dani inquired.

"Might not still be good, but cuz she's Claude's sistah, we might need to get ahold of her. If this don't work no more, contact the Nawlins Police," Mrs. Chalayne said before giving Dani another number.

When Dani ended the call, she took a minute and puckered her lips to exhale deeply before punching in the latest number, then doodling on her pad while she waited for someone to answer.

"Good afternoon, sugar," a smooth rich female voice answered. "This is Carlotta. How can I make your day sweeter?"

Taken aback, Dani sat up straighter and was certain she was blushing. "Hello," she finally managed, clearing her throat. "I was given this number for Courtney Chalayne. Is she there?"

"Have you used her services before, sweetie? Her clients include men and women. She's an equal opportunity provider," Carlotta said.

"I'm sorry, Carlotta. I just need to speak to her," Dani said, smiling as she covered her eyes.

"It's the same fee for just talking as any other service," Carlotta said calmly. "We accept cash as well as credit or debit cards. Shall I book you for an hour with Helena?"

"I won't need an hour," Dani said.

"Oooo, a fast worker, huh?" Carlotta rumbled with a deep laugh. "May I get your card number now? Helena is available this evening at seven."

"What's the fee?" Dani asked.

"One hundred for every hour," Carlotta continued as if it was an everyday thing, like picking up a loaf of bread at Wal-Mart or Target.

"A hundred bucks!" Dani exclaimed. When heads turned to stare in her direction, she ducked her head in embarrassment. "I only need fifteen minutes of her time."

"Do the math, sweetie," Carlotta said.

"Okay. Do I call this same number?" Dani griped.

"No, I'll give you her personal number after I get your card number," Carlotta hummed. "And just as soon as your purchase is approved."

Dani read off her number and expiration date before writing down yet another number. By then her curiosity was running rampant and she was almost looking forward to the seven o'clock telephone rendezvous with Courtney, or Helena, or whatever name she was using now. However, Dani seriously doubted the County Attorney would consider authorizing a reimbursement.

TIME WAS LITERALLY money as Dani rushed home after

work, dropped off a spaghetti dinner for her mother from her favorite Italian restaurant and prepared to place her call to Courtney Chalayne, AKA Helena.

"This is Helena. How may I please you tonight, darlin'?" a low whiskey smooth voice purred over the line.

After thinking for a second, Dani said, "This is Dani. I need to ask you a few questions concerning Maddie James. Take your time, but I only paid for fifteen minutes."

Helena chuckled. "That's too bad. I could probably make you go off like the Fourth of July in thirty."

"Already heard the sales pitch," Dani snapped. "Is your name Courtney Chalayne?"

"It is," Helena answered. "Who are you asking about again?"

"Maddie James," Dani repeated.

"Never met her," Courtney said blandly.

"She picked you up in Baton Rouge and dumped you in Wichita Falls, Texas about ten years ago. That's what the members of her band say. I've spoken to all of them and they certainly remembered you, Miss Chalayne."

"She didn't dump me, I split after she took off with some little loser she found outside their last venue. You can't believe a thing those bitches tell you," Courtney snapped. "They're all chronic liars."

"So you *do* remember Maddie James then?"

"Of course I do! Jesus! She used me to get drugs for her because, believe me, honey, she couldn't perform, on-stage or in bed, unless she was blasted. Without them, she was an incredibly disappointing lover, a fuckin' Girl Scout," Courtney answered hostilely.

"Did you abuse her sexually as well?" Dani asked.

"She liked it rough," Courtney gloated. "Came like a motherfucker and begged for more until she passed out. I could have done anything I wanted to her then, so I suppose it's possible I may have gotten a little carried away a time or two," she said without remorse.

"So carried away she couldn't get on-stage without assistance?" Dani asked.

"She *wanted* it and I gave her what she wanted," Courtney hissed. "Besides she was flyin' so high she didn't know the difference. It was more of a strange love-hate relationship than an intimate one. By the way, your time's up, lover," Courtney concluded and disconnected.

Dani pushed her hands through her hair and leaned back in her chair, suddenly feeling dirty, and tried to imagine the life Maddie had lived. It began with so much promise, then was destroyed by poor decisions that finally broke her, emotionally and financially.

A knock at her front door dragged Dani back into the present. She walked to the door, expecting to find her mother, but was pleasantly surprised to see Flo and Sal on her small porch.

"Y'all come on in," Dani invited as a chilly breeze danced inside. "I was just going to make some coffee," she said while they removed their parkas.

"Sounds real good to me," Sal said, briskly rubbing her hands together, while glancing around. "We didn't interrupt a private moment, did we?" she grinned.

"I haven't had a private moment in so long, I probably wouldn't remember what to do," Dani admitted with a shrug. "Hell, I even tried to seduce Maddie after our fishing trip, but she wasn't interested. How pathetic is that?"

Flo followed Dani into the kitchen and leaned her elbows on the counter, massaging her forehead with her thumb and index finger.

"Are you all right, Flo?" Dani asked.

"Not really," Flo answered. "I've been to the damn jail to see Maddie six times, but she won't talk to me. Don't want to see anyone. It ain't normal."

"I know. She won't see me either, and, unfortunately, I can't make her," Dani said.

"Sal says you're prosecutin' Maddie's case," Flo muttered.

"Yes, I am. I've already delayed it as much as I can, but the County Attorney told me to get in front of a judge and jury after the first of the year. Everything points to her guilt, Flo," Dani said sadly. "There's not much more I can do unless she talks to someone or starts defending herself."

A few minutes later, they carried three mugs of coffee into the living room.

"I have some files I need to print out tonight," Dani said. "Do you mind? I'll be right back."

Sal followed Dani into her office and leaned against the

doorjamb. "Why don't I keep an eyes on those while you talk to Flo. Maybe you can make her feel better," Sal said. "I won't read anything. I promise," she added with a smile.

"Doesn't matter, Sal. Probably won't amount to anything. Just wishful thinking on my part," Dani said, pausing to pat Sal on the shoulder as her printer started, before leaving the home office. "Might as well sit and make yourself comfortable. My printer's not the world's fastest. Holler if you need more coffee."

"Thanks, Dani," Sal said, sitting in Dani's office chair and leaning back.

"I need one of these," Sal said.

Almost half an hour later, Sal came wandering out of Dani's office holding a stack of printouts.

"What is this, Dani? Looks like inmate records," Sal asked.

"They are. Just set them on the coffee table and I'll get around to sorting them in a day or two," Dani said.

"What are they, really?" Flo asked.

"According to the warden at Sand Ridge, those are the inmates who were in a prostitution ring run by Sabreena Douglas. I was planning to take out the inmates still incarcerated. That should leave anyone besides Maddie who may have been out to seek a little revenge. She was never able to recruit Maddie, but tried by intimidation and at least one attempt on her life to keep the others in line," Dani explained.

"I say we divvy these up and get some more coffee," Flo said, her demeanor happier. "I can't stand just sittin' around."

"It might be nothing," Dani said, "but I'm running out of options."

"Then get the coffee, woman, and let's get on it," Flo said. "Tell me what I'm lookin' for, Sal."

Sal picked up a sheet and pointed at a box at the bottom of the second page. "Look for a box that says 'Disposition'. Most will probably say something like, 'Incarcerated—SR' for Sand Ridge. Ask me if the initials are different. They may have been moved and I'll tell you what the initials stand for. In fact, if it says incarcerated, just stick it on the throw away stack," Sal said, leaning over to kiss Flo on the cheek.

Three hours later, Sal stood up to stretch her back from hunching over to look through her portion of the stack. "You might have to massage my back tonight to get the kinks out, honey," she said.

"We're almost done anyway, babe," Flo muttered, setting another couple of sheets on their discard pile.

Sal sat back down. "I only found a couple who'd been released and they're both on parole, so they probably went back home," she said. "One, Delores Elizondo, is from El Paso and has a five-year-old son there. The second, Hilda Figueroa, is from Houston, but ICE picked her up as soon as she walked out the prison gates. We can probably rule them out."

"I've got one," Dani said. "Nope, can't be her. She's dead. A suicide about two years before our victim was killed. Unless you believe in ghosts, we can rule her out."

Flo grabbed the sheets from Dani to place them on the elimination stack in front of her, momentarily glancing at it. "I think I know this name," she said, handing the papers to Sal. Sal looked at it and shrugged, "Sandiford. Not ringin' any bells for me, but I don't go to most of the places you do."

"Does it say who claimed her body or where it was sent for burial?" Dani asked.

"Claimed by a sister," Sal said. "That's it."

"Can you get us more info, Sal? Like maybe an obituary," Flo asked. "I know I know that name. Now it'll drive me nuts until I can put it with a face."

"Let's go home, baby," Sal said. "I'm plum wore out and am on first shift tomorrow."

"Okay. Just let me clean up this mess we made first," Flo said as she picked up their coffee cups.

"Don't worry about that, Flo," Dani protested. "I've got all weekend to straighten this place up. Y'all get on home. It was worth a shot, so thank you."

Flo handed the paperwork to Dani. "Don't lose these until we can get more info, okay?"

"I won't," Dani promised, escorting the two women to the front door.

"I'll let you know if Sal finds anythin' useful," Flo said, hugging Dani quickly before stepping outside.

"Hey, Sal!" Dani called out.

"Yeah," Sal answered, hunching her shoulders against the cold.

"It might not do any good, but maybe you should pay

Maddie a visit. Flo and I are striking out. Maybe she'll talk to you," Dani said.

"Fat chance. We didn't get along that well," Sal snorted. "I didn't trust her and she knew it."

"She talked to you more than me," Flo said.

"That was mostly tossin' barbs back and forth. It wasn't exactly a bondin' experience. Besides, you're the one who told her to stay away from Dani," Sal said, her teeth chattering.

"What!" Dani barked.

"It was nothin'. I didn't want her to hurt you is all, so I told her to back off." Flo reached out and slapped Sal's arm. "Big mouth," she hissed.

"Will you try to talk to her, Sal?" Dani asked.

"If I get a minute, I'll try, but can't promise nothin'," Sal finally relented. She squinted at Flo. "Can we get home and warm up now, baby. Please. I'm shiverin' so much I'm liable to shake my bones apart."

"Poor baby. I know how to warm you up real quick," Flo crooned.

"P...promise?" Sal asked in a trembling voice.

"Just as soon as you promise to go see Maddie," Flo added.

Dani chuckled as she backed into her home and shut the door.

SAL'S SHIFT WAS relatively quiet all day, but as she was preparing to return to the police station to fill out her end of shift paperwork, she received a call from dispatch to go to a possible domestic disturbance reported by a neighbor. She responded, requesting backup. Sometimes domestic calls were nothing more than an argument over which channel to put on the television, but they could be unpredictable. Because she didn't ride with a second officer, it was better to be safe than sorry. The closest unit was finishing up working on a fender bender, but would join her as soon as possible.

Sal cruised slowly down the street where the disturbance was reported to be occurring, but didn't see anything unusual. She pulled to the curb in front of the house and radioed in her location, then stepped out of her unit, jammed her hat on her head, and adjusted her utility belt as she killed a little time, hoping her back-up would appear soon.

She glanced around the clean looking, middle class neighborhood as she strolled toward the front door of the red brick home. Just as she reached out to press the doorbell, she heard shouting from inside and the front door flew open. A large, angry looking man in jeans and a red and black flannel shirt loomed behind the glass storm door.

"What the fuck do you want?" he said loudly.

"Is everythin' okay here, sir? We received a report of a domestic disturbance and are just checkin'," Sal asked, her thumbs resting on her utility belt. She tried to see past the man, but his body completely shielded any view inside the home.

"How about I step inside and just take a quick look around?" Sal suggested.

To her surprise, the big man cracked a smile and pushed the storm door open to allow Sal to enter. "Sure, officer," he said. "No problem."

Now wary of his apparent change of attitude, she pushed the wooden door back all the way and stepped inside. "Anyone else in the house, sir?" she asked.

"My wife," he responded.

"Where?"

"She had a headache and is layin' down."

"Could you ask her to come in the livin' room, please?"

"For what?"

"I need to make sure she's okay, sir."

"I told you she's got a headache. Gets them all the time," he insisted. "She's fine, godammit!" He moved faster than Sal thought possible for such a big man, his arm cocked back and his hand fisted tightly. Her best hope of avoiding being hit was to close the distance between them and not give him enough room to throw a punch. She stepped into him and grabbed his arm, twisting it behind his back and sticking her leg in front of his to put him on the ground.

His weight helped take him down and his face slammed into the floor, followed by a howl of pain. Sal planted her knee in the middle of his back and slapped her handcuffs around his wrists. Then she pulled him up and shoved him against the nearest wall, leaving blood from his broken nose smeared over the painted surface. She kept a hand on his back and pressed the button on her shoulder radio.

"Where's my back-up for that domestic disturbance?" she demanded, trying to catch her breath and slow down her heartbeat.

"Turning on your location now. I see your unit," a voice answered.

"Just come inside. Door's open," she said. Before she could do anything else, she heard a scream behind her and a body slammed onto her back, arms wrapping around her neck, choking her. She took her hand off her prisoner and reached over her shoulder, grabbing the first thing her hand contacted. She bent forward and pulled the body over her. The woman landed on the floor on her back and the man leaned against the wall laughing. Grinning up at him was a woman almost as big as he was, wearing a thin housecoat that barely covered her large breasts.

"Best one yet, Wanda," he managed.

Wanda blinked up at him and smiled. "You okay, Big Willie? She didn't hurt you, did she, baby?"

"Not much," he shrugged.

Teddy Wilson, the back-up officer, pushed through the front door with his pistol drawn and stared at the sight before him. "Whatcha got, Sal?" he asked.

"Domestic disturbance and assault on a police officer...twice," Sal stated, still trying to breathe normally. She nudged Wanda with the toe of her boot. "What went on in here?" she asked.

"Can I get up now?" Wanda asked.

"Slowly," Sal warned.

Wanda stood up and sat down heavily on the couch, taking a deep breath and gazing at Big Willie. "It's a little embarrassing, officer, but me and Big Willie just got married a couple of weeks ago. We was in the middle of a little...uh...afternoon nookie call, y'know."

"We got this nosey old guy next door and Wanda's a screamer," Big Willie threw in with a stupid grin on his bloody face. He shook his head. "She really gets into it, but I never thought that old boy would call the cops. I wouldn't never hurt Wanda, officer. Swear to God, man."

"Why take a swing at me then," Sal asked. "You could have just told me the deal."

"I was pissed because we weren't done," Big Willie said. "I didn't hurt ya, did I?

"Why'd you jump me, Wanda?"

"Thought you was hurtin' my Big Willie," Wanda mumbled.

"Unfortunately, we'll have to take you both in, but you should be out soon on bail. I recommend you install some soundproofing material to prevent any more disturbance calls," Sal advised. "And Wanda, you might want to get dressed in somethin' less revealin'," she added.

"Can I clean up Big Willie's face first?" Wanda asked.

"Go ahead," Sal nodded. "Let us know when you're ready to go, okay?"

"Can we ride together?" Big Willie chirped. "Never ridden in a police car before."

"Will you turn on the lights and siren?" Wanda asked excitedly. "We'll be Wanda and Big Willie. Sorta like Bonnie and Clyde, only still alive," she grinned.

Sal and Teddy waited on the front porch for Wanda and Big Willie to come outside. They looked at each other and chuckled. "Well, that's a first," Teddy said.

"I'm tryin' to figure out what to put on the report," Sal said, rubbing her back. "That Wanda's a big girl. Damn near broke my back," she laughed as she stretched her back out. "Big Willie ain't no feather either."

SAL TAPPED HER pen on a worktable and glanced at her watch. She was supposed to be off shift at two, but after the escapade with Wanda and Big Willie, along with the accompanying paperwork, it was now five-forty-five. She had already sent Flo a text telling her she'd be late and to save her a plate. At six o'clock she signed her name to the final page of her reports and dropped them into her sergeant's in-box. She figured he'd at least get a chuckle out of the report on Wanda and Willie, the vocally amorous newlyweds.

She stopped on her way out of the police station and poured a couple of cups of coffee. Then she got in her vehicle and backed out, pointing the car toward the Wichita County Jail, something she wasn't looking forward to, but knew Flo would hit her with a thousand questions as soon as she walked in the house. Flo kept her promise the night before and the feel of her hands and body had warmed Sal most of the night, but the lack of sleep left her exhausted during her shift. Now she owed Flo and would try to get Maddie to speak to her, but wasn't ready to take any shit from their smart-mouthed boarder today.

Sal moseyed into the county jail, signed in, and locked her sidearm in a box before walking down the mostly empty line of cells in the women's section. She stopped in front of cell 12D and stared in at Maddie. She was lying on her back, staring at the ceiling, her arms folded under her head. She ignored Sal, but Sal knew Maddie had flicked her eyes in her direction for a second, then closed them.

"Go away," Maddie said.

"Looks like that sparklin' personality hasn't improved," Sal replied. "Brought you some coffee, James."

"Cop coffee? Prob'ly sucks," Maddie said and rolled onto her side to face the cell wall.

"Guess what smart-ass, I can still see you. Your lawyer been here?"

"Don't matter. I don't want to see him either. Now get the fuck outta here!"

"Yeah, I got that, but I promised Flo and Dani I'd drop in to talk to you. So, here I am, like it or not. They're real upset you won't see them."

"Nothin' to say and they got nothin' I want to hear."

"They're worried 'bout you. For some damn reason I can't figure out, they care."

Maddie rolled over and glared at Sal. "Flo only cares about losin' my rent money and keepin' her nose up my ass to make sure I don't molest anyone. She thinks I'm a sexual predator, bidin' my time until I can molest some innocent girl like Dani. But Dani isn't the sweet, innocent girl Flo thinks she is. Makes me sorry I didn't take her when I had a chance," Maddie snarled. "At least then there'd be a reason why my ass is sittin' in this damn cell. Dani's got a job that conflicts with my best interests. It's her fuckin' job to put me back in prison, but I'm sure as shit not gonna help her do it. That lyin' bitch told me she cared, but she lied just like they all did. I can't trust her. I can't trust anyone," she muttered.

"Must be why she's killin' herself tryin' to find a way to clear you, but isn't prison where you belong? I told Flo you was trouble, but she gave you a fuckin' place to lay your head. You seriously think we need your goddamn twenty bucks to survive? You're nothin' but a fuckin' ingrate, James! You're just damn lucky I don't open this cell and give you a personalized attitude adjustment."

Maddie launched herself off the small cot and wrapped her hands around two of the peeling bars on her cell. "Then do it, ya stupid fuckin' coward!" Maddie screamed at Sal. "You think you'd be the first one to work me over, bitch?" Unexpectedly, her arm shot out between the bars and slapped one of the coffee cups out of Sal's hand. "I don't need your damn help. Leave me the fuck alone," she mumbled as she backed away and dropped down on her cot, rolling over to stare at the wall.

"That was *your* cup of coffee, loser," Sal said.

"Figures," Maddie snorted.

A WEEK LATER, on Saturday morning, Flo drove the girls from her boarding house to the Salvation Army Thrift store to look for gently used coats that would keep them warm over the winter months. She'd heard the store had just received a new shipment of donated clothes, including coats. One of her girls had recently given birth and was looking for warmer sleepwear for her baby.

Flo was looking through the coats and loved the look and feel of a buckskin-colored, hip-length leather jacket. When she pulled it from the rack, it weighed a ton, and she checked the stitching to make sure the cold north Texas wind wouldn't penetrate the leather or lining. She had seen a similar coat in a higher-priced store in the mall for three-hundred dollars. The one in front of her was marked at sixty bucks and she couldn't pass it up. She stopped a worker who was hanging more clothes they'd just unpacked and asked, "I really want this coat, but don't have the full amount on me right now. Do y'all have a layaway or can you hold it for me until I come back?"

"No layaway," the woman responded. "Everthin' is first come, first serve, but that coat will probably go quick."

"Can I speak to your manager?" Flo asked.

"Ella's in her office, through those double doors," the woman said, pointing to the swinging doors into the back that said 'Employees Only'. "Can't promise nothin'," she said, continuing to hang clothes as Flo walked away.

Flo pushed through the swinging doors and knocked on the door that said 'Manager'.

"Come on in," a voice called out from behind the door.

Flo opened the door and peeked inside. "Mornin' Ella," she said with a smile.

"Haven't seen you in here for a while, Flo," the pleasant-looking woman behind the desk said with a smile.

"I brought my girls down. They need coats for this winter. Somethin' sturdy for the wind we always get and I found this coat. I love it, but I can't swing sixty right now and was hopin' maybe we could work out a way I could pay it off in a couple of payments or somethin'," Flo explained, crossing her fingers.

"I'd like to help you out, but it's not something we normally do," Ella said.

Flo pulled a chair in front of the desk and sat down. "I know, but I send quite a bit of business your way and I can pay half now."

"Best I can do is drop the price a few dollars. We just don't have the room to store anything similar to a layaway and if I do it once, I'd have to do it for everyone," Ella said, leaning back in her chair. "It would be a bookkeeping nightmare."

Flo lowered her head, trying to think. Then she noticed the nameplate sitting on the desk: Ella Sandiford — Store Manager. *Sandiford!* She glanced up quickly at the pleasant-looking woman sitting in front of her, but didn't say anything. She's known her for at least the last five years, but had never known her last name. She might have known it once upon a time, but had forgotten it long ago. "I'll call a friend. Maybe she'll loan me thirty bucks until next month. Guess I'll just wander around the store until I talk to her," she said.

"I'm really sorry, Flo. If I owned the store, I'd do it for you in a heartbeat," Ella said as she stood.

"No problem," Flo said. "Next time I'll bring more cash with me."

Flo handed the coat to one of the girls with her and stepped outside to make a quick call.

"Danielle Hunter."

"Dani, this is Flo. I need a really big favor," Flo said quickly.

"Whatcha need, Flo?" Dani asked.

"I need to borrow thirty dollars until the first of next month," Flo spat out.

"No problem. You can come over tonight and I'll have it waiting," Dani said.

"No, I can't wait. I need it right now," Flo responded.

Flo told Dani where to bring the cash as soon as possible. That she wouldn't be sorry. About thirty minutes later, Dani pulled into a parking slot next to the thrift store. She didn't see Flo and made her way into the store. She spotted Flo pacing back and forth between two circular clothing racks and pulled her wallet from her shoulder bag, prepared to hand Flo the money she'd requested. Flo waved at her and waited for Dani to join her. Flo stared at the money in Dani's hand and pushed it away.

"I don't need the money after all." She pointed at the leather coat and said, "But you might."

"I already have a coat," Dani frowned, slightly irritated at being called out for no reason. "It's nice, Flo, but not really my style."

"Thought you might want it for Maddie when she gets out. Hers is pathetic and this has her name written all over it. Very butch," Flo said excitedly.

"What the hell are you talking about?" Dani asked.

"I found Sandiford!" Flo hissed.

"Who?" Dani asked, looking confused.

"Sandiford, the inmate who killed herself. The manager of this store's name is Sandiford. I bet if you asked her a few questions, you'd find out they were related somehow," Flo said. "It's not a common name."

"Call Sal and see if she'll come down here. I'd rather she asked the questions," Dani said.

"Sure, sure," Flo nodded. "You gonna get the coat? It's a deal and would make a great Christmas present. It's practically brand new...unless you don't really like Maddie as much as I think you do."

"God. Is it that obvious? Okay, I'll get the damn coat if it shuts you up," Dani said. She ran her hand over the soft leather. "But it does feel nice," she admitted with a smile.

When Sal pulled up in her cruiser, Dani watched her and Flo

argue while standing on the sidewalk near the thrift store entrance. After a few minutes, Sal stomped into the store, shoved her hat back on her head, and walked to the back of the store as if she were on a mission, motioning Dani to follow her. Sal stopped before pushing the double swinging doors open and asked, "Now what am I supposed to be doin'?"

"What did Flo tell you?" Dani asked in return.

"That I wouldn't be gettin' any for at least a *month* if I didn't ask this woman some questions to find out if she's related to that inmate who killed herself," Sal spat out.

"I'm sorry, Sal. We probably should have met first to work up some questions for you," Dani said, concealing her grin.

"Oh, ya think!" Sal hissed.

"Look at the positive side," Dani offered. "Maybe you'll uncover the real killer and become the first female detective in Wichita Falls."

"Break through the good ole boy ceilin'?" Sal smiled. "That would be sweet. Let's go," she said, shoving the doors open and pulling her hat down again. She rapped on the manager's door and entered without waiting. Ella Sandiford looked up and saw Sal standing in her office with her thumbs stuffed in her utility belt. "I need to ask you a few questions, Miss Sandiford," Sal said.

"Of course, officer," Ella said, leaning back in her chair. "Is it about the coat Flo wants to buy?"

"What coat?" Sal asked, looking at Dani.

"Doesn't matter," Dani answered in a low voice. "Ask her if she was born in Wichita Falls?"

"This your home town?" Sal asked.

"No, I was born in Burkburnett."

"Are you an only child?" Dani asked. She decided there wasn't much sense in telling Sal the question and having her repeat it.

"No. I had a twin sister," Ella answered.

"Had?"

"She committed suicide a couple of years ago," Ella responded calmly.

"Did she leave a note saying why?" Dani asked.

"No, but I knew why," Ella answered, her eyes hard.

Dani's gaze scanned the office and landed on an older model

IBM Selectric typewriter on a typing table behind Ella's desk. Dani smiled. "I used to have a typewriter just like that. My parents bought it when I left home for college. I haven't seen one in years," she said.

"It was donated by someone, but we never could sell it because it's so heavy," Ella said. "So, I elected to keep it to type personal letters on."

"It has the interchangeable fonts, right?" Dani asked.

"This only has one, but it's good enough for me," Ella grinned slightly.

Dani reached into her shoulder bag and pulled out a copy of the bloody note found in Sabreena Douglas' pocket. "Did you use it to type this note to Sabreena Douglas?" she asked quietly. She watched a series of emotions work their way across Ella's face.

Ella clenched her jaw and stood up, placing her hands on her desk and leaning forward. "You're damn right I did! She killed Emma and deserved everything she got!" she ground out with hatred burning in her eyes. "I couldn't let her destroy anyone else," she added calmly.

Sal said, "Ella Sandiford, you're under arrest for suspicion of murder. Step around the desk and raise your hands," she ordered. While she handcuffed Ella, she recited her Miranda rights and led her away.

Flo stared at Dani. "It can't really be that simple, can it?" she asked.

Dani shrugged. "Apparently it is, but I'll have to read her statement to believe it," she answered. "My boss probably won't be happy, but it'll save the county a small fortune."

ELLA SANDIFORD SAT calmly on one side of a scarred wooden table in a small interrogation room. Sal stood next to the only door in the room, waiting to turn her prisoner over to Detectives Nolan and Suarez and trying to think of a way to remain in the room to observe their interrogation. Although Ella's statement had implicated her in the death of Sabreena Douglas, it wasn't a slam dunk by any means. Sal and Maddie gradually came to an arrangement they could both live with after Maddie moved in, but that didn't mean Sal trusted her any further than she could throw her smart-ass. However, Sal couldn't stand by and watch the detectives attempt to swing the case back around to Maddie as their killer. Sal had to admit that Ella Sandiford looked like an unlikely candidate for a murderer. Although she was a hard-nosed cop, Sal was an honest one and damn proud of it.

Nolan, followed by Suarez, finally entered the small room, pulled out two straight-back wooden chairs, and sat down opposite Ella Sandiford. "You can leave, officer," Nolan said.

"I'd rather stay, detective, if you don't mind, to observe your interrogation technique, sir," Sal said politely.

Nolan smiled. "Hopin' to make detective yourself someday?" he asked.

"Yes, sir," she said, returning his smile.

"Then just stand against the back wall and don't talk," he said.

"Thank you, sir," Sal said.

Nolan flipped open the file folder he'd carried into the room and settled it between himself and Suarez. "Have you been apprised of your rights, Miss Sandiford?" he started.

"Yes, I was," Ella answered. "And yes, I understood them completely. I don't need a lawyer."

"Do you know why you were taken into custody?" Nolan asked.

Ella nodded. "Because I admitted that I typed a note to Sabreena Douglas."

"How did you get that note to Miss Douglas?" Suarez asked.

"I mailed it to another inmate Emma and I knew and asked her to give it to Bree. I'm assuming she did because Bree showed up in Wichita Falls not long after she was paroled," Ella answered. "I knew she would, so all I had to do was bide my time."

"Did Maddie James ask you to lure the victim to Wichita Falls for her?" Nolan asked.

Ella laughed. "God, no," she said.

"How did you know Bree Douglas then?" Suarez asked.

"My sister, Emma, was incarcerated at Sand Ridge. Emma pointed Bree out to me and said Bree was trying to recruit her into her prostitution ring. Tried the same thing with Maddie, according to my sister, but Maddie fought back. When Emma refused to join Bree's group, Bree had her beaten up. Emma was never a fighter and eventually acquiesced, but hated being used that way. It drove her nuts and when she couldn't take it anymore, she killed herself," Ella explained. Tears dribbled down her cheeks, but she wiped them away quickly. "Emma was only thirty. Just got mixed up with the wrong crowd when she was younger," she added. "And the prison officials wouldn't do a damn thing about it!" Ella took a deep breath to calm herself, sitting there and staring blankly at the wall.

"Eight years later, when Maddie walked into my store, I knew she was a messenger from God, and I could finally avenge Emma's death," Ella said with a smile. "That's when I sent the note telling Bree where Maddie was. I knew she wouldn't be able to resist coming after the one who got away. And I was right," she laughed. Her face looked as if she was re-living everything that had happened the night Bree Douglas lost her life, taken by someone she didn't even know existed.

"Did Maddie James assist you in killing Bree Douglas?" Nolan pushed.

Ella shook her head. "She was out cold after one of Bree's goons hit her. Bree told them to leave and said she'd finish Maddie off. Well, I couldn't let that happen, so just as Bree was getting ready to sexually assault Maddie, I whacked her with a tire iron. Then I don't really know what happened. I just went crazy and beat Bree to a pulp, but it felt damn good letting all that frustration and anger out. I thought she was dead, but she groaned, so I wrapped her in a tarp and rolled her onto one of those things they use to work under a car..."

"A mechanic's creeper," Suarez said.

"I guess," Ella shrugged. "I grabbed something off a work table and put it in my coat pocket, then pushed Bree down a back alley and hid her body under a pile of debris, but not before I did to her what she'd forced on my sister. Probably got a little carried away, but I don't regret any of it. She got what she deserved. I didn't think it out too well though because I never meant for Maddie to get blamed for any of it. If she'd gone to trial, I'd have had to suck it up and come forward," Ella apologized.

"Any other questions, Suarez," Nolan asked.

"We didn't find any of your prints anywhere," Suarez said.

"I wore gloves," Ella said. "I burned them when I got home. They couldn't be salvaged. Unfortunate because I really liked them," she frowned.

"Officer," Nolan said. "Would you escort Miss Sandiford to booking? We'll be down with the paperwork shortly."

TWO DAYS LATER, Saul Orbach followed the jailer to Maddie's cell.

"Get your shit together, James," the jailer said as he unlocked the door of the cell.

"What the fuck are you talkin' about?" Maddie snapped. "And what's he doin' here?" she asked, pointing at Orbach.

Orbach stepped around the jailer and said, "You're being released, Maddie. You're free. I came to escort you out and have the paperwork to prove it. So unless you've grown accustomed to this cell, let's get out of here," he smiled.

"Is this a trick or somethin'?" Maddie asked. "Am I gonna walk out of here and then get yanked back inside again?"

Orbach pulled a folded court order out of his pocket and handed it Maddie. She sat down on her cot and looked at the paper in front of her. "I don't know what any of this means," she finally admitted.

Orbach sat beside her and gently removed the paperwork from her hands. He flipped to the last page. "This is the most important part," he said. "Someone else confessed to killing Sabreena Douglas; therefore, all charges against you were dropped. The judge authorized your immediate release."

"Will this still be on my record?" Maddie frowned.

"No. Your record has been expunged...um...erased," Orbach explained.

Maddie stood. "Then let's get the hell outta here," she said.

Dani stood next to Flo, anxiously waiting for Maddie to be released from the County Jail. Saul preceded Maddie, who stopped to sign for her personal belongings. Saul strode to where Dani waited and accepted a warm hug.

As soon as Maddie stepped away from the discharge counter, carrying a small paper bag, Dani noticed how much she'd changed since her release from the hospital nearly a month earlier. Maddie had lost a noticeable amount of weight and her clothes seemed to hang from her body. She needed a haircut, and her eyes seemed to have sunken into their sockets. Dark rings were evident beneath her eyes and she looked broken. A healing bruise marred one side of her face.

Maddie stopped to wait for an officer to unlock the gate between her and freedom before stepping out into a gray, overcast day. Flo wrapped her arms around Maddie and whispered, "Let's go home, honey."

Maddie nodded and made an attempt at a grin. Dani couldn't stand not touching Maddie again, but she looked so frail and beaten down, that Dani was afraid she might hurt her. Maddie stepped closer to Dani and stopped. She raised a hand and trailed her fingers slowly down the side of Dani's face. "Hi," Maddie said.

Tears ran down Dani's cheeks as she embraced Maddie and dropped a soft kiss on Maddie's dry lips. "Hi," Dani smiled. "I missed you so much."

Dani slid an arm around Maddie's waist and guided her toward her car.

Maddie slid into the passenger seat, but only sat stiffly, gazing out the side window as Dani got in and started the car. After about a mile, Dani couldn't stand the silence any longer.

"Sal told me you believed I lied to you," she said.

Maddie finally looked at her. "I did," she acknowledged. "I'm sorry. Maybe it was the stress, the concussion, or somethin'."

Dani slid her hand across the front seat and slipped it into Maddie's. Maddie squeezed Dani's fingers. "I thought you betrayed me," she said. "Just like everyone else always did."

"Why would you think that, Maddie?"

"Because my ass was sittin' in a fuckin' jail again and *you* were bein' paid to make sure I stayed there," Maddie answered. Her voice started softly, but seemed to grow tenser as she spoke, gripping Dani's hand tighter.

"I would *never* do anything to hurt you, Maddie," Dani said, ignoring the pressure on her fingers. "I don't know exactly how or why others hurt you because you aren't ready to tell me yet, but I've *never* lied to you. I've *never* betrayed your trust. I care about you though because you sacrificed your life for mine eleven years ago. Let me be your friend now and trust me."

Maddie nodded. "What do we do now then?" she asked.

"Well, I've still got to bake all those damn cookies my mother was complaining about. Will you come to my place this weekend and help? Perhaps we can talk then, too."

"I can do that," Maddie smiled.

Chapter Thirteen

MADDIE RANG THE doorbell, expecting to see Dani's mother again. When the door opened, she was surprised to see Dani, an apron covering her jeans and T-shirt. There were smudges of flour on Dani's face and hands. Maddie grinned, finding the scene before her unexpectedly sweet and incredibly sexy.

"Looks like you started without me," Maddie said, stepping inside the small duplex apartment. She looked around and saw the Christmas tree, loaded with a plethora of multi-colored ornaments reflecting the lights embedded in the branches. "I thought having the tree up would inspire us while we made the cookies," Dani explained nervously. She seemed mildly uncomfortable being alone with Maddie for the first time in what seemed like an eternity.

Maddie took a step closer and began removing her jacket. "Where's your mother?" she asked with a crooked half smile.

"Visiting my aunt for the weekend," Dani answered with a laugh. "She'll do anything to avoid baking cookies."

"What will I do if you decide to take advantage of me...since it's just you...and me?" Maddie teased, stroking her hand slowly down Dani's arm.

Dani turned away quickly and said, "I made coffee." She walked into the kitchen and poured steaming coffee into two mugs, adding cream and sugar before sliding one in front of Maddie.

Maddie took a small sip and asked, looking at Dani over the rim of the mug, "Well, what should we do first?"

"I was thinking...hoping really...that you might consider...perhaps...uh...kissing me," Dani stuttered as she played with her mug without looking at Maddie. "I know I must look a mess, and you might not be interested, but—"

"Is that what all lawyers do? Talk somethin' simple to death?" Maddie interrupted as she moved closer to Dani and brought her hand up to play with her hair for a moment before slipping it to the back of her neck. She smiled when she saw the vein along the side of Dani's neck begin pulsing wildly. She raised her hand to brush a smudge of flour from Dani's cheek before running a finger down the throbbing vein. "Do I make you nervous?" Maddie asked softly.

"Very," Dani muttered when Maddie began teasing her ear, outlining it with her tongue.

"Why?" Maddie whispered, moving her mouth lower to suck lightly at the vein below Dani's ear.

"I...I don't know...ooo... that's so...nice," Dani said, tilting her head slightly. Her hands gripped Maddie's waist as Maddie moved closer and pressed her thigh against the vee of Dani's crotch. When Dani's legs parted slightly, Maddie slid her lips over Dani's, stirred by the heat her tongue felt as it glided smoothly into her mouth to explore. Dani groaned as she sucked Maddie's tongue farther into her mouth and deepened the kiss. When the kiss ended, Dani rested her forehead against Maddie's and smiled.

"What...cookies...were you plannin' to make first?" Maddie's voice cracked. There was something different, calmer, about the way Dani was looking at her.

"Touch me," Dani breathed out slowly, her fingertips outlining Maddie's jawline.

Maddie blinked, watching the woman in front of her transform from a frightened sixteen-year-old into a grown woman who knew what she wanted and wasn't afraid to ask for it. Maddie's eyes drifted down Dani's lush body for a moment. When she looked into Dani's eyes again, she opened her mouth to speak, but her mouth was dry. She finally managed to swallow and ask, "Here?"

Dani moved away a step and pulled her apron over her head. She tossed it on the counter and took Maddie's hand, leading her down a short hallway. She opened a door and backed into a dark room. "Here," she said, pulling her sweater over her head.

Maddie could barely see in the darkness with only the light from the front room filtering in. But it was enough to see the fullness of Dani's breasts. They were glorious and she ached to feel their weight in her hands. She watched them sway gently as Dani bent over to push her jeans down her legs. Dani smiled and walked toward Maddie, pausing to kiss her again, slowly and deeply. "Your turn," she said. "I want to see you now."

When Maddie made no move to remove her clothing, Dani pulled her shirt from her jeans, unbuttoned it, and pushed it down her arms, stopping to kiss the skin just above her cotton sports bra, teasing the nipples pushing against the material. She smiled when she straightened up and looked into Maddie's eyes. "Nervous?" she asked.

Maddie grabbed Dani and pulled her into a hungry kiss, running her mouth down her neck as her hands found Dani's breasts, squeezing the pliant skin gently. "You're killin' me, baby," Maddie said, pressing her hands in the middle of Dani's back and taking a breast into her mouth, teasing it with the flat of her tongue. "I'm so hungry for you," she said, walking them toward the bed.

Dani reached for Maddie's jeans, but before she could lower the zipper, Maddie grabbed her hand and leaned over her until they were both lying on the bed with Maddie on top. "I need to... touch you," Dani groaned. "Please, Maddie...let me...," she started before Maddie's fingers stroking between her legs prevented her from speaking coherently. "Oh, yes, baby...right there...feels so good." She attempted to twist away when Maddie slid down on the bed, her mouth replacing her hand.

Dani's body began to buck when Maddie's tongue pressed into her. Dani covered her face with her hands. "Oh, God...I can't stand it...almost there...you're so good." Maddie slipped smoothly into her, sucking hard on Dani's engorged clit while her hand thrust in and out of the tight muscles clasping her fingers. She looked up at Dani, breathing heavily, "Let it go, baby. I gotcha. I'm ready to go off, too. Just let it go."

Dani pumped her hips and forced Maddie deeper. Maddie felt Dani's muscles clamp down on her fingers, followed by a wave of heat flowing over them. The feeling overpowered Maddie and she reached a hand between her own legs and worked her fingers quickly up and down her throbbing clit. Without removing her fingers from Dani's body, she drew her knee up and jerked into a powerful release that left her weak, barely strong enough to crawl up to cradle Dani in her arms. Dani rolled onto her side and buried her face against Maddie's neck. Her hand brushed lazily down Maddie's chest and abdomen, her fingertips sliding onto Maddie's pubis before Maddie stopped it and said, "Don't."

"Why?"

"I don't want it. I don't like it," Maddie said.

"Well, I love it when you touch me," Dani said, hugging Maddie tightly. "You have no idea what you're missing."

But Maddie did remember. Not long after she came out, she and a teenaged friend, Jenny Farrell, had been playing around and became unexpectedly intimate. Although, they were young, inexperienced, and clumsy, she remembered how wonderful Jenny's soft touch made her feel and her body's reaction.

As if reading her mind, Dani asked, "When was the last time you let anyone touch you intimately?"

"Long time ago," Maddie answered.

"Do you remember how it made you feel?"

"Yes," Maddie answered quietly, but now she refused to trust anyone, even Dani. She sat up and leaned back against the headboard. Dani draped her arm over Maddie's waist and snuggled against her. Her hand skimmed down Maddie's side and stopped when she found a rough raised area not far from Maddie's breast. She sat up and pulled Maddie over to look at a jagged scar.

"Where did you get that?" she asked, running a finger down the scar's length.

"Got shanked in prison after a disagreement," Maddie answered dully. She closed her eyes and remembered getting shoved on the rec yard, falling, and feeling the smothering weight on her body as everyone around her dog-piled on top of her. Before Aggie and the guards could break it up, Maddie lay at the bottom of the pile, with a homemade shank protruding from between her ribs, bleeding profusely, and unable to draw a full breath. No one was ever accused of the stabbing, but Maddie was certain that Bree ordered it done to warn everyone what happened when they didn't go along.

"I'm sorry," Dani muttered softly before leaning over and dropping kisses along the thick, raised scar tissue.

"You didn't stab me, so you've got nothin' to be sorry for," Maddie said.

"I don't like the idea of anyone hurting you," Dani murmured between kisses.

"Eventually everyone does, even if they don't mean to,"

Maddie said, pulling Dani's hair back and kissing her neck. "Can we talk about somethin' else, or maybe not talk at all?" she asked.

Dani sat up and smiled. "Do you have something in mind?"

Maddie nodded and pulled Dani up to straddle her hips. She drew Dani against her and sucked her breast into her mouth, biting the nipple lightly, releasing it to shift her mouth to its neglected twin. Dani threw her head back and arched her back as Maddie's mouth claimed her. She held Maddie's head tightly against her breast and moaned. "Oh, God, I've waited so long for you."

When Maddie responded by sucking harder and sliding a hand between their bodies to stroke through Dani's slick folds, Dani whimpered, "Oh, yes, baby. I'm yours." Her hips began slowly rotating against Maddie's hand and she brought her mouth to Maddie's, enveloping her in a devouring kiss, pressing her pelvis against Maddie's seeking contact.

"No!" Maddie said harshly, breaking the kiss abruptly and pushing Dani away. She quickly sat up, breathing heavily. "I can't. I'm sorry," she mumbled as she buried her face in her hands, reflexively fisting her fingers in her hair.

Dani sat up behind Maddie and wrapped her arms around her shoulders. "You can trust me, sweetie. I won't hurt you...ever. I love you," she whispered.

"I've heard that before," Maddie laughed humorously. "But it was always a lie. I was just somethin' that needed to be controlled until I was no longer a real woman, but a *thing* to be controlled and used."

Dani circled her hand across Maddie's back to soothe her. "Please trust me, baby," she whispered. She had an idea what Maddie had been through with Shay, Courtney, and Bree, two of whom had claimed to love her. "Let me show you how you should have always been loved. I know you remember how it should have been. Let me give that feeling back to you. Don't be afraid, darling. Please let me love you."

"I can't," Maddie snapped, whipping her head around to glare at Dani, tears running down her cheeks. "What part of that can't you fuckin' understand?"

While Dani continued to lightly run her hand over Maddie's back and sides, gazing at her calmly. Maddie avoided her eyes and wiped her tears away. "I'm sorry," she said. "I should go."

"You don't have to, baby. We still have to bake all those damn cookies," Dani chuckled.

Maddie looked at her. "You're kiddin', right?"

Dani shoved her playfully in the back. "You have a problem with naked, or half-naked in your case, baking?"

"Betty Crocker never does it."

"Then she has no idea what she's missing."

"How the hell do you expect me to get anythin' done when you're jigglin' around in front of me buck naked?"

Dani hopped off the bed and sashayed toward the hall. "Not my problem, studly," she said over her shoulder. "And I *don't* jiggle."

Maddie pulled her shirt back on and walked to the kitchen in time to see Dani bending down in front of the oven, sliding a cookie tray in, her naked butt sticking out temptingly. When she stood, Dani wiped her hands on the apron, once again tied around her neck and waist. "If you'll take those out when the timer goes off, I'll get the next sheet ready to go in. Okay?" Dani asked.

"I think I can do that. Do you want me to put the cookies on that rack to cool? My mother used to do that."

"Sure. Then we can keep a pretty steady pace going."

"Are you mad at me?" Maddie asked softly.

"Why would I be?" Dani answered with a shrug, then added, "Maybe a little disappointed, but I'll get over it."

"Did I disappoint you?"

Dani whirled around and looked at Maddie tenderly. "God, no, baby. Don't ever think that. I'm just sorry I couldn't satisfy you. It's a trust thing and hopefully one day you'll be able to trust me."

"Thank you," Maddie mumbled.

"But that doesn't mean I plan to give up," Dani snickered.

"Great," Maddie said under her breath just as the timer for the oven buzzed. She carefully pulled the cookie sheet out and used a spatula to move the cookies onto the cooling racks. She scooped up a cookie and stuffed it into her mouth before carrying a second one to the counter where Dani was working.

"They taste good to me," Maddie said, waving the cookie in front of Dani. "Take a bite," she said, her other hand brushing over the soft, smooth rise of Dani's butt.

Dani turned and chewed the cookie thoughtfully. "They're perfect, but don't steal a couple from every sheet." Cookie dough coated both of her hands thickly and before she could turn away again, Maddie drew her into a deep, searching kiss.

"So sweet," Maddie said as the kiss ended, her hot breath mingling with Dani's.

Dani leaned back and smiled. "Don't try to distract me or we'll never finish these cookies. But I love the way you kiss me...everywhere."

"Where do you enjoy bein' kissed the most?" Maddie asked as she nuzzled against Dani's neck.

"In the bedroom, of course," Dani teased with a grin. "Turn off the oven, baby," she whispered.

A few minutes later, Maddie followed Dani down the hall for the second time. Dani removed her apron, then approached Maddie to push her shirt off again and leaned over to suck in her breast. "Wanting you so much makes me feel...absolutely wanton," she muttered, covering Maddie's mouth with her own. Her hand roamed smoothly over Maddie's torso, gradually venturing to her crotch and cupping it. Maddie attempted to move away, but Dani wrapped her leg around Maddie's calf and held her in place.

"Please don't," Maddie said, her voice strained. "I don't want to hurt you or be hurt."

"I won't hurt you, baby," Dani whispered as her fingers pressed against Maddie's crotch. She could feel the damp heat through her jeans.

"But you are," Maddie croaked. She grabbed Dani arms and forced her away. "Why can't you understand that?"

"I only want to please you, Maddie. I can't just lay there like a box of rocks and not touch you," Dani said.

"Then I'm not the one you want," Maddie said flatly. "I won't let you hurt me like the others. I can't take it again!" She slapped her hand against her chest. "This is who I am now. It's my *choice*, but I'm not a fuckin' *freak*!" She grabbed her shirt and pulled it on, then left the bedroom and walked out of the house, slamming the front door.

THE NEXT MORNING, although she was exhausted, Dani

drove to Flo's place, carrying a couple of containers of cookies. When Sal opened the door, still in her robe and house shoes, a mug of coffee in her hand, Dani went inside and glanced around. "Brought you and the girls some cookies," she said with an attempt at a smile. "Happy Holidays. Where's Flo?"

"In the kitchen fixin' breakfast," Sal said after swallowing a gulp of coffee. "We slept in a while and got a late start. Want some coffee?"

"I can get it, thanks," Dani said and carried the containers of cookies into the kitchen.

"Mornin', Dani," Flo said cheerfully as Dani set the containers on the counter and took a mug from the cabinet above.

"Morning, Flo," Dani responded as she sipped her coffee.

"Have you had breakfast yet? We have plenty," Flo offered.

"No, thanks. Is Maddie sleeping in?"

"She's gone, honey. Came home last night, packed her shit, and split with zero explanation. Looked a little upset, but didn't want to talk."

"We had an argument. Where did she go?"

"Don't know and she didn't say. Paid me for this week and called Oscar to quit her job. Woke the poor man up. Made a couple of other calls and left. Tried to get her to talk to me, but she was closed down tighter than a damn clam," Flo said as she heaped scrambled eggs, bacon and buttered toast onto five plates. "I don't wanna crawl up in your bus'ness, but what did you argue over?" she asked.

"It was personal, Flo," Dani answered sullenly. "I...I love her."

"But you can't accept her, right?"

"Not all of her," Dani confessed.

"I don't know what happened to her in the past, but whatever it was, she's decided to shut herself off so it don't happen again," Flo said.

"I know, but I would never hurt her, Flo," Dani said with tears in her eyes.

"In her mind I reckon you already have, honey," Flo consoled.

"I know," Dani said, breaking down and sobbing. "I ruined her life and have to find a way to make it up to her. I...I'm the only...one who can...fix it," she hiccuped. "But I don't know what to do, Flo."

"We'll figure it out, honey," Flo said, hugging Dani.

"I need to own up to what I did and turn myself in," Dani muttered miserably. "Then maybe Maddie will be able to forgive me."

"For what?" Flo asked.

Dani looked at her friend and forced herself to say, "*I* killed Bryan Melendez. Maddie told the police she was driving to protect me, but she wasn't. I was and she did ten years for a crime she didn't commit. I owe her at least that much."

"Why do you think she did that, honey?" Flo asked.

Dani shrugged.

"How old were you?"

"Sixteen," Dani admitted. "I was a scared kid."

"Takin' the blame for Bryan's death was the only good thing Maddie James ever done," Flo insisted. "She was a drug addict and tearin' up the road to nowhere. She'd have died within a few years if she hadn't gone to prison and got herself straightened out."

"It wasn't worth being beaten and stabbed," Dani argued. "I can clear her name and give her her life back."

"Do you really think you would be better off if you'd gone through what she did?" Flo asked. "She gave you the chance to do somethin' good with your life and you have. Don't let Maddie's sacrifice be for nothin', Dani," she said. "She chose to do a good thing, so just accept it for the gift it was."

Chapter Fourteen

TWO DAYS BEFORE Christmas, Buck and Alice sat next to one another, huddled close to a fire. "Should be ready in a little bit," Alice said. "Damn wind's not helpin'."

Buck rubbed his gloved hand briskly up and down her back. "I gotta fix your damn stove in the trailer soon so we won't have to act like a couple of freakin' Eskimos," he said, looking at the sky. "Snow'll be here b'fore long."

"Get me the parts, old man, and I'll fix it for ya," a familiar voice behind him said. "Ya look like a couple of popsicles sittin' out here."

"Maddie!" Alice squealed as she jumped up and flew to the younger woman, taking her in her arms in a crushing embrace. Maddie dropped her duffel bag and guitar case to hug Alice warmly.

"Where the hell ya been, kid?" Buck asked gruffly, spinning his wheelchair around.

"Workin' down in Wichita Falls," Maddie answered.

"Ain't a damn thing in Wichita Falls," Buck huffed. "We got coffee. If you want some, he'p yourself."

Maddie released Alice and rubbed her hands together, moving closer to the fire and filling a blue porcelain cup. "Appreciate it. Pretty nipply out here," she smiled.

"It's a fuckin' cornfield," Buck coughed. "Ain't much else in damn Iowa."

"Got a gig?"

"Carson was offered a chance to do a winter festival, so here we are, freezin' our asses off. Openin' the day after Christmas. Locals swear this'll blow over in a day or two. If it don't we'll need blow torches to get the gears on the rides to move. After this, we're done for the season and are headin' south to spend the winter gettin' the equipment back in shape before spring."

"Need a mechanic?"

"Always need a *good* mechanic. Know any?" Buck jibbed. "I was pretty pissed when ya up and split like ya did," he added.

"Took me a few days to cheer Alice up. Hell, I almost starved to death," he grinned.

"Yeah, sorry about that, but there was somethin' I needed to do," Maddie said.

"Get it taken care of?"

Maddie nodded. "Yeah, it's done."

"Well, sit down and eat breakfast. You're lookin' a little skinny," Alice said, handing Maddie a loaded plate.

"Isn't this yours?" Maddie asked.

"I can make more in a jiffy. Eat!"

"How'd ya get here?" Buck asked.

"Hitched and walked mostly," Maddie answered, stuffing her mouth with eggs and biscuits and gravy. She looked at Alice and grinned. "Really missed your cookin'," she hummed with happiness.

"Got a special job for ya tomorrow, kid," Buck said, winking at Alice while he washed his food down.

"What's that?" Maddie asked, running a chunk of toast over her plate to sop up the remaining gravy.

"I need ya to take the lift off my old trailer and put it on Alice's." He reached out and grasped Alice's hand, tugging her into his lap. "Me and Alice got hitched a couple of weeks ago and I'm gettin' tired of draggin' my horny ass inside ever night to be with my woman."

Maddie swallowed hard. "Congratulations. It's about damn time, old man," she said with a broad smile.

"Well, I didn't wanna saddle her with someone who wasn't whole, but she convinced me she didn't care and I finally gave up. Besides, she knows how to satisfy me in ever way possible," he chuckled.

Alice smacked him on the chest, blushing furiously. "She don't need to know *that*, Buck."

"She don't care, my dove," Buck responded, pulling Alice into a hungry kiss and skimming his hand over her full breasts.

Maddie smiled, finishing her coffee. Like Buck, she wasn't whole. Like Alice, Dani had tried to find a way to satisfy her completely, but Maddie hadn't been brave enough to let go of her fears. Instead, she'd chosen to run away again. "Where are your tools? I can get Alice's stove workin' today and move your lift tomorrow," she said. "Did you get a new trailer?"

He swept his arm around and asked, "Ya like it? Much roomier than Alice's old one."

"Looks good. When did you get it?"

"Two or three months ago. It was used, but we like it. I checked ever damn thing on it, except the stove, before we bought it. I replaced the propane lines and tank, the water lines, and the compressor in the a/c. By the time I pointed out what needed to be replaced, the price dropped so much the guy made a package deal for the SUV to tow it. Overall, it was a doable deal. Alice sold her old trailer to a new guy who joined the carnival down in Missouri. We did a few things to make it suit our needs better. Even got us a king-size bed," he added with a wink. "Got a damn grill and sink built into the side. Slides out so we can cook outdoors when the weather gets warmer."

"Fancy," Maddie grinned. "If you decide to retire, you can park it anywhere."

"That's the plan in a couple of years," Alice nodded.

"Me and Alice don't need two trailers," Buck said, nuzzling Alice's neck. "If you're stickin' around, ya can bunk in mine. Might need to fix it up some, but we've already moved most of my stuff to Alice's."

"Dependin' on how much ya want, I might could buy it and the truck from ya. Let me know what you want for 'em and I'll let you know if I can swing it," Maddie said.

Buck nodded and patted Alice on the butt when she stood up. "We got work to do, woman, and better get to it," he laughed.

"I'm tired from all that walkin' and now I've got a full belly. I might need a quick nap, so get me up in about an hour, will ya?" Maddie asked.

"Sluffin' off already, huh?" Buck chuckled. "Go stretch out, kid. You're lookin' a little droopy. Trailer's open."

MADDIE BLINKED HER eyes open and let them adjust to the dim light finding its way into Buck's old trailer. "Fuck," she muttered, running a hand over her face to wake up. She threw off the blanket she'd wrapped over her body, swung her feet to the floor, and shook her head. She pulled her work boots on and charged out the door of the trailer, running across the grounds to Alice's. No one was outside and she banged on the door with her fist, looking at the blinking Christmas lights that outlined the door and side windows. Alice's smiling face greeted her a moment later. "Dinner will be ready as soon as the cornbread comes out of the oven. Sleep well?"

"You or Buck were supposed to wake me up so I could fix your stove," Maddie groused. "Not let me sleep all damn day, Alice."

"Buck checked it out and it was only a gummed-up pilot light, so he fixed it. Don't you get grumpy with me, kid," Alice admonished.

"Sorry, but I promised to look at it. I hate people who make promises, then don't keep them. Guess I ate too much, got warm, and couldn't stay awake."

"Buck's washin' up. Come on in. Chili this evenin'," Alice said. "The carnival won't even open until the day after Christmas. There'll be plenty of time to get everthin' goin'."

A small Christmas tree was on a table beneath the side windows. Little Christmas ornaments and figurines were scattered throughout the front living area. "Nice tree," Maddie commented.

"Thanks. I love decoratin' for Christmas, but not that crazy about puttin' it all away afterward," Alice said as she opened the oven to check her cornbread.

"Hey!" Buck said loudly. "It's Sleepin' Beauty," he laughed.

"I'll get on that lift tomorrow mornin'," Maddie said. "Shouldn't take too long."

THE DAY BEFORE Christmas, Maddie joined Buck and Alice for an early Christmas dinner at their trailer since on Christmas Day they would all be busy setting up the rides and games for opening day. Maddie couldn't remember the last time she'd seen so much food. Probably not since the Christmas before her parents died. Seeing everything laid out, she suddenly felt overwhelmed by loneliness, something she'd rarely felt before. She'd had glimpses of how real people lived occasionally, had allowed her fears to stop her from fully engaging. As she blinked to clear her mind, every time she blinked, a picture flickered through her mind like a slide show. She saw the gruff, but gentle face of Flo, the obvious love when Flo and Sal gazed at one another, the red, unforgiving face of Natalie Melendez who was still letting her anger control her life.

Then Maddie smiled at the memory of Dani wearing nothing other than her apron as she made cookies the night Maddie stormed out of her house, unwilling to be touched by another woman who claimed to love her. She rubbed her fingers together, feeling the soft warmth of Dani's skin as she gave herself freely to Maddie. All Dani had asked in return was to touch Maddie. But after being hurt and used so many times, how could Maddie trust her? Now she was where no one judged her and accepted her unconditionally. Wasn't that enough? All she really wanted or needed?

Early Christmas morning, Maddie ran cold water in the kitchen sink and splashed it on her face. She lit a cigarette and inhaled a long drag. After she dressed, she pushed the trailer door open and felt a cold breeze on her face. She started down the metal steps to examine how the lift was connected under the trailer. She glanced down and saw a round metal tin with a large bow attached to the lid. She picked it up and shook it before popping the top open. A note rested on top of the cookies inside. Probably Alice, she thought, as she flipped open the note.

You helped bake them, so I thought you should have a few. Merry Christmas. D —

Maddie squinted into the sun, her eyes searching the campgrounds, her heart beating against her chest. Finally, she spotted Buck, directing carnies who were unloading and hauling brightly painted booth sections to the eventual Midway area. She trotted over to him, but before she could speak, he reached into the tin and grabbed a cookie.

"Did you see who left these outside the trailer?" she asked.

"Yeah. Pretty brunette lady," he answered around a mouthful of cookie. "Not a bad cookie," he nodded, reaching for another one.

"Take them all," Maddie said with a hint of urgency in her voice as she deposited the tin in his lap. "Just tell me where she went."

"Somewhere with Alice," he answered with a shrug. "Car's still here, so look around," he said, continuing to direct workers in various directions.

Maddie loped down the center of the gradually rising

Midway, twisting her head from side to side. Halfway down the open walkway, she spotted Alice hanging stuffed animals. Maddie stopped and walked casually toward the booth. What would she say if Dani was there? What could she say?

"Need help?" Maddie asked as she approached Alice.

"Thought you was movin' Buck's lift this mornin'," Alice said, hanging another large stuffed Panda.

Maddie shrugged and shoved her hands into her jean pockets. "Just checkin' to see what else needed to be done," she said, glancing around, trying not to appear obvious, but failing miserably.

"She's out back unpackin' the last of the prizes for me, if that's who you're lookin' for," Alice said with a smile.

"Thanks," Maddie replied.

Alice reached across the booth counter and grabbed Maddie's arm. "Don't you hurt that girl, kid."

Maddie frowned. "Too late. I already have," she muttered. She vaulted over the counter and started toward the rear of the booth. When she pulled the back curtain aside, Dani stood in front of her, her arms loaded with plush animals. Only her eyes showed above the prizes. She was dressed in old faded jeans, a flannel shirt covered by a quilted vest, and scuffed boots. To Maddie, she looked adorable.

"Merry Christmas!" Dani chirped with a smile. "Did you get your cookies?"

Maddie nodded. "You didn't have to drive across three damn states to bring them to me. How the hell did you know where I was anyway?"

Dani leaned forward slightly and lowered her voice. "Don't tell anyone, but I have some connections with the local police department back home," she said. "I knew you'd run back to somewhere you felt safe."

Maddie stared at the ground and pushed dirt around with the toe of her work boot. "I wouldn't call it runnin'. I was comfortable here," she said.

"Well, whatever you call it, I'm sorry I tried to push you into something you didn't want," Dani said.

"Old Buck sort of confiscated my cookies, so you might have to bake another batch," Maddie grinned. "Thanks for helpin' Alice get set up."

"No problem. It's kinda fun," Dani said. "Oh, and there's a Christmas present for you in the trunk of my car. Remind me later," she said as she pushed her way around Maddie.

Maddie took a deep breath. "Okay. I've got somethin' I promised to do this mornin', so I gotta get on it. Maybe we can talk later."

"I'd like that," Dani said with a soft smile.

"Hey, Alice!" Maddie called out, "Can I borrow your wagon to haul Buck's lift to your place?"

"Of course, honey. We're almost through here anyway," Alice called back.

BY THE TIME Alice and Dani finished Alice's booth and walked back to Alice's trailer to warm up, Maddie was laying under the trailer door using a ratchet to tighten down the bolts that would hold the wheelchair lift firmly in place, using her long legs to push her body farther beneath the trailer. The metal steps that hung below the door were lying on the ground near Maddie's leg.

"How the hell are we s'posed to get in the damn trailer?" Alice asked sharply.

"Lift your leg higher and pull yourself in," Maddie answered with a chuckle.

"I'm not six-feet-tall like you, dummy. These old stumpy legs don't cut it, smart-ass," Alice chided.

"Okay, okay. Hang on and I'll lift you into it," Maddie said as she started scooting from under the trailer.

"Besides, unless you want to starve to death, I have to get inside," Alice said.

Maddie stood up and brushed her hands over her butt to knock off loose grass and dirt. She bent over and scooped Alice up, setting her inside the trailer. "Happy?" she asked.

"Thrill of my life, sugar. If you see Buck, tell him lunch will be ready in about an hour."

"Okay," Maddie said before turning to Dani. "Need a lift into the trailer too?" she asked.

"No thanks. I can make it," Dani answered, shaking her head. As Dani brought a leg up to enter the trailer, her jeans stretched tightly across her ass. Maddie swallowed hard, the memory of running her hands over Dani's soft, yet firm ass clear in her mind. Her fingers twitched and she quickly crawled beneath the trailer again.

In less than an hour, Maddie wiggled her body into the open again, opened the trailer door, and reached inside to flip a switch she'd installed earlier. She watched the lift slide smoothly out and lower to the ground before rising slowly until it was level with the trailer door. She flipped a second switch to reverse the process. The only thing left was to weld the folding steps for the trailer back in place.

She placed a final weld, flipped up her mask, and turned the torch off.

"I think your weldin' technique is gettin' better," Buck said. "Very neat work, kid."

"Thanks. Wanna try out the lift?" she asked with a smile.

"Sure. I don't mind livin' dangerously," he laughed. Maddie reached inside and flipped the switch again. The lift slid out and lowered to the ground. Buck rolled onto the heavy metal grate that formed the bottom. A minute later, the lift rose slowly. "I gave it a delay in case you needed to take something in with you and had to load it," she explained.

"Hadn't thought about that, but not a bad idea," Buck nodded.

As soon as the floor of the lift was even with the trailer door, he called out, "Honey! I'm home! Start gettin' nekkid!" Peels of laugher from Buck and Alice carried through the surrounding area. Buck looked at Maddie. "Thanks, kid. Think we can rig up a remote for this critter?"

"I'll work on it, old man. Give me a day or two. Merry Christmas," Maddie smiled.

AFTER A FILLING lunch, Maddie began checking the mechanical parts of the rides and making a few adjustments while Dani went with Alice to continue setting up booths and stringing lights throughout the Midway. It was nearly six in the evening before Maddie saw Dani again, but she had been thinking about her most of the afternoon. They had dinner with Alice and Buck again that evening. They all talked congenially, except Maddie, who remained relatively quiet through the meal.

After listening to the other three exchange stories over dinner, Maddie strolled with Dani back to her car to get the present out of the trunk. Then she detoured them toward her trailer.

"I can make coffee, if you want," Maddie said with a grin. "I even have cream and sugar," she added.

"Oh, now you've really hit the big time," Dani kidded.

"I've missed you," Maddie blurted out.

Dani patted Maddie on the chest. "I've missed you, too, Maddie."

"How 'bout that coffee and we can talk," Maddie said, the beginnings of discomfort running through her body.

Dani shrugged. "Okay. Then you can open your present."

Maddie unlocked the old trailer and stepped inside before offering Dani a hand. Dani looked around. "This has really changed since the last time I was here," she said, looking around while Maddie started the coffee.

Maddie laughed. "Yeah, it's clean and you can actually see the damn floor," she huffed. "It's mine now and as soon as I can get a driver's license, I'll tune up Buck's old truck to tow it with. We're moving south for the winter. He said he'd tow it for me until I get my license."

"Buck and Alice are nice people," Dani stated.

"The best," Maddie agreed. "If you treat them right, they'll do the same...for anyone regardless of their past." She took two mugs from the cabinet over the sink and filled them with coffee. She set cream and sugar on the table, followed by the mugs, and sat across from Dani.

After several minutes without talking, Dani cleared her throat and said, "Open your present. Hope you like it."

"I feel bad," Maddie said. "I didn't get you anything."

"Just seeing you again and knowing you're safe and happy, is present enough," Dani said as she sipped her coffee. "Plus, this is great coffee."

Maddie ran her hands over the metallic looking paper and felt the lacey filigreed ribbon. "Seems like a shame to mess up this paper. It's nice," she said softly. Dani watched Maddie blink several times. "It's pretty. This is the first gift I've had in...eleven years, maybe more," she shrugged.

"I didn't mean to upset you," Dani said.

"I don't have anything for you though. Doesn't seem fair."

When Maddie looked at her again, Dani would have sworn she saw tears shimmer in her eyes.

"You're killing me, Maddie. Just rip it open," Dani said, reaching over the table to touch Maddie's hand.

Maddie smiled and ran her finger under a flap of the paper, tearing it while Dani yanked the bow that encircled the box. Maddie jiggled the top off and lifted a piece of white tissue paper up to reveal what was inside. Her face filled with wonder as she fingered the buttery soft leather nestled inside. She stood up and lifted the jacket away from the box. "It's beautiful," she muttered.

Dani stood up and took the jacket, holding it for Maddie to slip her arms into. "Perfect fit," Dani laughed. "Merry Christmas, Maddie," she said softly against Maddie's shoulder.

"Buck will be so fuckin' jealous," Maddie grinned. She wrapped her arms around Dani. "Thank you," she whispered.

Dani ran a hand down the front of the jacket and looked up at Maddie. "It's warmer than that old denim jacket you have now," she said.

"How long will you be here?" Maddie asked as they sat down and she continued running her hands over the leather.

"I took the week off between Christmas and New Year's. It's a long drive home, so I can only stay a couple of days," Dani shrugged.

"Was the trip worth it?" Maddie asked.

Dani nodded and slid a hand across the table to cover Maddie's. "I had to know you were all right. I couldn't stand the thought that something else terrible would happen to you because of me."

Maddie pulled her hand away and rubbed both hands up and down her thighs. She looked at Dani and began to feel her body tremble. She knew the feeling, but couldn't stop it as her pervasive fear began to take control. Control. Wasn't that what she cared about most? Why she refused to allow anyone to get close to her? By giving control to anyone else, she would be giving up a priceless part of herself, perhaps forever. She was allowing her fear to control her. She gritted her teeth and tried to calm her body. But the fear of giving permission for someone to hurt her was so strong that she began to shake. Dani must have noticed because she moved to sit beside Maddie and slipped her arm under the jacket and around Maddie's waist.

"What's wrong, Maddie?" Dani asked tenderly. "You're shaking, baby."

Maddie turned to look at Dani and brought her trembling hand up to trace Dani's lips. Dani took Maddie's hand, parted her lips, and sucked Maddie's fingers into her mouth one at a time. Maddie leaned closer to kiss her firmly. Her hands slipped under Dani's shirt and ran up and down her back and sides. Dani deepened the kiss and buried her hands in Maddie's hair eliciting a deep groan.

When the kiss ended, Maddie clung to Dani. "I love the way you kiss me. Like you own me," she whispered. "I never wanted anyone to own me before." She finally leaned away and cupped Dani's chin, her thumb brushing over her lips. "Is the bedroom still your favorite place to be kissed?" she asked with a devastating smile.

Dani nodded mutely and stood. She removed her quilted vest and tossed it aside. In the short distance to the bedroom at the rear of the trailer, she shed most of her clothes and stretched out on the bed. To Dani's surprise, Maddie stared at her almost nude body and began removing her own clothes, leaving only her cotton boxers on. She crawled beside Dani, kissing her way up the length of her body, stopping to lavish attention on her breasts. Maddie brought her leg up to drape it across Dani's thighs. Maddie pushed her body up, her arms trembling, and stared into Dani's eyes to read what was hidden there. "I care about you more than I should, Dani," she said before kissing her deeply again.

"Please, baby. I need you so much," Dani begged.

Sucking up every ounce of courage hidden inside for so long, Maddie embraced Dani and with a shaky voice forced herself to say, "T...touch me."

Dani's eyes widened. "Are you sure? You're trembling."

"I'm af...raid," Maddie managed, swallowing hard. "Just p...please don't...don't hurt me."

"I won't. I promise," Dani said softly, stroking the side of Maddie's face, then whispered, "You can trust me, Maddie."

Maddie locked her eyes with Dani's and nodded before burying her face against Dani's neck, holding her breath. Dani could feel Maddie's body stiffen as she ran a hand down her back and slowly slipped it beneath Maddie's boxers to massage her butt, easing the boxers down. "I won't hurt you, sweetie," she breathed, hoping to reassure the woman she'd fallen in love with. She drew her hand up to Maddie's hip and gradually pushed her over onto her back. Maddie tightened her grip on Dani's arm and stared up at her, the fear obvious in her eyes.

"You're so beautiful, Maddie," Dani said before leaning over her to kiss her as she moved her hand to slide her fingertips along the crease between Maddie's hip and thigh. Maddie twitched and grunted, grabbing Dani's hand and pulling it away. "N...no, wait," she said.

"Did I hurt you, honey?" Dani asked, alarmed.

"No," Maddie said.

"Good," Dani said as she moved down Maddie's body and pressed her face into Maddie's crotch, inhaling deeply. Looking up at Maddie, she said with a smile, "You smell so sweet. I really want to taste you. Will you let me, sweetheart?"

Maddie nodded, her knuckles white from gripping the sheet beneath her. She closed her eyes and took a deep breath. "I trust you," she ground out tightly, more to convince herself than anything else.

She was awed as Dani parted her folds with her tongue and gently stroked the length of her sex for the first time. Her body tensed at the tender touches as she opened her fists and groaned, "Oh, Jesus, baby." Snapshots flickered through her mind. It always started this way, tender and pleasurable, but the pain began soon afterward making her feel like she was being devoured by a wild animal. Memories of how Shay had touched her before the pain began as she seized Maddie's engorged clitoris and pinched it painfully between her fingernails until Maddie begged her to stop. The anticipation of that pain coursed through Maddie and she began twisting her body to escape, breathing harder, her chest rising and falling rapidly as the panic and need to flee overwhelmed her. There were no drugs to dull her pain now. She reached down and pushed Dani away, rolling onto her side and drawing her legs up tightly against her heaving chest, gasping to take a breath.

Dani slowly kissed her way up Maddie's shivering body to comfort her. Starting at Maddie's head she began gently scratching her scalp, then lightly stroking down her back until she felt her tight muscles begin to relax. "Talk to me, Maddie. Tell me how to please you, baby," she whispered while gradually pulling Maddie into her arms.

Maddie looked up at Dani, her eyes brimming with tears, and managed to rasp, "I...I'm sorry," before burying her face in Dani's neck and crying.

"You don't have anything to be sorry for, honey," Dani reassured her as she continued to scratch Maddie's head and stroke her body tenderly. "I don't know exactly what Shay or Courtney did to you, but I promise no one will ever hurt you again...*I* will never hurt you." She made Maddie look at her. "Do you believe me?" she asked, wiping Maddie's tears away with her thumb.

"I...don't know...if I can ever be...what you need me...to be," Maddie hiccupped. "I can't...promise to...make you happy."

Dani smiled and stroked Maddie's face. "However long it takes, you're worth waiting for. So until you're ready, let's just agree to take it one day at a time...one step at a time, okay?"

"If I kissed you again, that would be a good first step, right?" Maddie asked, looking up at Dani hopefully.

"I'd like that, baby," Dani smiled as Maddie's lips hovered close to hers. "It's my very favorite step."

About the Author

Originally from the Appalachian region of Eastern Tennessee, Brenda recently moved from Central Texas, where she had lived for over sixty years, to Central Michigan, due to health and to be closer to one of her daughters. She began writing in junior high school where she wrote an admittedly hokey western serial to entertain her friends. Completing her graduate studies in Eastern European history in 1971, she worked as a graphic artist, a public relations specialist for the military and a display advertising specialist until she finally had to admit that her mother might have been right and earned her teaching certification. Following twenty-nine years teaching world history and political science, she retired in 2013. Brenda and her wife, Cheryl, have four grown children and ten grandchildren. They celebrated their twentieth anniversary together in June, 2017 by getting legally married with all their children and grandchildren in attendance. Rounding out their home are a cat named Tootie and a dog, a Puggle named Peanut. When she is not writing, Brenda putters around the house and reads, enjoying her retirement. She may be contacted at adcockb10@yahoo.com and welcomes all comments.

More Brenda Adcock titles:

Unresolved Conflicts

*The long awaited sequel to *Redress of Grievances**

Thomas Wolfe said: "You can't go home again," and most of us know that, but it doesn't mean wanting to recapture just one good memory about our family isn't powerful enough to draw us back over and over again.

Harriett Markham and her lover, Jess Raines have finally settled into a comfortable relationship together following a harrowing and disturbing case when their peaceful life is interrupted by a plea from a high school friend of Harriett's, who has been arrested for the murder of a fellow teacher. Their investigation drags them both into a past they'd rather forget and forces them to acknowledge their seemingly perfect life might not be quite so perfect to the rest of their family.

Every family has secrets they'd prefer to not share, even with the people they love most. A trip to Harriett's home town re-opens old wounds for both Harriett and Jess that will either force their families together again or rip them apart forever.

ISBN 978-1-61929-374-8
eISBN 978-1-61929-375-5

Redress of Grievances

Harriett Markham is a defense attorney in Austin, Texas, who lost everything eleven years earlier. She had been an associate with a Dallas firm and involved in an affair with a senior partner, Alexis Dunne. Harriett represented a rape/murder client named Jared Wilkes and got the charges dismissed on a technicality. When Wilkes committed a rape and murder after his release, Harriett was devastated. She resigned and moved to Austin, leaving everything behind, including her lover.

Despite lingering feelings for Alexis, Harriett becomes involved with a sex-offense investigator, Jessie Raines, a woman struggling with secrets of her own. Harriett thinks she might finally be happy, but then Alexis re-enters her life. She refers a case of multiple homicide allegedly committed by Sharon Taggart, a woman with no motive for the crimes. Harriett is creeped out by the brutal murders, but reluctantly agrees to handle the defense.

As Harriett's team prepares for trial, disturbing information comes to light. Sharon denies any involvement in the crimes, but the evidence against her seems overwhelming. Harriett is plunged into a case rife with twisty psychological motives, questionable sanity, and a client with a complex and disturbing life. Is she guilty or not? And will Harriett's legal defense bring about justice — or another Wilkes case?

ISBN 978-1-932300-86-4

Gift of the Redeemer

Jourdaine Troyce is the commandant of the Guardians, her entire life spent training to kill, literally, anyone that poses the slightest threat to her emperor or the royal family. Killing is as natural as breathing.

Ambreen Prins is a pacifist by nature, killing only as a last resort as she and her young companions fight against the tyranny of the emperor.

Rowan Shayne is the captain of an Intergalactic ship crewed by all the misfits the Fleet can't put anywhere else. They aren't expected to do great things. They're not even expected to function well enough to do their jobs.

Alec Travers is one of the best fighter pilots the Fleet has ever seen, especially when flanked by her two closest friends, creating what they call The Furies. But being posted to Captain Shayne's ship of misfits, out where there are no enemies to fight, is stifling. All she and the other Furies want is to get out there and take down the enemy. Whoever that enemy might be.

Heartbreak, treachery, evil, and the need for justice bring these four together on an adventure to discover the gift of the Redeemer, and the heroines they are destined to become.

ISBN: 978-1-61929-360-1
eISBN: 978-1-61929-361-1

The Heart of the Mountain

Lucinda "Lu" Calder is an experienced miner, sent to investigate possible irregularities at Brushy #3, a coal mine owned by her step-father, in eastern Kentucky. Acting as a transfer from another mine in the West, she is hired as a general miner and mechanic. As the first, and only, female miner at Brushy #3, she puts up with some distrust and hazing from her male counterparts to test her mettle.

One of the first people she meets is an attractive woman in personnel named Regina Kinlaw. Regina is the single mother of a nine-year-old daughter, who is relentlessly curious. When Regina's van breaks down, Lu stops to assist and is drawn to the young woman. Even though Regina seems stand-offish and secretive, something about her intrigues Lu. But she has a job to do and can't allow herself to be distracted by wishful thinking.

The area surrounding Brushy #3 is a close knit, rural community and Lu finds herself thrown into situations that bring her into more frequent contact with Regina than she planned. They also bring her into contact with a man who believes Regina is his future wife and resents the time Regina spends with Lu. It's a situation that jeopardizes Lu's mission, and eventually her life.

ISBN: 978-1-61929-330-4
eISBN: 978-1-61929-331-1

Untouchable

Dr. Emma Rothenberg is the most feared professor at Overland University because of her failure rate. Laramie "Ramie" Sunderlund is a senior art major, desperate to earn three lousy English credits to graduate.

Thrown together in a battle of wills, the two women grudgingly establish a measure of respect for one another during one long semester. Emma is a lonely woman of forty-five who occasionally risks her career with dangerous liaisons.

Ramie faces unwanted advances from Rothenberg's graduate assistant, resulting in an assault that threatens her future as a sculptress. Relieved when the semester ends and Ramie leaves to recuperate at home, Emma is suddenly faced with the fact that she misses the woman with curly blonde hair and deep blue eyes who occupied an aisle seat on the third row. She was also a young woman half her age, virtually a child. The notion of anything between them is ridiculous.

When Ramie returns to the university a decade later as the artist-in-residence, Emma is shocked that the younger woman seems interested in actively pursuing her. Against the objections of parents, friends, and colleagues, and despite their own reservations, what are these two very different women willing to sacrifice to find the happiness both are seeking?

ISBN: 978-1-61929-210-9
eISBN: 978-1-61929-209-3

In the Midnight Hour

What happens when you wake up to find the woman of your dreams in your bed? All-night radio hostess Desdemona, Queen of the Night draws her listening audience with her sultry, seductive voice, the only thing of value she possesses. During the day she becomes an insecure, unattractive woman named Marsha Barrett, living in a world with too many mirrors. She is comfortable with her obscurity until she meets Colleen Walters, a tall, attractive woman hired to expand her listening audience by selling Desdemona to new markets. When she wakes up in bed with Colleen after a night at a club, Marsha is terrified. A woman like Colleen would never go to bed with a woman like Marsha. She might dream about such a thing, but in the harsh reality of daylight, it would never happen. Beauty is only drawn to beauty and Marsha refuses to believe beauty could ever be drawn to anyone who looks like her. Just as she begins to believe happiness may be possible, the past returns determined to destroy them.

ISBN: 978-1-61929-188-1
eISBN: 978-1-61929-187-4

The Chameleon

Six years ago Detective Christine Shaw left her happy life and a good job in Texas to follow her libido to New York City. She's still a cop, but her stewardess girlfriend has flown the coop and Chris hasn't been able to fill the void. Everything in her life begins to change when she and her partner are assigned to a high profile case.

The murder of Broadway star Elaine Barrie propels Chris into a whole new world. A fan of the murdered actress since she was a teenager, Chris isn't prepared for the secrets she uncovers during their investigation, including her attraction to the daughter of her number one suspect.

Was the victim any of the personalities witnesses describe, or was the real person a chameleon, satisfying the expectations of each person she met?

ISBN 978-1-61929-102-7
eISBN: 978-1-61929-103-4

The Game of Denial

Joan Carmichael, a successful New York businesswoman, lost the love of her life ten years earlier. Alone, she raised their four children, always cherishing her deep love for her wife. Her memories of their life together come back even stronger as one of their daughters prepares to marry. Joan and her four adult kids fly to Virginia to meet the groom's family and attend the ceremony at the small horse farm owned by the mother of the fiancé.

Evelyn "Evey" Chase, also a widow, has secrets in her past, and her memories of her dead husband aren't pleasant. She's concerned about meeting her future daughter-in-law's family, certain that she and her three kids will have little in common with the wealthy New Yorkers. Besides, the thought of two women in a relationship bringing up a family together makes her uncomfortable, even though her daughter-in-law assures her that lesbianism is not hereditary or catching.

When the two women meet they are drawn to one another in a way neither anticipated, and the game of denial begins. Evey fights her attraction and doesn't realize the effect she has on Joan. Joan tries to shake off her feelings, seeing them as a betrayal to the memory of her wife. Besides, isn't Evey Chase straight? After Evey and Joan share an intimate moment at the wedding reception, they are both emotionally terrified and Joan flees. Will Joan overcome the feeling of betraying her former mate and stop denying her desire to be happy again? Can Evey finally face her past in order to accept the love of another woman and the desire to live the life she had once dreamed of?

ISBN: 978-1-61929-130-0
eISBN: 978-1-61929-131-7

The Sea Hawk

Dr. Julia Blanchard, a marine archaeologist, and her team of divers have spent almost eighteen months excavating the remains of a ship found a few miles off the coast of Georgia. Although they learn quite a bit about the nineteenth century sailing vessel, they have found nothing that would reveal the identity of the ship they have nicknamed "The Georgia Peach."

Her rescue at sea leads her on an unexpected journey into the true identity of the Peach and the captain and crew who called it their home. Her travels take her to the island of Martinique, the eastern Caribbean islands, the Louisiana German Coast and New Orleans at the close of the War of 1812.

How had the Peach come to rest in the waters off the Georgia coast? What had become of her alluring and enigmatic captain, Simone Moreau? Can love conquer everything, even time?

ISBN 978-1-935053-10-1
Available in print and eBook formats

Pipeline

What do you do when the mistakes you made in the past come back to slap you in the face with a vengeance? Joanna Carlisle, a fifty-seven year old photojournalist, has only begun to adjust to retirement on her small ranch outside Kerrville, Texas, when she finds herself unwillingly sucked into an investigation of illegal aliens being smuggled into the United States to fill the ranks of cheap labor needed to increase corporate profits.

An unexpected visit by her former lover, Cate Hammond, and the attempted murder of their son, forces Jo to finally face what she had given up. Although she hasn't seen Cate or their son for fifteen years, she finds that the feelings she had for Cate had only been dormant, but had never died. No matter how much she fights her attraction to Cate, Jo cannot help but wonder whether she had made the right decision when she chose career and independence over love.

ISBN 978-1-932300-64-2

Available in print and eBook formats

Reiko's Garden

Hatred…like love…knows no boundaries.

How much impact can one person have on a life?

When sixty-five-year old Callie Owen returns to her rural childhood home in Eastern Tennessee to attend the funeral of a woman she hasn't seen in twenty years, she's forced to face the fears, heartache, and turbulent events that scarred both her body and her mind. Drawing strength from Jean, her partner of thirty years, and from their two grown children, Callie stays in the valley longer than she had anticipated and relives the years that changed her life forever.

In 1949, Japanese war bride Reiko Sanders came to Frost Valley, Tennessee with her soldier husband and infant son. Callie Owen was an inquisitive ten-year-old whose curiosity about the stranger drove her to disobey her father for just one peek at the woman who had become the subject of so much speculation. Despite Callie's fears, she soon finds that the exotic-looking woman is kind and caring, and the two forge a tentative, but secret friendship.

When Callie and her five brothers and sisters were left orphaned, Reiko provided emotional support to Callie. The bond between them continued to grow stronger until Callie left Frost Valley as a teenager, emotionally and physically scarred, vowing never to return and never to forgive.

It's not until Callie goes "home" that she allows herself to remember how Reiko influenced her life. Once and for all, can she face the terrible events of her past? Or will they come back to destroy all that she loves?

ISBN 978-1-932300-77-2
Available in print and eBook formats

Tunnel Vision

Royce Brodie, a 50-year-old homicide detective in the quiet town of Cedar Springs, a bedroom community 30 miles from Austin, Texas, has spent the last seven years coming to grips with the incident that took the life of her partner and narrowly missed taking her own. The peace and quiet she had been enjoying is shattered by two seemingly unrelated murders in the same week: the first, a John Doe, and the second, a janitor at the local university.

As Brodie and her partner, Curtis Nicholls, begin their investigation, the assignment of a new trainee disrupts Brodie's life. Not only is Maggie Weston Brodie's former lover, but her father had been Brodie's commander at the Austin Police Department and nearly destroyed her career.

As the three detectives try to piece together the scattered evidence to solve the two murders, they become convinced the two murders are related. The discovery of a similar murder committed five years earlier at a small university in upstate New York creates a sense of urgency as they realize they are chasing a serial killer.

The already difficult case becomes even more so when a third victim is found. But the case becomes personal for Brodie when Maggie becomes the killer's next target. Unless Brodie finds a way to save Maggie, she could face losing everything a second time.

ISBN 978-1-935053-19-4
Available in print and eBook formats

Soiled Dove

In 1872, sixteen-year-old Loretta Digby fled her home in Indiana to escape an abusive step-father. Rescued from the streets of St. Joseph, Missouri by brothel owner Jack Coulter, she turns to the only work available. By twenty she became a much sought after prostitute catering to St. Jo's most influential men and dreaming of the day she can leave her past behind and start her life anew. Working with teacher, Hettie Tobias, who is traveling west for a teaching position in Trinidad, Colorado, Loretta and Amelia leave their former lives behind.

In the foothills of the Sangre de Cristo Mountains outside Trinidad, Clare McIlhenney has been struggling for years to make her father's dream of owning a cattle ranch in the west come true. Working with a few ranch hands and her foreman, Ino Valdez, Clare has slowly built the ranch over the last twenty years while overcoming everything that should have stopped her.

In the spring of 1876 Loretta and her friends arrive in the dusty Colorado town. Her first meeting with Clare McIlhenney is less than inspiring. When Clare is injured, over her strenuous objections, Ino hires Loretta as a temporary cook and housekeeper for the ranch. Over the next few months, Clare struggles with her unwanted attraction to the much younger woman, unable to forget the events of her past that led to the deaths of everyone she had been close to. Determined to never lose anyone else, Clare closed off her emotions and became a distant and disliked stranger to everyone around her.

Will Loretta be able to keep her past a secret and find a new life? Will Clare open herself up to loss yet again and put her own prejudices behind her? In a story of the struggles in a harsh and unforgiving time will the two women find peace at last?

Recipient of a 2011 award from the Golden Crown Literary Society, the premiere organization for the support and nourishment of quality lesbian literature. *Soiled Dove* won in the category of Historical Romance.

ISBN 978-1-935053-35-4
Available in print and eBook formats

The Other Mrs. Champion

Sarah Champion, 55, of Massachusetts, was leading the perfect life with Kelley, her partner and wife of twenty-five years. That is, until Kelley was struck down by an unexpected stroke away from home. But Sarah discovers she hadn't known her partner and lover as well as she thought.

Accompanied by Kelley's long-time friend and attorney, Sarah and her children rush to Vancouver, British Columbia to say their goodbyes, only to discover another woman, Pauline, keeping a vigil over Kelley in the hospital. Confronted by the fact that her wife also has a Canadian wife, Sarah struggles to find answers to resolve her emotional and personal turmoil.

Alone and lonely, Sarah turns to the only other person who knew Kelley as well as she did — Pauline Champion. Will the two women be able to forge a friendship despite their simmering animosity? Will their growing attraction eventually become Kelley's final gift to the women she loved?

ISBN 978-1-935053-46-0
eISBN: 978-1-61929-032-7

Picking Up the Pieces

Athon Dailey hasn't had many breaks in her life other than the ones she made for herself by living up to her reputation as a tough girl until she meets Lauren Shelton, a new girl at school in Duvalle, Texas. Tamed by Lauren's affection, Athon begins to believe there could be a brighter future. When Lauren's parents discover the growing relationship they send her away, making sure the two girls never have contact, leaving Athon alone and abandoned.

Twenty years later the two women meet again. Athon has established a successful military career as a helicopter pilot while Lauren has returned to Duvalle to teach. It doesn't take long for them to rekindle their feelings for one another and they finally get the chance to rebuild their teenage dreams. Permanent happiness is within their grasp when Athon's unit is deployed.

Athon comes home in a coma, diagnosed with a traumatic brain injury. She awakens to find Lauren by her side to welcome her home. When Athon chooses to retire and return to Texas, neither realizes the twists and turns the journey home will take. The Athon Dailey who returned to Lauren is not the woman she remembers. In order for their relationship to survive, Lauren begins her search for the woman she loves. Will Athon finally find her way back to Lauren and the dream they both once had? Does Lauren have the courage to live with a woman who is now a stranger?

ISBN 978-1-61929-120-1
eISBN: 978-1-61929-121-8

OTHER REGAL CREST PUBLICATIONS

Brenda Adcock	Soiled Dove	978-1-935053-35-4
Brenda Adcock	The Sea Hawk	978-1-935053-10-1
Brenda Adcock	The Other Mrs. Champion	978-1-935053-46-0
Brenda Adcock	Picking Up the Pieces	978-1-61929-120-1
Brenda Adcock	The Game of Denial	978-1-61929-130-0
Brenda Adcock	In the Midnight Hour	978-1-61929-188-1
Brenda Adcock	Untouchable	978-1-61929-210-9
Brenda Adcock	The Heart of the Mountain	978-1-61929-330-4
Brenda Adcock	Gift of the Redeemer	978-1-61929-360-1
Brenda Adcock	Unresolved Conflicts	978-1-61929-374-8
Brenda Adcock	One Step At A Time	978-1-61929-408-0
K. Aten	The Fletcher	978-1-61929-356-4
K. Aten	Rules of the Road	978-1-61919-366-3
K. Aten	The Archer	978-1-61929-370-0
K. Aten	Waking the Dreamer	978-1-61929-382-3
K Aten	The Sagittarius	978-1-61929-386-1
Georgia Beers	Thy Neighbor's Wife	1-932300-15-5
Georgia Beers	Turning the Page	978-1-932300-71-0
Lynnette Beers	Just Beyond the Shining River	978-1-61929-352-6
Sharon G. Clark	A Majestic Affair	978-1-61929-177-5
Tonie Chacon	Struck! A Titanic Love Story	978-1-61929-226-0
Cooper and Novan	Madam President	978-1-61929-316-8
Cooper and Novan	First Lady	978-1-61929-318-2
Sky Croft	Amazonia	978-1-61929-067-9
Sky Croft	Amazonia: An Impossible Choice	978-1-61929-179-9
Sky Croft	Mountain Rescue: The Ascent	978-1-61929-099-0
Sky Croft	Mountain Rescue: On the Edge	978-1-61929-205-5
Cronin and Foster	Blue Collar Lesbian Erotica	978-1-935053-01-9
Cronin and Foster	Women in Uniform	978-1-935053-31-6
Cronin and Foster	Women in Sports	978-1-61929-278-9
Jane DiLucchio	A Change of Heart	978-1-61929-324-3
Anna Furtado	The Heart's Desire	978-1-935053-81-1
Anna Furtado	The Heart's Strength	978-1-935053-82-8
Anna Furtado	The Heart's Longing	978-1-935053-83-5
Anna Furtado	Tremble and Burn	978-1-61929-354-0
Melissa Good	Eye of the Storm	1-932300-13-9
Melissa Good	Hurricane Watch	978-1-935053-00-2
Melissa Good	Moving Target	978-1-61929-150-8
Melissa Good	Red Sky At Morning	978-1-932300-80-2
Melissa Good	Storm Surge: Book One	978-1-935053-28-6
Melissa Good	Storm Surge: Book Two	978-1-935053-39-2
Melissa Good	Stormy Waters	978-1-61929-082-2
Melissa Good	Thicker Than Water	1-932300-24-4
Melissa Good	Terrors of the High Seas	1-932300-45-7
Melissa Good	Tropical Storm	978-1-932300-60-4
Melissa Good	Tropical Convergence	978-1-935053-18-7

Melissa Good	Winds of Change Book One	978-1-61929-194-2
Melissa Good	Winds of Change Book Two	978-1-61929-232-1
Melissa Good	Southern Stars	978-1-61929-348-9
Jeanine Hoffman	Lights & Sirens	978-1-61929-115-7
Jeanine Hoffman	Strength in Numbers	978-1-61929-109-6
Jeanine Hoffman	Back Swing	978-1-61929-137-9
Jennifer Jackson	It's Elementary	978-1-61929-085-3
Jennifer Jackson	It's Elementary, Too	978-1-61929-217-8
Jennifer Jackson	Memory Hunters	978-1-61929-294-9
K. E. Lane	And, Playing the Role of Herself	978-1-932300-72-7
Kate McLachlan	Christmas Crush	978-1-61929-195-9
Kate McLachlan	Hearts, Dead and Alive	978-1-61929-017-4
Kate McLachlan	Murder and the Hurdy Gurdy Girl	978-1-61929-125-6
Kate McLachlan	Rescue At Inspiration Point	978-1-61929-005-1
Kate McLachlan	Return Of An Impetuous Pilot	978-1-61929-152-2
Kate McLachlan	Rip Van Dyke	978-1-935053-29-3
Kate McLachlan	Ten Little Lesbians	978-1-61929-236-9
Kate McLachlan	Alias Mrs. Jones	978-1-61929-282-6
Lynne Norris	One Promise	978-1-932300-92-5
Lynne Norris	Sanctuary	978-1-61929-248-2
Lynne Norris	The Light of Day	978-1-61929-338-0
Paula Offutt	Butch Girls Can Fix Anything	978-1-932300-74-1
Kelly Sinclair	Getting Back	978-1-61929-242-0
Kelly Sinclair	Accidental Rebels	978-1-61929-260-4
Schramm and Dunne	Love Is In the Air	978-1-61929-362-8
Surtees and Dunne	True Colours	978-1-61929-021-1
Surtees and Dunne	Many Roads to Travel	978-1-61929-022-8
Rae Theodore	Leaving Normal: Adventures in Gender	
		978-1-61929-320-5
Rae Theodore	My Mother Says Drums Are for Boys: True	
	Stories for Gender Rebels	978-1-61929-378-6
Barbara Valletto	Pulse Points	978-1-61929-254-3
Barbara Valletto	Everlong	978-1-61929-266-6
Barbara Valletto	Limbo	978-1-61929-358-8
Barbara Valletto	Diver Blues	978-1-61929-384-7
Bonnie Wormsley	The Cursed Heart	978-1-61929-400-4
Lisa Young	Out and Proud	978-1-61929-392-2

Be sure to check out our other imprints,
Blue Beacon Books, Carnelian Books, Mystic Books, Quest Books,
Silver Dragon Books, Troubadour Books,
and Young Adult Books.

VISIT US ONLINE AT
www.regalcrest.biz

At the Regal Crest Website You'll Find

~ The latest news about forthcoming titles and new releases

~ Our complete backlist of romance, mystery, thriller and adventure titles

~ Information about your favorite authors